THE
TRAVELLER

AND

OTHER STORIES

STUART NEVILLE

D1025823

Published by
Soho Press, Inc.
227 W 17th Street
New York, NY 10011

Library of Congress Cataloging-in-Publication Data
Names: Neville, Stuart, author. | Connolly, John, writer of foreword.
Title: The traveller : and other stories / Stuart Neville ; [foreword by John Connolly].
Description: New York, NY : Soho Crime, [2020] Identifiers: LCCN 2020015489

ISBN 978-1-64129-295-5
eISBN 978-1-64129-204-7

Classification: LCC PR6114.E943 A6 2020 | DDC 823'.92—dc23

Interior design by Janine Agro

Printed in the United States of America

10 9 8 7 6 5 4 3 2 1

For Juliet

Table of Contents

THE TRAVELLER

AND OTHER STORIES

Introduction by the Author

At the time of writing, it is ten years since my debut novel, *The Ghosts of Belfast*, was first published by Soho Press. That decade has seen huge change in my life, both professionally and personally. I became a full-time writer within a year of that book's publication, got married not long after that, and became a father to two children. I've published eight further novels in that time, and the writing of each has been its own unique journey. Some novels were written in a matter of weeks, others took years. None have been easy. There have been times when I've questioned the sanity of what I do, and even considered quitting. At those times, one has to consciously remind oneself of the pleasure of writing, no matter how lost it seems.

Thank the writing gods for short stories. While writing a novel has become ever more grinding, it's the short form that reminds me why I do this in the first place. The thrill of discovery, the delight of letting an idea spool out until it becomes something more, a real and tangible thing that can be shared with others. I am always bemused by those authors—and there are many—who say they struggle with short stories, that they can't write within that structure. For me, the short story has always been a pleasure, both as a reader and a writer. Even as a child, I devoured anthologies and collections, and continue to do so as an adult. Alas, the publishing industry doesn't agree; collections and anthologies are rarely a profitable enterprise, even for those authors at the top of the food chain. I must therefore express my gratitude to those publishers who still release them into the wild, including my own.

Every story has its own origin tale, a genesis, and those in this collection are no exception. Please indulge me while I share a glimpse of how the sausage is made . . .

PART I: NEW MONSTERS is an assortment of stand-alone short stories I have published over the last decade, some crime, others reflecting the more supernatural reading I did in my teenage years.

"Coming in on Time" is kind of an accidental story. It was originally written for a charity anthology with books as a theme, but for reasons too tangled to get into here, a completely different story wound up in that book. This story was inspired by a song of the same name by John Martyn, an aching ballad that uses a boat coming in after a long voyage as an allegory for the mother who abandoned him as a child.

Like most eighties kids, I grew up reading Stephen King,

and although I consider myself a crime writer, that horror influence still lingers today. "The Green Lady" builds on a local legend from my hometown. I grew up close to the Folly River and played in the woods there nearly every day. As children, we whispered of the Green Lady, a witch who haunted the ruins of the Old Mill. Woe betide any child who fell under her spell, including Billy, who is fishing for sticklebacks when a mysterious woman calls to him.

I was enduring a year-long spell of writer's block (yes, it's a real thing) and desperate to find a way out when late one sleepless night I had the idea for a character: Echo, a young boy who is raised as the reincarnation of his own dead sister, Melody. I got out of bed, went to my office, and started typing. Over several weeks, the story got longer and more convoluted until I didn't know what I had. Was it a novel? If so, what kind? Or maybe a novella? Stumped, I set it aside, occasionally opening the file over several years and wondering what to do with it. Skip forward to 2017 when I was contacted by the immensely talented Lucy Caldwell, originally from these shores, who was editing an anthology of Irish writing for Faber called *Being Various*. I happily accepted her invitation to submit a story, but soon realised I didn't actually have anything. Then I remembered poor Echo, sitting lonely and neglected on my hard drive. I opened the file, and thought, I wonder? Over a few days, I pared it down from almost 15,000 words to just under 6,000, finally getting to the nub of the story. "Echo" was always meant to be a short story; it just took a prompt from someone else to make me realise that.

"London Safe" was written for an anthology inspired by a song by Frank Turner in which the singer-songwriter described a box of postcards, reading the inscribed messages, and summed them up as Ten Word Tragedies. Each author was sent a postcard from the box and asked to write a story based on the message. Mine said, simply, "Don't worry about me in London. I'll be safe." Simple as that.

"Queen of the Hill" was the first story I was ever asked to submit to an anthology. The brief for *Requiems for the Departed* was an interesting one: a crime story based on Irish mythology. The obvious choice for me was Queen Macha, the warrior chieftain after which my hometown was named; Armagh comes from Ard Macha, meaning Hill of the Queen. The Christmas Eve setting meant it was also an obvious choice for Soho Press's holiday anthology, *The Usual Santas*.

"The Night Hag" is a new piece written specifically for this collection. It is inspired by the phenomenon of sleep paralysis, something I have experienced repeatedly over the years. Many people have been visited by the Night Hag at one time or another, and her manifestation varies from person to person. The protagonist's experience of her closely resembles mine, but with added murderous guilt and invasive fingers.

"Black Beauty" is an odd little story. I and a bunch of

other authors were asked to write a piece of flash fiction to celebrate the three-hundredth edition of the men's lifestyle magazine, *Shortlist*. There were two very specific requirements: the story had to be exactly three hundred words long, and it had to feature the colour black. Noir, in other words. That was quite a challenge, but in the end I was able to tie it into my life's passion: the guitar. The 1957 Gibson Les Paul Custom earned the nickname Black Beauty for its lustrous ebony finish, and it plays a starring role here.

PART II: OLD FRIENDS contains what my editor has dubbed "fan favorites"—each story ties into characters who have appeared in one or more of my novels.

Several of my novels began as short stories, including "Followers," which will be very familiar to anyone who has read *The Ghosts of Belfast*. I woke one Sunday morning in 2007 with an image in my head: a man getting drunk in a bar, surrounded by all the people he'd killed. At the time, I had a mobile phone with a word processor app, so I began writing the story then and there, and finished it later that day. A month or so passed, and the story continued to nag at me, telling me there was a novel here. That novel became *The Ghosts of Belfast*, and "Followers" is essentially the first chapter.

As with some other stories in this collection, being asked to contribute to an anthology allows a writer to find a home for an idea that's been nagging at them. In the case of "Faith," it was the question of what might a man of God do if his belief evaporates? If a man has lived his life in avoidance of sin, what happens if he suddenly comes to believe there is no such thing? What sins might he then commit? When I was asked to contribute a story to be broadcast on BBC Radio Four, that was the perfect opportunity to finally explore the idea. Not only that, but the resulting story wound up being the basis for my novel *So Say the Fallen*.

If you've read my novel *Ratlines*, then you'll be familiar with the characters of Albert Ryan and Celia Hume. But that book was not their first appearance. They actually started as an elderly couple living outside Dublin. They share a terrible secret, and when they risk being found out, Albert must make an awful choice. "The Craftsman" first appeared in *Down These Green Streets: Irish Crime Writing in the 21st Century*, edited by Declan Burke.

"The Catastrophist" is unusual in that it began as a title in search of a story. The story itself came from an earlier idea I'd had, involving a senior republican paramilitary travelling to the Irish border to investigate a murder within the ranks. "The Catastrophist" was written for the Irish crime anthology *Trouble Is Our Business*, edited by Declan Burke, and is one of four stories in this collection in which Gerry Fegan makes an appearance.

"The Last Dance" is one of the oldest stories in this book, and it was written a few months after completing *The Ghosts of Belfast*. At the time, I simply wanted to revisit Gerry

Fegan, see how he was getting on. When I sold the story to the online crime zine Thuglit, I couldn't have guessed that it would be read by Nat Sobel, one of New York's preeminent literary agents. This story, set in a grimy Irish bar in Boston, literally changed my life.

This collection closes with a novella that's never been published elsewhere, and it's the only story I've ever written specifically at the request of readers. *The Traveller* is a response to the messages I've received over the years asking what happened to Jack Lennon and his daughter, Ellen, after the events of *The Final Silence*. Although I've always known exactly where Jack wound up—the coastal village of Cushendun, working as a security guard—I'd put off writing about it for several years. This collection offered the opportunity to finally put that right, as well as tie up several loose ends, including the eponymous villain coming back to take his revenge.

THIRTEEN STORIES IN TOTAL, representing more than a decade of work. I sincerely hope you gain some pleasure from them, and perhaps the occasional chill.

Stuart Neville
Fall 2019

Foreword

About twelve years ago, in a very different world, an author handed me his as-yet-unpublished manuscript following a literary event in Dublin. Now there are many occurrences that may cause a writer's heart to sink—we're sensitive, delicate creatures—but high among them is being handed an as-yet-unpublished manuscript after a literary event. Why? Because chances are that the writer in question has, only moments before, been broadcasting his own credentials as an open-minded connoisseur of new fiction, a supporter of budding talent, and a friend to small animals, children, and the poor. At that instant, he is at his most vulnerable. If his bluff is called, he has nowhere to hide.

Thus I left the event carrying, somewhat grudgingly, the as-yet-unpublished manuscript of a book entitled *The Ghosts of Belfast*, also known as *The Twelve* outside North America for reasons far too complex and arcane to be entered into here, unless one is desperate for a disquisition on the difficult history of Northern Ireland, its tortured relationship with the rest of the United Kingdom and the Republic of

Ireland, and how these factors may sometimes color the perceptions and attitudes of certain sections of the reading public.

To be honest, it took me a while to get around to *The Ghosts of Belfast*. My house will never be short of books to be read, and I am resigned to the fact that I will go to the grave with that situation largely unaltered. Many of those books I have chosen for myself. Some I may even have paid for. In 2008, *The Ghosts of Belfast* did not fall into either of those categories.

Yet—and this is most unlike me—I started to feel guilty for not giving the manuscript a chance. The author, after all, had seemed most personable, and his initial approach was admirably unassuming. In fact, had he been any less forward, I wouldn't have been in possession of the book at all. I knew that the novel was scheduled for publication in 2009, so clearly someone, somewhere had decided it was worth a considerable investment of time and money. The least I could do was give it a few hours, and bask in my magnanimity forever after.

I read most of *The Ghosts of Belfast* on a flight to New Jersey, and finished it on the airport station platform while waiting for my train to New York. That same evening, I met Joe Long, my oldest American friend, and a great proselytizer for Irish fiction. I told him that I'd just read the best post-Troubles Irish novel yet written, which was also the finest Irish mystery novel of the century so far, and therefore one of the great Irish mystery novels, period. It was no exaggeration, and I stand over those comments more than a decade after the fact. *The Ghosts of Belfast* was uniquely Irish in its mood and setting, but its prose style boasted the muscularity of the American crime tradition, while its generic influences were also wide enough to encompass elements of the British police procedural and the gothic—the latter a field in which Irish writers had excelled for much of the nineteenth century, but which had been neglected for much of the twentieth.

The Ghosts of Belfast, therefore, provides a useful touchstone for this volume of Stuart Neville's short fiction. The Canadian-American mystery novelist Ross Macdonald once noted that a writer's first novel tends to function as an index to his or her subsequent career. In other words, everything that follows can probably be detected in nascent form in the debut work. This collection conforms, in the best possible way, to Macdonald's observation. Here are monsters, both human and non-human. Here are hauntings, real or imagined. Here are old friends and older fiends. Here is the work of a prodigiously talented writer, one who has more than fulfilled the promise of his first book.

Here, then, is *The Traveller and Other Stories*.

—John Connolly

PART I:

NEW MONSTERS

COMING IN ON TIME

Barry Whittle asked, "Is she coming in on time?"

Old Man Gove, the loading officer, said, "Aye."

"Good weather today," Barry said.

"Aye," Old Man Gove said.

"Nothing to hold her up," Barry said.

"No," Old Man Gove said.

"She'll not be long," Barry said.

"She'll not be long," Old Man Gove said.

Barry stepped back, looked out across the channel. Saw the Sapphire cracking the flat table of water. Coming fast like it always did. Once a day, here in the morning, and back again in the evening. Tourists and locals, all of them squashed together, in and out of their cars. The ferry would spill them onto the slip soon. Just wait.

Barry watched.

He didn't know if today was library day or not. He wasn't good at telling the days yet. Mum had been teaching him: Monday, Tuesday, Wednesday, then . . . Barry wasn't sure. He always got Saturday and Sunday mixed up. Without

Mum to help, he couldn't say them all in the right order, even if he counted on his fingers.

Barry thought there had been three sleeps since Mum went. And he thought the last day he'd seen her had been library day, when the van came off the ferry and stopped in the small car park. Mum had brought Barry on board that day, like she always did, and let him take as long as he wanted to look at the books.

Josie, who worked on the van, sometimes read books to him. *The Tiger Who Came to Tea, Winnie the Witch, The Gruffalo*. She would sit on the floor, her legs folded to make a nest for him, and he would let himself be swallowed by her. He liked the way she smelled, and the feel of her breath on his cheek when she leaned in close and read the words, her fingertip following the letters that he didn't understand.

He knew some words and letters. Mum had been teaching him. He could recognise DOG, Duh-Oh-Guh, and CAT, Cah-Ah-Tuh, and some more. Numbers too. But not well enough to read all by himself. Not yet.

Mum would sit at the back of the van, reading grownup books. Or sometimes Josie would leave Barry to look at the books on his own and she and Mum would talk in low voices, their heads close together. Then, when it was time to go, Barry could choose six books to keep until the van came back. Mum did the same, and they would walk home to their house on the other side of the island.

Sometimes, if they were too heavy, Mum would carry his books for him.

Mum didn't say bye-bye. No kisses or anything.

"She left," Dad said.

Barry had come downstairs after waking up. Normally, Mum would come and get him, but not that morning. So he had walked into the kitchen, still in his pyjamas, the floor cold on his bare feet. Dad was sitting at the table. He looked like he'd been crying. He had taped some tissue to his hand, across his knuckles. The paper was stained reddish brown.

There was broken glass on the floor. Barry was careful not to step on it as he moved farther into the kitchen.

"Where'd she go?" he asked.

Dad didn't answer, so Barry asked again.

"To the mainland," Dad said.

"On the ferry?"

"How else would she get there?"

"When's she coming back?"

"Dunno," Dad said. Then after a while, he said, "Soon."

Dad smelled funny. He always smelled of beer and ciga-rettes, but that morning there was something else. Something Barry couldn't name. He had dark stains on his shirt.

"You want breakfast?" Dad asked.

Barry nodded.

"Toast? Cornflakes? What?"

"Mum gives me Weetabix," Barry said.

Dad got up from the table, fetched a bowl and spoon

from the dish rack, placed them on the counter. He opened one cupboard after another before asking, "Where are they?"

Barry pointed to the cupboard beside the washing machine.

Dad found the box, put two biscuits in the bowl, took a bottle of milk from the fridge.

Barry opened his mouth to tell Dad he always had warm milk, but it was too late. Dad poured cold milk into the bowl, dropped the spoon in, then set them on the table.

"Can you turn the TV on yourself?" Dad asked.

"Yeah," Barry said.

"I'm going back to bed. Don't make any noise."

Dad left him in the kitchen to eat.

Barry thought about Mum. He wasn't surprised that she'd left. Not really. The way Dad hit her when he was angry and had been drinking beer. Sometimes he hit Barry too. Dad's hands were hard and heavy. They sometimes knocked Barry off his feet.

It happened more often now that Dad didn't have a job anymore. Barry used to like the mornings when Dad was out working on the fishing boat. He and Mum had the house to themselves, and they would cuddle and read stories, and Barry would touch her bruises and kiss them better.

Why didn't she say bye-bye? It was okay that she left because she didn't want to get hit anymore, but why didn't she say bye-bye? Why didn't she take Barry with her? He

supposed it was because she left late at night and didn't want
to wake him up.

But the ferry didn't go in the middle of the night, did it?

When he finished his breakfast, Barry dressed himself
and left the house without telling Dad. He went out the
back door, which was never locked, and walked around
the house to the patch of gravel and weeds that was their
front garden. He knew the way to the ferry slip, so he didn't
need Dad to take him. Not that he would, even if Barry asked.

It felt like a long time, that first morning when he walked
there alone. Old Man Gove asked if his parents knew he
was there, so Barry lied and said yes. He remembered the
things Mum would say while they waited for the ferry: Is she
coming in on time? The weather's good. Nothing to hold
her up. And Old Man Gove grunted the same replies.

Barry knew the library van wouldn't be on the ferry that
morning because it had been just the day before, so he didn't
bring his books. But anyway, that wasn't really why he
walked to the slip. He went there in case Mum came back.
If she came back, he knew she would be happy that he was
there waiting for her.

But she didn't come back. Not that morning, or the next,
or the one after that. He had gone to Mum and Dad's bedroom while Dad lay snoring and gathered up the books she
had borrowed. One of them had her favourite bookmark
still stuck between the pages, so Barry slipped it out and put
it on the bedside locker. He took the books and put them

in a plastic bag along with the ones he'd borrowed and carried them all the way to the ferry slip. This was the third morning he'd done that, and they were so heavy, but he did it anyway because he wanted to bring them back to Josie so she could read some more to him.

The first morning he carried them, the plastic bag's handles cut into his palm and fingers, and he cried. The next time, he put them in a backpack he found under the stairs. That was easier, though it did hurt his shoulders.

Now he watched the ferry approach, and he could see the cars and one small bus on its bottom deck, a few passengers leaning on the rails of the top deck. He lifted his hand and waved. Some of the passengers waved back, smiling.

The library van wasn't there. Mum wasn't there.

Barry said goodbye to Old Man Gove and headed home.

DAD WASN'T THERE WHEN Barry got to the house. He looked in the cupboard and found the last slices of bread. There was no more butter in the fridge, so he ate them dry along with water from the tap. That done, he took the backpack up to his bedroom and removed the books. He set Mum's aside and opened the first of his own.

He'd borrowed this one before and he knew nearly all the words from memory. The pictures of the little boy in his bed, then falling.

"Did you ever hear of Mickey, how he heard a racket in the night?"

Barry worked his way through the book, touching the words, saying them out loud. Almost like proper reading. He did the same with the others, though he didn't know them so well.

He hoped the library van would come tomorrow so he could get some new ones. He hoped Mum would come back soon and take him away.

Sometime later, Barry heard Dad arrive home. He went to his bedroom door, opened it a little, and listened. Keys dropped on the table. The rustle of plastic bags. Things getting put away. The snap and hiss of a beer can being opened.

Barry went back to his books.

HIS BELLY GRUMBLED LOUDER as the day went on. He heard bad words and stumbling from below, then crying.

"She's a demon," Dad said. "A demon."

Barry wondered if he should go down there and tell Dad it was all right, Mum would be home soon to look after them. But he knew when Dad was like that he would be angry, and he might hit. So he stayed in his room until he smelled something bad, a burning kind of smell.

He opened his door and the smell got worse. He saw wisps of smoke in the air. The stairs creaked under his feet. From the hall, he saw Dad in the kitchen, his head resting on his forearm, spit hanging from his lips. Rows of empty cans on the table, and a half full bottle with an orange label.

Dad always called it wine, but Barry thought it wasn't real wine, not like people drink on TV.

Smoke billowed from a pot on the stove. Two slices of charred bread stood up in the toaster. An open tin of beans on the counter.

Barry went to the cooker. He thought he should probably turn it off the way Mum did when something was getting too hot. One of the big knobs on the front was turned all the way round. He turned it back until it clicked. Still, the beans in the pot burned, more smoke filling the air. It made his eyes water, and he wanted to cough.

He reached for the pot handle to lift it away. His fingers released it before he felt the burning heat, and the pot clattered on the floor, spilling hot beans across the tiles.

Dad's head jerked up, his eyes wide, his mouth open.

Barry put his hands up, backed away, saying, "Sorry, sorry, sorry, I didn't mean it, sorry."

Dad blinked at him, then coughed, waved the smoke away. "What happened?" he asked.

"I'm sorry," Barry said, the tears coming. "I didn't mean to spill it. It was an accident. I'll clean it up, I promise."

Dad looked at the mess. He looked at Barry.

"The beans were burning," Barry said. "I lifted the pot off but it was too hot and I dropped it. I'm sorry."

Dad crossed the room and Barry backed as far into the corner as he could go. He held his hands up, crouched down, made himself small, saying, *sorry sorry sorry . . .*

Dad got down on his knees, took Barry's hand, and pressed his lips to the hot palm. Barry felt the stubble of his chin, saw tears fall from Dad's eyes. Then Dad wrapped his arms around him, pulled him in close, hugged him for the first time he could remember.

"No, I'm sorry," Dad said. "I'm so sorry. I did a terrible thing and I can't take it back. I'm sorry. I'm sorry."

And Dad held Barry like that for a long time, so long that Barry had to push Dad's arms away. Then they cleaned up the mess together. Later, Dad made them both toast, and opened more beans, and they ate them cold straight from the tin.

After they'd finished, and they'd been sitting quiet for a while, Dad started to cry again. It occurred to Barry that he should hold Dad's hand, even though he knew how hard and heavy it could be. He did it anyway. Dad squeezed Barry's fingers between his.

"I should end it," Dad said as his eyes gazed at something very far away. "I should just end it, but I'm too scared."

"End what?" Barry asked.

Dad didn't answer. He let go of Barry's hand, stood up from the table, and fetched another can of beer. As he drank it, staring out of the kitchen window, Barry left him there and went to bed.

"EVERYTHING ALL RIGHT, SON?" Old Man Gove asked.

He hardly ever looked at Barry, but he did this morning, his eyes small and watchful.

"Yeah," Barry said.

"You sure? I saw your dad yesterday afternoon. He didn't look too well."

"He's been sick," Barry said, not sure if it was a lie.

"Where's your mum these days?"

"She left," Barry said.

Old Man Gove's face went loose. He looked away and said, "Sorry to hear that, son."

He didn't say anything else.

It had been three sleeps since the night Barry and Dad ate together. Barry had hardly seen him since. Only heard him staggering and bumping into things, and the cursing and shouting, and the crying, saying, *demon, demon.* So Barry had eaten dry bread, and Weetabix from the packet, and drunk water from the tap once the milk was done. Each morning, he washed his face at the bathroom sink, even brushed his own teeth. He'd been wearing the same clothes since Mum left, but he did change his underpants one day because they had gotten stained and smelly.

He didn't see Dad at all yesterday, and hadn't heard him since the evening. The back door had slammed sometime after dark, and that was all.

The house had felt empty as Barry came downstairs this morning and into the kitchen. A piece of paper lay on the table, some writing on it that he couldn't read.

"Is she coming in on time?" Barry asked.

"Aye," Old Man Gove said.

"Good weather today."

"Aye."

"Nothing to hold her up."

"No."

"She'll not be long."

"She'll not be long."

And there she was. The Sapphire, gliding across the water. Barry felt hope in his chest, just like he'd done every morning since Mum left. And every morning, as the ferry had come closer, he'd felt the hope wash away when he saw no library van on the bottom deck. And his Mum never waved at him from the top deck because she wasn't there.

But maybe this morning.

He shielded his eyes from the sun, but its reflection on the water made him squint. The ferry appeared as a black shape against silver, nothing Barry could make out. As it came closer, he saw the forms of people on the upper deck, but still the lower deck remained obscured by the glare. Then a cloud passed across the sun, and he saw the reds and blues of cars, a white delivery van, and there, to the back, the bright splashes of colour on the library van.

Barry couldn't help but giggle. The smile felt strange on his mouth after so many days without. He found himself jumping on the spot, a dizzy feeling behind his eyes like when Mum would spin him around, his hands clasped in hers.

Then a dark feeling pierced the joy.

Mum should be here too.

Old Man Gove trudged down the slip as the ferry's apron ramp lowered. The metal met the concrete with a clang and clatter, and Old Man Gove waved the first of the cars off the boat. Barry waited by the railing at the edge of the car park, the vehicles passing him one by one.

At last, the library van climbed the slip, up and into the car park, to the far side where it would stay until the ferry made the return journey that evening.

Barry ran to it, the backpack full of books slapping against his shoulders. He reached the side door and knocked it hard enough to hurt his knuckles.

The door opened, and Barry's heart felt like it might burst when he saw Josie on the top step, smiling down at him.

"Hiya, Barry," she said. "Up you come."

She reached down, took his hand, helped him up and into the van. Rob the driver already had his newspaper open on the steering wheel and was pouring himself a cup of tea from his thermos.

Josie looked past Barry, out into the sunlit car park, the smile falling away from her lips.

"Where's your Mum?" she asked.

Barry shrugged the backpack off, unzipped it, and emptied the contents onto the floor. "I brought her books back. Mine too."

Josie hunkered down in front of him. "Barry, where's your mum?"

"Can you read my books for me?" Barry asked.

Josie got on her knees and took hold of Barry's arms. "Tell me, where's your mum?"

He didn't want to tell her, but she looked him in the eye.

"She left," he said.

And then it all came out. All the worry. All the pain. All the fear. It gushed out of him along with the tears he'd been holding back. He collapsed into her arms, and she gathered him up, and he cried and cried as she rocked him, saying, "Oh sweetheart, oh darling . . ."

THE VAN RATTLED AND juddered along the road to Barry's house. Rob drove, his newspaper stashed into a pocket in the door. Barry sat on Josie's knee, the seatbelt strapping them both to the passenger seat. She had insisted they come here. Rob had argued, said they couldn't leave the car park, but Josie had shouted at him, and Rob had said, *okay, okay, don't get your knickers in a twist.*

The engine grumbled as the van climbed the steep lane to the house before the ground flattened out. It occurred to Barry for the first time that it wasn't a nice house. It was small and old and dirty looking with a garage that had never had a car in it.

"You wait here," Josie said to Rob. "I'll find out what's going on and then we'll head back, all right?"

"Just don't be long," Rob said.

Josie helped Barry climb down from the van and onto the

gravel with its tufts of moss and grass. She held his hand as they walked to the front door.

"Will your dad be home?" she asked.

"Dunno," Barry said. "I don't think so."

She knocked on the door and listened to the quiet. After a while, she asked, "Do you have a key?"

"No. But the back door's open."

Josie took his hand again and said, "Lead on, then."

She glanced back at the van where Rob watched and waited. Barry brought her around the side of the building, and she sniffed at the air as they passed between the garage and the house.

At the back, the door was shut. Barry pressed down on the handle, and it swung inward. He stepped inside first, and Josie followed, his hand still in hers. The kitchen smelled bad. He hadn't really noticed before, but now that Josie was with him, in his house, he felt embarrassed and sad.

Josie looked around at the dishes piled in the sink, the stack of dirty clothes on the floor by the washing machine, the rows of empty cans and bottles on the counter.

She squeezed his hand tighter and he saw a glisten in her eyes. He knew she felt sorry for him and it caused hot anger in his heart. Even though she was being kind, it made him feel small and stupid, like a baby. He let go of her fingers, shoved his hands down into his pockets.

"Mr. Whittle?" she called.

No one answered. She tried again.

"I don't think he's here," Barry said. "He went out last night. He left that."

Barry pointed to the piece of paper on the table.

Josie approached it, leaned down so she could read the words. He watched her lips move, his anger forgotten.

"Oh Christ," she said, then she covered her mouth with her hand. She looked to the back door, still open, then at Barry. "Stay here," she said.

Josie rushed out through the door, into the back garden. Barry went after her, out onto the step. She glanced back at him, told him to stay there.

He didn't. He walked along the back of the house, keeping her in view. She opened the side door of the garage and stumbled back, her hands over her nose and mouth. Flies, black and fat, tumbled through the air around her.

Josie looked back at him once more. "Stay there," she said. "Don't come any closer."

She stepped into the dark.

Now Barry stopped. He watched the dim throat of the doorway, listening hard.

Josie screamed. She lurched out into the light and fell to her knees. Vomit spilled from her mouth and nose.

Barry stood still, unsure what to do. He wanted to go and help her, tell her everything was all right, but he was too scared to move. So he stayed there just like she'd told him to, even as she wept and threw up and spat, even as Rob came running from the van.

HE WOKE UP IN the strange bed, Josie beside him. Mrs. McCue in the village had given them a room and Josie had insisted she stay with Barry, said she didn't want him to be alone.

The police had come in a helicopter. It had made a big noise as it landed in the field behind the house. Two policemen and a pilot. The policemen went into the garage, and when they came out, their faces were different. Like they'd grown older in there.

They asked lots of questions. When did Barry last see Mum? Had her and Dad been fighting? Was Dad angry lately? More police came, some without uniforms, and they all needed to talk with Barry. And two different doctors. Low voices and warm hands. They told him things he didn't understand, about Mum, about Dad, big words that didn't make any sense. So he stopped listening.

Josie stayed with him all the way through the questions, and eventually she told the policemen to stop. They could do more tomorrow. And then they talked about where Barry could stay for the night. Josie knew Mrs. McCue had a big house, so she got Rob to drive her into the village to ask.

As Barry got out of the library van, people on the street looked at him strangely and whispered to each other. Josie gathered him in close, let him hide his eyes in the billows of her cardigan.

She sent Rob back to the mainland, said she'd stay here with Barry, he needed someone to look after him. So they slept in the big old bed in the draughty room, Josie still wearing her clothes, Barry in the pyjamas she found in his bedroom.

Now it was light outside and he was wide awake. Josie snored softly, the kind of sound a cat makes, he thought. He lay still and quiet for a long time until he could see the sun through the crack in the curtains.

Barry realised it would soon be time for the ferry, and Mrs. McCue's house was only a couple of streets away from the slip. It wouldn't take long to get there. Of course, the library van wouldn't be on the ferry this morning, it had only been here yesterday.

But maybe Mum would come back.

Barry knew something bad had happened at the house. Something to do with Dad. But he didn't know what. People in the village seemed to know. Maybe Mum had heard about it and she'd come back to take him away.

The idea grew in his mind.

Yes, she would surely know something bad had happened and she would come back this morning. Barry was certain of it.

He slipped out of bed, found his shoes on the floor, and carried them out of the room. The door creaked as he pulled it to, and he froze, watching Josie. She huffed and rolled over.

Barry went down the stairs and paused at the bottom to put his shoes on. He didn't know how to do up the laces, so he tucked the loose ends down the sides of his feet. The front door didn't make a sound as he opened it. He stepped through, but didn't close it all the way, in case the noise would wake Josie.

The streets were empty on the short walk to the slip, no one to stare, no one to whisper about the boy in the pyjamas.

Old Man Gove saw him approach. The loading officer's shoulders slumped.

"What are you doing here, son?" he asked, his voice softer than Barry had ever heard it.

"I'm going to wait for the ferry," Barry said.

Old Man Gove shook his head and looked sad. "Why?" he asked.

"Mum'll be on it," Barry said.

And when he said it out loud, it made him even more certain, because now it was a real thing, not just an idea in his head.

Old Man Gove breathed out long and slow, and he blinked tears out of his eyes.

"Ah, Jesus, son," he said.

Then he looked away, out across the channel as he wiped at his red cheeks.

"Is she coming in on time?" Barry asked.

Old Man Gove sniffed hard and said, "Aye."

THE GREEN LADY

Billy dipped his bucket in the water as the bright dart of a stickleback flashed against silt and pebbles. Too quick, it zipped past, lost amid the blinding patterns on the stream's surface. The sun warmed Billy's shoulders through his Starsky & Hutch T-shirt.

"You near had him, then."

Billy fell back at the sound of the voice. The bucket slipped from his fingers and the stream's plucky current snatched it away.

The old woman resting on the opposite bank clucked. "Ah, now you've lost your bucket too."

The orange plastic vanished around a bend in the stream. He'd only got it a couple of weeks ago when he went on a Sunday School trip to Portrush.

"That's a pity," the old woman said, drawing her green shawl around her shoulders.

Billy wondered how she didn't melt. The telly said it would be the hottest day of the summer, and here she sat with a shawl and big layered skirts. Her shoes looked funny too; more like the kind of boots the soldiers wore when they patrolled the streets.

The old lady smiled. "Have you no one to play with today?"

Billy shielded his eyes from the sun and shook his head.

"Speak up, wee man. Don't be shy."

Swiping dust from his jeans, Billy got to his feet. "I called for my friend, but he wasn't in. His daddy took him to Belfast."

"Have you no other friends?" She tilted her head as she studied him, her grey-green eyes picking over every bit of him.

Billy sucked on his lower lip and looked at the baked earth beneath his feet. His mum had taken him out of the Drelincourt School where all the other kids on the estate went and made him go to the big school in town. Because he was smarter than the others, she said. Now he had no one on the estate left to play with.

The old woman clucked and smiled, showing her stained teeth. Midges swarmed around her head, mingling with the loose silver strands of her hair to make a shifting halo in the sunlight. Somewhere in the trees a bird called. Billy looked around him. Down here at the water's edge he couldn't see the playground up above, or the houses beyond.

"I remember when this was a real river," the old woman said. "It stretched from yon houses up there, all the way back to the houses on the other side. It cut this big bowl through the earth. But there were no houses then. Except mine."

Billy looked downstream, wondering if the bucket might have snagged on some rocks. He should go after it.

"I'm going to get—"

"It's gone, wee darling. Sure, it'll be halfway to the sea by now."

Billy knew that was nonsense. He wasn't sure how far away the sea was from the Folly River, but he remembered it took the bus ages and ages to get to the seaside. His Mum had always told him to be polite to old people, so he didn't want to argue. Instead he chewed on his lip and picked dirt from under his fingernails.

"Where's your house?" he asked.

"Oh, just down the river a wee bit," she said. "The Old Mill."

Billy stopped picking at his fingernails. "No one lives there. It's got no roof or doors or anything."

"Is that right?" She laughed and slapped her thigh, the sound muted by the layers of skirt. "And how do you know that?"

Billy went back to picking at his nails.

"Have you been there?" she asked.

He scuffed at the light brown earth with his worn plimsolls.

"Does your mummy let you play there?"

Billy raised his eyes to meet hers and shook his head.

"I bet she doesn't." Her smile dripped away. "Did you go on a dare?"

"Yeah," Billy said.

"And did you get scared?"

Billy shrugged.

Her smile returned. "Did you cry?"

Billy's cheeks grew hot. Sweat licked at his forehead and made the thin cotton of his T-shirt stick to his back. He sniffed and wiped his nose on his forearm.

"No need to be ashamed, love. Sure, everyone gets scared." She pointed over Billy's shoulder. "Even Michael there, and he's a big boy."

Billy spun on his heels to see a boy, about twelve, sitting cross-legged in the dirt. "Hello," Michael said.

He wore strange clothes, like the olden days photos Billy's grandad kept in a big book. A plain jacket and short trousers, with a collarless shirt. "What are you staring at?" he asked.

"Be civil, Michael," the old lady called from across the stream. "This wee man needs someone to play with."

"He's too young to play with me," Michael said, scowling.

"Michael's a bold boy," the old lady said. Billy turned back to her, and his tummy fluttered up to his throat. Another boy sat next to her, and a girl just behind, peeking over her shoulder. "Never did learn his manners," she said. "Not like wee Kevin here."

Kevin looked about Billy's age, but his clothes were

different. Not like Michael's, but still strange. Still somehow
. . . wrong. Billy couldn't think why.

"Hello," Kevin said. He lifted his small hand and waved.
Billy waved back.

"You can play with me," Kevin said. He smiled.

Billy smiled back.

The little girl peered over the old lady's shoulder, her
blonde hair catching the sunlight. "What games do you
know?" she asked.

Billy hesitated for a moment before counting on his fingers. "Ring-a-ring-a-rosies, hide and seek, tig—"

"I like tig." She stepped out from behind the old lady.
Her clothes looked normal, not olden days clothes, and
Billy knew her face.

He thought hard about it for a few seconds before he
remembered where from. The image formed in his mind.
Mum at the kitchen table reading the newspaper, crying.
Was it last summer or the one before? Billy had climbed
up into her lap and looked at the newspaper while Mum
wrapped her arms around him. Her cheek was warm and
damp against his neck. She smelled of apples.

There was a picture of a little girl in the newspaper. Billy
traced the headline with his finger, saying the words out
loud. He didn't get very far before he had to ask his Mum
what some of them said.

"Community," she said.

"Shocked," she said.

"Disappearance," she said.

The girl walked to the water's edge and put her hands on her hips. "Who'll be It?"

Michael sprung to his feet. "Me!"

The old lady laughed. "So, you're not too big to play after all?"

Michael grinned.

Billy's heart drummed in his chest. He looked back up the bank to where the trees heaved and whispered. The houses of Ballinahone stood just beyond them, and Orangefield, where he lived, just beyond that. Mum would have lunch ready soon. Jam sandwiches. *Playschool* would be on TV, and cartoons a bit later. *Scooby-Doo*. He never missed *Scooby-Doo*.

But he could play Tig for a little while. Mum might be cross if he was late for lunch, but he'd say sorry, and she'd give him his jam sandwiches anyway.

Michael crouched, his hands forming claws, bearing his teeth. "Ready or not," he said.

A dizzy giggle escaped from Billy's stomach. "Wait," he said, and hopped across the river, using the stepping stones. When he got to the other side, another boy and girl were waiting. They looked like brother and sister, and wore clothes like Michael's. But Billy had stopped caring about clothes, and tingled with the excitement of the coming chase.

The old lady hunkered down so Billy could see the red lines around her green irises, criss-crossed and snaking through the yellow. She brought her hand to his cheek and her skin felt like paper.

"Better run," she said.

An animal howl came from the other side of the stream, and the children squealed as Michael took it in one leap. They scattered into the trees and Billy bolted after them. He heard Michael's ragged laughter behind him and churned his arms and legs, ignoring the whipping of branches.

"I'm going to get you!"

Billy chanced one look over his shoulder and saw Michael's teeth bared, his tongue lolling. Spit slopped from the corners of his mouth. Billy laughed and ducked to the left between two trees whose branches intertwined to form a low tunnel. He had to keep his head down, his knees bent, to fight his way through. Branches crunched behind him and Billy heard Michael swear as he got tangled up in leaves and twigs.

Billy burst out onto an open path, one he didn't recognise, and broke into a sprint through the clear air. Laughter bubbling in his chest, the breeze on his cheeks.

He didn't know how far he'd run before he had to stop. His chest heaved, making him bend over, his hands on his knees, breathing deep until the dizziness passed. His thighs quivered with spent energy, his nerves jangling in the same way they did when he went on the Cyclone ride at Barry's Amusements in Portrush.

Billy listened.

Quiet all around, not even the chirp of a bird. He turned in a circle. There, off in the distance, he could see the rooftops of Ballinahone and Orangefield. Miles away, it seemed. How could it be so far? The Folly wasn't that big.

"You're a fast runner for such a wee boy."

Billy gasped and spun around.

The old lady stood there, a few feet along the path, her shawl still wrapped around her.

"How fast can you run?" she asked.

"Dunno," Billy said.

"Bet you can run faster, anyway."

The voices of the other children rang through the trees, echoing along the path. The old lady's eyes sparkled.

First Kevin, then the girl erupted from the dense growth on either side. They charged past the old lady, looking back over their shoulders at Billy, smiling, laughing. Then the other children, all shouting, telling him to come on, come on, run, run, run!

From behind, Michael's hand slammed into Billy's shoulder, almost knocking him off his feet.

Michael shouted, "You're It!" as he tore past.

His laughter receded along the path.

The old lady reached out her hand to Billy.

"You heard him," she said. "You're It. Come on. You can catch them. A fast runner like you. Run as fast as you can."

Billy stood quite still, watching her.

"Come on," she said, rippling her outstretched fingers.

Billy looked back towards the distant rooftops, barely visible above the trees.

So far away.

"You've no one to play with back there," the old lady said. "Come on with us. You'll have so much fun."

Billy took small steps closer to her. He let her take his fingers in hers.

"Come on," she said again. "Let's catch them. Let's run."

She took off, dragging Billy after her. So quick, her strange olden days boots barely touching the ground. Billy ran too, faster, until he kept pace with her, then faster, pulling her along behind him.

Up ahead, the other children, laughing and laughing.

And more, dozens now, all calling his name, all shouting can't catch me, can't catch me.

Deeper into the trees until he didn't know where he was, until it he could no longer see the sky above, until he couldn't have found the path home if he looked for a hundred years, or a thousand years, or a million years. Still he giggled, the old lady's hand in his.

So far away now, so far he would never hear his mum's voice, no matter how loud and how long she called. Even if she searched all day and all night, she would never find him, not out here, not so deep and lost among the trees.

Billy felt like he could run for ever and ever and ever.

ECHO

I'm lucky. I have two birthdays. The ninth of March and the second of September. Two cakes and two presents. On Christmas Morning, there are two piles in the living room. I don't know if I get more things than other kids. Maybe I just get the normal number of presents split in two. One pile is always girls' things, but that's okay.

Today is my twelfth birthday. The second one. The real one.

There are bottles on the coffee table in the living room when I come downstairs. The lino on the kitchen floor is cold on my bare soles, so I walk on tippy-toes. Angus looks up from his bed in the corner, blinking. He sighs and huffs, buries his nose between his paws, and goes back to sleep.

The Crunchy Nut Corn Flakes are kept in the top cupboard, out of my reach. I bring a chair from the table, careful not to scrape it across the floor, and place it beneath my target. I climb up, open the cupboard, and grab the box.

Later, I'll have Weetabix without sugar, and I won't

complain. Mum will be happy, and Dad will wonder how he gets through the Crunchy Nut so quickly.

I wash the bowl and spoon, dry them, and put them back.

Not a word.

Back in bed, the sheets are cool. Dry, thank God. The first time in weeks. I burrow in, like a worm through soil. I flex my toes between the cotton.

Clanking bottles wake me up. Mum sings to herself downstairs, "She's a waterfall."

The Stone Roses, I think. She only plays them when she's had some wine. On LP, spinning on the old turntable that Dad bought at a vintage fair.

I like the crackle and hiss, but you can only hear them when you're up close. Close enough to see your reflection wavering in the black vinyl.

For the second time, I get out of bed and go downstairs.

I do lots of things twice.

"Morning, sweetheart."

Mum takes a bowl from the cupboard, drops two Weet-abix in, and a splash of milk.

I eat at the table, in the same seat as earlier.

"Do you think the postman will have anything for you?"

I shrug.

She strokes my back.

"Bet he will."

I look up at her. Her face is dry and lost. Her eyes are red.

Today will not be a good day.

"Where's Dad?" I ask.

"He's having a lie-in," she says, and clears the last of the bottles into the recycling bag. "Are you looking forward to your party?"

"Yeah," I say, but I'm not.

Two hours of forced smiles and thank-yous. No school friends will come because I don't go to school. Mum teaches me. She used to be a primary school teacher. There's a blackboard in the front room, but it's rarely used. Mostly, I read books. People from the education authority come round sometimes. Mum smiles for them. So do I. They go away happy.

The only guests at my birthday party will be my parents, Aunt Laura and her latest new boyfriend, and Granny Carol.

Granny Carol will get weepy. Aunt Laura will put an arm around her. Mum will start clearing up while they're still eating. Dad will wait for them to leave, then he'll excuse himself and go back to his office upstairs in the attic.

That's the easy part. Before that, it'll be the photo album. I wonder how long she'll go before she gets it out. Maybe an hour or two, if I'm lucky.

"Can I walk Angus?" I ask.

"Your dad walks the dog," she says, sitting down opposite.

"He could walk him again," I say. "Later on. Angus wouldn't mind."

"No, sweetheart. It's too dangerous. Those roads. And you can't go into the Folly on your own."

"You said I could walk him when I was old enough."

"Twelve isn't old enough. What if you fell in the river?"

I realise my mistake.

"I couldn't lose you again," she says.

"Mum," I say, trying to undo what I've done.

Too late. She's gone.

She stands, goes to the bookcase against the far wall. I watch as she finds the darkest spine on the shelf, lifts it out, brings it back to the table. She tightens her dressing gown around herself, sits down, opens the photo album to the first page.

A baby, pink and blind, in a clear plastic crib, white bands on its ankles. Its head lies to the side, a puff of dark hair on its scalp.

"Eight pounds," she says. "You were a good weight. Healthy. You came out at two in the morning. Like a purple mole, you were. But, Christ, you screamed the place down. Me and your dad in floods."

She touches the photograph.

"No medication at all. I took the pain, every bastard bit of it."

More pictures. Dad holding the baby. Aunt Laura and some other boyfriend, Granny Carol with tears in her eyes. Stronger and bigger before the cancer broke her.

The baby grows, gets longer in the limbs, fatter. The eyes open, first blue, then deep green. A helpless thing, held in someone's arms, then sitting up and smiling, pink gums.

Then one tooth. Then the single photograph of the child clinging to the edge of an armchair, standing, turned to the camera, grinning with that one tooth.

Then still and pale in a box, a white gown, flowers all around.

Mum weeps.

I want to leave the table. I can't. Not now. Her tears smack the plastic that covers the photograph.

Finally, she sniffs. Exhales. She reaches across and squeezes my arm.

"Thank God you came back," she says.

THEY SING "HAPPY BIRTHDAY" in the front room. The school things, the blackboard and the desk, have been cleared away. Mum sets the cake in front of me. I blow. Twelve flames die.

"What did you wish for?" Granny Carol asks.

"Can't tell you," I say.

Can't. Won't.

Mum would slap me around the ear if I said the wish out loud. Then she would go to her bedroom and wail loud enough for me to hear through the burn and the sting.

The cake is from Sainsbury's. It's not bad. The use-by date was yesterday, but it isn't dry.

Granny Carol has a sherry. She asks to see the photo album. Mum says not now, maybe later. Granny Carol goes quiet and faraway.

Aunt Laura's new boyfriend is called Trevor. He is very polite, always apologising and stepping out of people's way. Always offering to carry things, or tidy things away, or give up his seat.

I think he wants everyone to know how polite he is, which means he's not really polite at all.

The talk has gone on for an hour, and I am half asleep, when Trevor says, "I was sorry to hear about your first child . . ."

His words trail off like someone falling. I look up, a sudden hollowness in my middle.

Everyone is quiet for a moment, then Mum says, "Thank you. We don't talk about it much."

Aunt Laura's face is pale, her mouth a perfectly straight line.

Trevor shifts in the hard chair. "Sorry, I didn't mean to . . ."

His apology dies in his mouth.

Granny Carol clears her throat and says, "I'd like to see the photo album, please."

Mum nods. She stands, goes to the kitchen and the bookcase there, and returns with the leather-bound album in her hands. She places it in Granny Carol's lap.

Granny Carol takes a breath, then opens the album. She stares at the first photograph, her lips rubbing against each other.

"Such a wee dote," she says. "So content. Most content child I ever saw in my life. She hardly cried at all."

She touches the picture, just like Mum did earlier.

She turns the stiff pages, one picture after another. She cries.

Mum watches me.

I say nothing.

AUNT LAURA HUGS ME before she leaves. She hugs me hard, like she means it. I go upstairs. Angus follows, nuzzling my heels.

Mum and Dad argue. I hear them barking at each other from below.

I lie on my bed, grab Dad's iPod from the bedside locker. He hasn't noticed it's missing yet. It usually takes him a week or two before he comes looking for it. I push the earbuds in as far as they'll go. I choose a Led Zeppelin album.

They're from the olden days, but I like them. The singer has a squeaky voice. The song is called "Black Dog." Angus is black, apart from the white patch on his chest. He curls up at my feet.

Melody sits on the end of the bed.

I ignore her.

I sing to myself, a hoarse whisper about big-legged women and their lost souls.

Melody stares. And stares.

"Piss off," I say.

She does not.

I kick her lower back. Angus hops off the bed. She stares harder.

I groan and pull the earbuds out.

"What?"

She smiles. "Happy birthday."

I turn over on my side, face the wall. But I still feel her there.

"What do you want?"

She lies down beside me, her back against mine. Her bare toes seek the gaps between my jeans and my socks. They tickle, but I don't tell her to stop.

"Just to say happy birthday. No need to be a pishmire about it."

I think about getting up and leaving the room. Maybe see if Dad will let me use his computer. Instead I say, "You'd be fourteen by now."

"Thirteen and a half," Melody says. "You can't count."

"Mum doesn't really do sums."

"It's called maths."

"Whatever. We just do reading."

Melody asks, "Do you wish you could go to proper school?"

"Sometimes," I say. "The other kids would pick on me, though."

"They might not."

"They would. Definitely."

I had a friend once. Just for a few days, summer before last. His name was Dale. He used to walk past our house

when I was playing in the front garden. One time he stopped
and asked what I was doing.

"Building a fort," I said.

Four chairs from the kitchen arranged in a square, and a
tablecloth over the top.

"Can I come in?" he asked.

We played all day until Mum realised I'd taken the chairs.
She would've slapped me if Dale hadn't been there. She
asked his name. She asked who his parents were.

"Yes, I know them," she said, like it mattered.

Dale came back the next day. I took him up to my bedroom. He said "Wow" when he saw the toys. There were
dozens of little men, a couple of women, and some robots.
And a big spaceship. They had been my dad's. He found
them in the attic when Granda Tom died and Granny Carol
wanted somewhere smaller. The attic that he made an office
when we took the house. I don't remember very well, I was
small. But he gave me the toys.

I explained all this to Dale. He picked up two almost
identical figures.

"You've got two Boba Fetts," he said.

"Two what?"

"Boba Fett," he said. "The bounty hunter. He was in *Episode Five. The Empire Strikes Back*."

"The what?"

"*Star Wars*," he said, laughing like I'd said something
crazy. "The films. You know, the movies?"

I shook my head. Fear crept up inside me, fear that I had failed some test, that he would walk out thinking me a fool for not knowing what he was talking about.

"You've not seen them?" he asked. "Seriously?"

I shook my head again, felt my eyes go warm, something thick in my throat.

Do. Not. Cry.

He smiled. "Look. This is Luke Skywalker." He picked up one figure after another, showed them to me. They looked very small in his thick fingers. "He's a goodie. He's a Jedi Knight. But not yet, not in this outfit. And this is Darth Vader. He's the main baddie. But he's kind of a goodie as well. And this is Han Solo, and Chewbacca, and these are stormtroopers, they fight for Darth Vader. And you know what this is?"

He pointed to the spaceship. I shook my head.

"It's the *Millennium Falcon*."

We played for three hours. Space battles. Dale was good at the noises. Pew-pew-pew! Vvvooommm! Grraarrr!

He said I could come round to his tomorrow to watch *Star Wars. Episode IV*, he said, the best one.

I told Mum at dinner that night. I told her Dale's house was just around the corner, number twenty-three. I asked please, could I go, please? Dad watched Mum across the table while she sat there quiet. After a while, he put his hand on hers.

"It's just around the corner," he said.

I wanted to get up from my chair and hug him.

"You can walk him round," Dad said. "The film's, what, two hours? Walk him round then go back and get him."

I wanted to say I could go by myself, but I knew to keep my mouth shut.

Eventually, she nodded once and said, "All right. Two hours."

Dad smiled at me. Mum's hands shook.

I woke up early the next morning, my tummy full of scratchy things. I couldn't hold a thought in my head other than *Star Wars*. Dale had said it was brilliant, told me the entire story, but I didn't care if I knew how it ended. I wanted to see it anyway. I went to the toilet so many times, Mum asked me if I was ill. She picked out my clothes for me. She took a long time about it, crying when she couldn't find the socks she wanted me to wear.

I told her it didn't matter about the socks.

"Of course it fucking matters," she said, her voice high and cracking.

We found them at the bottom of the laundry basket half an hour later.

At five minutes to two, the socks still warm and damp from sitting over the radiator, Mum closed the front gate behind us. We didn't speak as we walked to the end of our road, and turned into the next street.

Number twenty-three stood at the far end. It looked like a nice house. A nice garden. Flowers and all. The gate didn't have any rust on it, didn't squeak when Mum opened it.

The doorbell worked. I heard it chime inside. I saw the shape of a woman through the frosted glass, and Dale beside her. I saw their hands moving. I heard them whispering hard. Then Dale walking away.

The door opened. Dale's mum was pretty, like in television adverts. She looked at my mum, then at me.

"Hello," she said. Her smile looked like it didn't belong on her face.

Mum nudged me.

"Is Dale in?" I asked, even though I'd seen him through the glass. "He asked me to come round. To watch *Star Wars*."

Her smile looked like it hurt. "I'm sorry, love, Dale's not well today. Bit of a cold. Sorry."

Mum took my hand in hers. "It was just for a couple of hours," she said.

"I know," Dale's mum said. "But honestly, he's got an awful dose. I wouldn't want your lad to catch anything."

Mum's hand squeezed mine tight, squishing my fingers together.

"He was so excited," she said.

"I'm sorry," Dale's mum said, easing the door over. "Honestly."

My mum said, "You bitch."

Dale's mum stopped the door a few inches from its frame, her pretty face suspended between. "Excuse me?"

"You fucking bitch."

I started to walk away, but she kept hold of my hand.

Dale's mum said, "Look, there's no call for that kind of language. Not on my doorstep."

"He's not good enough to play with your lad. I know. He's got a nutjob for a mother, and a failure for a father. You don't want the likes of him around your boy. That's it, isn't it?"

"Listen, Mrs. Chaise, I know you've had some problems, and I do sympathise, but that doesn't give you an excuse to go around abusing people in their own homes. Now, I'd like you to leave."

I tried to pull my mum away. She stood firm.

"You're a fucking stuck-up cunt," she said.

Dale's mum stayed quiet for a moment, her mouth open, before she said, "Get out of here now or I'll call the police."

She slammed the door.

Mum let go of my hand.

"Please, Mum," I said. "Let's go. Please."

Mum stood there, breathing hard. Then she looked around the garden until she saw a big green ceramic flower-pot. She picked it up, grunting at the weight of it.

"Please, Mum, don't."

She threw the pot at the door. Bang. Compost and green ceramic fragments scattered. A crack in the glass.

Mum grabbed my hand, hauled me back home.

The police came half an hour later. A man and a woman. The woman did the talking. Small voices. Kind voices.

No charges. Just stay away. You and the boy.

Mum stayed drunk for a month. Dad did the cooking.

The next time I saw Dale, he called me a fucking weirdo, said my mum was a mental hippy, and hit me so hard in the stomach that my pee was red for a whole day.

Melody stayed away for ages. Because I was angry, she told me later. She doesn't like me when I'm angry.

I don't know if she really likes me the rest of the time. She says she does, but I'm not sure. Sometimes she calls me the Walrus. Not because I'm fat. I'm not. Because of the song by the Beatles.

I am the Walrus.

I am he as you are me, or something like that.

It's on Dad's iPod. My back to hers, I take one earbud out and hand it over. She pushes it into her ear.

We listen to olden-days music together until it gets dark and I get hungry. By then, she's gone, but she'll be back tomorrow.

MUM SAYS SHE'S TOO tired to do school stuff today. I can go and play in my room if I want. She sleeps on the couch. Dad stays up in his office.

He says he's working, but I don't hear the clatter of his keyboard when I listen at the bottom of the narrow stairs that lead up to the attic. I'm not allowed to disturb him when he's up there. That's the worst thing I could do. It would break his concentration.

Dad hasn't written a book in years. He's started lots, but not finished any. He used to talk to Mum about it. Now he just stays in his office.

I go to Mum and Dad's bedroom.

The curtains are closed, and the bed isn't made. Clothes on the floor. The room smells like sweat and warm earth. I turn on a bedside lamp, the one on Dad's side, with all his notebooks and the scribbles I can't read.

I cross to the big chest of drawers. The second drawer down is open a little bit, clothes spilling out over its lip. I open the bottom drawer and smell something like old damp towels.

There are clothes in here that haven't been worn in years. And broken things, a hairdryer without a lead to plug it in, a razor with no batteries. An old passport. It's Dad's. I've looked at it before. It has stamps from America and Australia and other places. He used to travel a lot for his books. Now the passport's out of date.

What I'm looking for is at the bottom. A folder made of orange card.

Inside there are pages from newspapers. Some of them proper famous papers, like the *Sun* and the *Mirror*, but most of them are local papers like the *Belfast Telegraph* and the *News Letter* and the *Ulster Gazette*. The pages have turned yellow. They all have that same photograph from Mum's album, the baby holding on to the chair, smiling. That one tooth.

TODDLER SWEPT AWAY BY RIVER
SWOLLEN RIVER CLAIMS LITTLE MELODY
LOCAL CHILD DROWNED, FAMILY DEVASTATED

I read one of the stories.

An Armagh family is in shock today as it comes to terms with the drowning of toddler Melody Chaise. The mother had removed the child from her buggy to walk along the bank of the Folly Glen River, known locally as the Folly, which had swollen due to recent heavy rainfall, when Mrs. Glenda Chaise reportedly slipped and fell, losing her grip on the child's hand.

I read another.

The grandmother of local toddler Melody Chaise has spoken of her family's utter devastation at the child's tragic drowning. Carol Mawhinney said the little girl, an only child, will be desperately missed by all who knew her. Mrs. Mawhinney said, "I don't know how we'll get over this. I'm so worried for her mummy and daddy. How can they survive it?"

And another. This one has a photograph of the funeral. Dad carrying the white coffin, his face all crumpled up. Mum looking like a ghost.

The Coroners Service for Northern Ireland has ruled that the recent drowning of a fourteen-month-old girl was a tragic accident. The coroner stated that weather conditions in the days previous to the incident contributed not only to deeper and faster-moving water at the Folly Glen River, but also to poor footing along the path that runs alongside.

I know the river. I've been there lots of times.

Once, Mum took me. She walked me along the path to the fence made of wire and wood with the steep drop on the other side. Mum said the fence didn't use to be there. She stood beside me, holding my hand tight, looking at the water. It moved slow and lazy.

She asked me if I remembered. I said no, I didn't.

I've gone back other times. Sometimes if Mum has a nap, and Dad's upstairs working, I go to the river. It's only a few minutes away from our house. Some days I go to that spot, where the fence wasn't before, and other times I don't. I like the trees and the quiet. In the autumn, the squirrels run and hop through the leaves on the ground. I wish I could bring Angus so he could chase them.

I think he could catch one. I would watch him eat it, his teeth red. The guts spilling out.

I'm kneeling by the chest of drawers, the newspaper pages on the floor in front of me, picturing the dog eating the raw meat. The tiny bones breaking. It gives me a feeling that I think I shouldn't like.

A movement in the corner of my eye. I spin around, fall on to my arse.

Melody sitting on the edge of Mum and Dad's bed.

"You were touching yourself again," she says.

"Piss off," I say. "I wasn't."

"Yes you were. Pervert."

I stand up. I cross the few feet of floor to the bed. I open my hand and slap her cheek. Her head rocks back. She closes her eyes for a few seconds. I feel the burn on my own face, and the heat on my palm.

When she opens her eyes again, she asks, "Do you want to bite me?"

She reaches out her bare forearm. I take her skin between my teeth, close them until I can't stand the pain anymore. Tears roll down her cheeks, and she wipes them away. I see the twin red crescents on her forearm, exactly the shape and colour of the ones that have appeared on mine.

She looks down. I know what she's looking at. I want to hit her again, but instead I walk towards the door.

"Hey, Walrus."

I stop. My insides are hot with anger. "What?"

"You're forgetting something."

I turn and see her pointing to the newspaper pages on the floor. "Shit," I say. I go back and gather them up, put them in the folder, return the folder to the drawer, arrange the old clothes and broken things as they were before I disturbed them.

Melody asks, "Why don't you ask Mum if you can look at the papers? She'd probably let you."

"I don't want her to know I'm looking at them," I say.

"Why?"

Her cheek has a red handprint on it. I can still feel the sting of it on my own skin. The anger that burns my insides turns to something else, something heavier.

"Because she'd look at them with me, and then she'd start crying again."

Melody shrugs. "Why do you want to look at them anyway?"

"Dunno." I sit on the bed beside her. "To see if I remember."

"Remember what?"

"Falling in," I say. "Drowning. What it felt like."

She takes my hand in hers. "But you didn't fall in. I did."

"But I am he—"

"—as you are me. I know."

We sit quiet for a while. Her fingers aren't warm or cold on mine. They're just there. I ask, "Do you remember what it felt like? When you fell in. When you drowned."

"No," she says.

"You'd think you'd remember something like that."

"Well, I don't," she says.

"Why not?"

"Because I am he—"

"—as you are me—"

"—and we are always together."

Those aren't the real words, but it doesn't matter. They're still true.

Quiet again. Then I say, "Sorry for hitting you."

"S'all right," she says. She leans close to me. "Do you want to go to the river now?"

"Yeah," I say.

I PEEK INTO THE living room. Mum is lying on the couch, her breath raspy in her throat. A bottle of red wine is open on the table, a mostly empty glass beside it. I leave her there and close the front door as quietly as I can. The garden gate squeaks. Inside the house, Angus barks like he does at the postman. I know if he wakes Mum, she'll just shout at him to shut up before she rolls over and goes back to sleep.

I go to the end of our road, turn back into the Crescent, then into the Ballynahone estate. The houses here are smaller than ours, newer, and uglier. I've been beaten up here a couple of times. Today it's all right, though, because most of the kids are at school. Except the ones who mitch off, but they aren't around either.

There's a playground down some concrete steps. Mum used to take me here when I was younger. She says I'm too old for swings and slides now.

The Folly is on the other side of the playground. You have to open the gate and go through. A path leads down into the trees. Soon, you can't see the houses, only the brown and grey trunks, and the leaves, still green. Conkers, hidden in their shells, lie on the ground. I kick at them as I walk. Some of them I stamp on. Like little skulls crushed under my feet.

The river cuts through our side of town. It used to be bigger. It carved a bowl out of the earth, Dad told me, and that's where the trees grew. The ground slopes down towards the water until you reach the gravel path at its bank. Today, there isn't much here. Just a stream. It smells of chemicals, and suds clump on the surface, foaming around the stones that poke up out of the water. Dad told me there used to be fish here. Tiny ones called sticklebacks, he used to catch them in buckets when he was a kid, but they're all gone now.

Melody walks behind me.

"Are you going to that place?" she asks.

"Maybe," I say.

I walk towards the bridge. Halfway across, I stop and look over the railing. I see a wheel off a bike gathering mud and weeds. Rusty beer cans and plastic bags. Next big rainfall, when it turns from a dirty stream back into a proper river, the rubbish will be washed away. Like old memories.

"Come on," Melody says.

I follow her across the bridge to the gravel path on the other side. She stays ahead of me. The ground dips up and down. We pass the picnic area with its benches and burnt patch in the grass. Where the path cuts closest to the river, there are fences of wood and wire. Melody stops at one.

I put my hands on the fence. Look over. There's a drop

on the other side, straight down into the water. Even if there wasn't enough water to drown in, you'd break your head on the stones. I lean a little farther.

I imagine my head hitting the stones, going blind from the pain and the shock of it, warm things spilling out.

Dad says imagination is a curse. Picturing the worst horrors you can think of, then writing them down. Maybe that's why he doesn't want to write anything anymore.

The water moves like a fat snake.

"It was summertime when you fell in," I say.

"Was it?"

I imagine what it felt like. Slipping, falling away. A hand holding my hand, then not, then down into the water.

"I think it must have been cold," I say. "Even if it was summer."

And how fast the water. Swept away, just like that. They found the little body half a mile downstream, snagged on fallen branches.

"Why don't we remember?" I ask.

"Maybe we were too young," Melody says. "Or maybe we don't want to remember."

"Maybe," I say.

I know Melody isn't real. Not real in the way Mum and Dad are, or even Angus. I know she lives in my head. I know the real Melody I talk to has never been, never grew up like that, never learned to talk and run and hit and bite and all the things she does.

But still, there she is. And she is we and we are all together. Melody stands close. "I think what Mum says isn't true."

"What?" I ask.

"About you and me."

"What about you and me?" I ask.

"About you being me."

I don't answer. I look at the water, the fat snake.

"What if you're not me?" she asks. "What if I'm not you?"

"Shut up," I say.

"What if you're just you and nobody else?"

"Fucking shut up," I say. Loud enough so my voice comes back to me through the trees.

"I think she didn't slip," Melody says. "I think I didn't fall."

"Stop it," I say.

"I think she carried me down the bank," Melody says. "I think she brought me down there, and she put me in the water."

"Stop," I say.

"I think it was cold," Melody says. "So cold. Right to the bones of me. I think she held me under. I was scared. I looked up and I could see her face through the water. Her hands were hard on my shoulders. I think I could hear her screaming. I tried to cry but I was too cold inside and it hurt."

"Shut your fucking mouth," I say.

I turn to look at her, to slap and bite her, but she isn't

there. Instead, along the path, Mum stands staring back at me. Slippers on her feet. Her coat buttoned tight. Her eyes wide. Her mouth turned down, her lip shaking.

I try to think of something to say. Some reason I can give her.

Mum marches towards me, her open hands cutting through the air. I open my mouth. She raises her fist. It hits me below my eye, a hard slam against my cheekbone. I fall down, my head light.

"What are you doing?" Her voice is high and shaky.

I scramble back. The gravel is wet and stinging on my palms. The heat beneath my eye grows hotter and heavier.

She follows me. "What are you doing here?"

I try to speak, but I can't find the breath.

"You're not allowed to come here on your own."

"I'm sorry," I say. It comes out as a whisper.

"You're sorry?" She shakes her head. "You're fucking sorry? You little . . . you . . ."

She falls on me.

I bring my forearms up, try to keep her hands away, but it's no good. The nails and the knuckles, the ring she wears on her left hand.

I wish someone would come, pull her away, make her stop. But no one does.

Hot, hot pain above my eyes, and they fill with blood. I am blind. I cover my face with my hands. Her weight shifts on me as she leans back.

"Oh my God, sweetheart, I didn't . . . I didn't . . ."

I hear her voice. Know her position. I take my hands away from my face, blink, see light and shade. Push myself upright.

Her voice wavers as she touches my cheek.

"Sweetheart, I—"

I put my shoulders and my neck into it. My head snaps forward. I feel her nose crushed against my brow. She rocks backwards and I feel the heat of her blood on my chest. I roll sideways, and she topples over.

She cries out. I wipe at my eyes, regain something of my vision. She falls back against the fencing, nothing more than sticks and wire. It cannot hold her weight. The sticks and wire give way, and she tumbles back.

I wipe at my eyes again, watch her fall, taking the fence with her. As she slides down the bank, her foot catches in the wire, whips her body back and down.

The sound of her head meeting rock echoes through the trees like a gunshot.

I stand, wiping more blood from my eyes, blinking it away. At the edge, at the torn-away fence, I look down. Her eyes are open wide. Her mouth is working, like she's trying to tell me something. The shallow water around her head swirls with red.

Melody stands beside her, looking.

Mum's eyes turn to where Melody stands. Wide and wild. Melody says nothing, only watches as Mum becomes very still. Then she climbs the bank, up to where I wait. I follow her home.

I GO TO THE bathroom, undress, and clean myself up. The cut on my forehead isn't as bad as I thought. I hold a wet facecloth against it, and the bleeding slows.

When I go downstairs, still in my underwear, Melody sits beside me on the couch. We watch cartoons on the television. Old ones and new ones. Most of them I'm not allowed to watch, but I don't care, I watch them anyway. Melody holds my hand, the one that isn't holding the facecloth against the cut.

We know this time is precious. We know it will end soon and we will have to talk to the police and think of lies to tell.

But for now, there are cartoons.

LONDON SAFE

Jason McCoubry's mother stared at the postcard in his hand, her mouth a thin straight line. Her window didn't allow much light into the room, and sometimes he thought that a blessing. The drab painted walls, the bed with its rails to prevent her from falling in the night, the vase of plastic flowers. They had to sell her house to pay for this place, and she had wept when he first helped her through the door. The carers did their jobs well, but still, leaving his mother here had been about the hardest thing he'd ever done. Until now.

"Why didn't you tell me?" he asked.

"There was nothing to tell," she said, her voice as dry as the card in his hand.

"Nothing to tell? You said he'd left us."

"And that was the truth."

"Not the whole truth, though, was it?"

He was getting angry. He'd promised himself he wouldn't. She was a frail woman, mostly intact upstairs, but her body had failed her long ago. It wasn't fair to harangue her. But it wasn't fair that she'd lied to him. He swallowed the anger, pushed it down as far as he could.

"He left us," Margaret McCoubry said. "That's all you needed to know."

"But we never knew why," Jason said.

She lay back in the bed and looked up at the ceiling tiles. "What difference would that have made?"

"At least I could have understood. Maybe I wouldn't have wound up hating him the way I did. Thirty years, carrying that around with me. Thinking he didn't want us."

"He didn't," she said. "If he cared about you or me, he would never have done what he did."

What he did.

Informant was one word for it. Snitch was another. Or around here, in the towns and villages, in the cities like Belfast or Derry, the word was tout.

Touts out. Snitches get stitches.

He remembered the graffiti on the gable walls of the estate. Keep your mouth shut. Say nothing.

When Jason was eleven years old, one week after he started at the local grammar—the first in his family ever to pass the exams and get into a good school—his father wasn't at the breakfast table. Jason and his little sister, Claire, had sat in silence as their mother filled the bowls with cereal and milk, radiating fury and pain. She didn't have to say anything. He and Claire both knew something was terribly wrong.

Margaret told them that evening. Their father, Dan McCoubry, had abandoned them. Just gone. No explanation, no warning. Jason knew his father hadn't been himself this last while. He had become sullen and withdrawn when he'd always been jovial and outgoing. Everyone knew Long Dan, so-called because of his six-foot-four height married to a painfully slender frame. Long Dan the Handy Man. Those words were hand-painted on the side of the little Renault van he drove about the town, doing odd jobs, clearing gutters, papering walls, painting doors. He worked hard to feed his family, some years even made enough to pay for a stay in a guesthouse in Portrush in the dying days of August.

Long Dan McCoubry was a good man. Jason had been certain of that until his mother told him otherwise. That had been a Monday. On the following Friday, they moved house, moved town, moved county. Not even a chance to say goodbye to their friends. Barely even two weeks at the good school before Jason had to leave, starting over again at a place where he knew no one.

Six months ago, Jason had had to clear out his mother's house before it went on the market, and boxes full of letters and documents had been stacked in his garage ever since. Two days ago, he began sorting through them, filling bags for recycling, shredding the more private correspondence. He had found the postcard, dry and yellowed, in the bottom of a biscuit tin. It was bound up with a rubber band along with a selection of old photographs and envelopes. Blue ink in a meticulous script. He read it once, twice, three times before he understood.

> *Maggie—*
>
> *I'm sorry. I had to do it. They would of put me in jail if I didn't and told them I touted anyway so I have to go. You know its for the best. Tell the wee one's I love them and I will always miss them. Try to make them understand its for there own good. I don't want them to see me shot in front of them. Don't worry about me in London. I'll be safe.*
>
> *Dan*

Jason held it now in his hands, read it again.

"What did he do?" he asked.

"He turned on his own," Margaret said, "that's what he done."

He waited until she glanced at him. "Tell me. I deserve to know. So does Claire."

"What have you told her?"

She seemed concerned now, her face darkening. Her daughter had always been the delicate one, the one who needed protecting.

"Nothing," Jason said. "Yet."

Margaret let the air out of her chest, deflating, withering beneath the bedclothes.

"They came for him in the middle of the night," she said.

"Near kicked the door in before he got to it. They never explained anything, just told him to get dressed, follow them in his van. He didn't come home till the morning, after youse had gone to school. I never asked him what happened, but he told me that afternoon.

"They'd got a boatload of weapons in from South Africa. Rifles, he told me, pistols, all sorts. Dozens of them, he said. They'd got some stupid so-and-so to store some of them, but they needed to put up a false wall and none of them knew where to start. So they came for you father.

"There was a building supplies place they could take stuff from. Timber, plaster, whatever it was they needed. Took your father all night, but he got it done. They gave him fifty pound and two hundred fags for his trouble. Wasn't bad for one night, I suppose. But he didn't like it. He'd never got mixed up in that sort of carry on, but he put it out of his head and just got on with things.

"Then we were at our tea one night, maybe you remember it. The news came on the wireless, and they said they'd gone into a wee grocery shop on the other side of town and shot the owner dead. His daughter came out from the back, so they killed her too. They put out a statement saying the owner was in the IRA, but the police said that was nonsense. Anyway, your father said nothing, just put his knife and fork down and got up from the table, left his food sitting there."

Jason remembered. It had been summer, light outside as they ate, gammon and chips, slices of tinned pineapple rings on the kids' plates, fried eggs on their parents'. His father's seat suddenly empty for no reason, his mother silent and far away. He didn't remember the news. The killings happened so often, almost daily, that they barely registered. Just another dead girl he didn't know.

"So he went to the police?" Jason asked.

"Aye," Margaret said. "Not straight away. It took him a while. He was very quiet those few days, hardly spoke, didn't eat. Then he went out one evening, and when he came back he told me what he'd done. That he'd gone to the police station and told them everything, where the guns was hid, who had brought him there, all of it. Next evening, on the news, they said about the raid, showed the guns all lined up on the television. Said they'd arrested five men.

"We got the first bullet in the post a couple of days later. I went down to the shop at the end of the road for milk and they refused to serve me. Every job your father had lined up just disappeared. You and your sister never knew about any of that. I made excuses to keep you inside so you wouldn't realise the other wee'uns weren't allowed to play with you anymore. He told me that weekend that he had to go, that the police or MI5 or whoever had got him a place in London, and we couldn't go with him. I begged him not to leave us, for all the good that did me. And away he went."

Jason sat quiet for a time, staring at the picture on the postcard. The Strand at Portstewart, sand and sea stretching away into nothing. He remembered paddling there, the water splashing up around his knees, as his father held his hand. Hard skin and bones, the fingers yellowed by nicotine.

"Why didn't you tell us?" he asked.

"Tell you what? That your father was a tout?"

"He did the right thing."

She shook her head, her mouth downturned as if tasting something burned and bitter. "There's nothing right about turning on your own sort. No matter what they done. You don't turn on your own. And you don't run off on your family."

"Did you ever hear from him?"

"Just the once," she said. "That first Christmas. A card came with a hundred pound in it, saying get something for the wee'uns. I threw it on the fire."

Jason felt the familiar ball of hate in his chest, the same one he'd carried for thirty years. It weighed as much now as it had before he'd found the postcard, regardless of the truth he'd learned. But it weighed a fraction of the hate his mother carried; he could see it on her, feel the heat of it.

"I'm going to find him," Jason said.

Margaret said nothing.

"I'm going to find him and bring him home."

"Don't bring him anywhere near me," she said.

"Don't worry," Jason said, standing. "I won't."

They exchanged no goodbyes as he left her there.

THE MAN WHO HAD once been Long Dan the Handy Man walked through the morning crowds on his way to the little newsagent on Lupus Street. His name was still Dan McCoubry, they'd never given him the option of changing it, but no one here had ever known him as Long Dan. He remained slender, but his shoulders had slumped, his back hunched, so that nobody could see the tall man he used to be. And that was just as well, probably.

It was Imran behind the counter today. Sometimes it was his older brother, occasionally his father, but Dan liked Imran the best of them. The father was a decent sort, but the older brother was surly and watchful, as if every customer was a potential thief. There was a Tesco Express up the way a little, much closer to Dan's flat, but he didn't like the self-checkout.

"Good morning, my friend, how are you today?"

Imran smiled as he spoke the same eight words with which he always greeted Dan.

"Not too bad, not too bad."

Always the same reply. And the same two packets of cigarettes waiting on the counter, forty Mayfair, the same *Daily Mirror* along with them. Dan handed over the twenty-pound note, waited for his change, and said his thank yous and goodbyes.

Dan McCoubry had become a man of small routines and rituals, his days shaped by a strict schedule that rarely varied. Fags and paper in the morning. An hour in the gardens of St. George's Square if the weather was dry, back home in the kitchen with a cup of tea if it wasn't. Cheese on toast and an apple for lunch. The William Hill bookies by the tube station at two, then over to the White Swan on Vauxhall Bridge Road for a pint at three. Maybe a second pint, but never more than that. After that, he'd head home for his tea, apart from Fridays, when he'd buy fish and chips on the way. Then an evening spent with four cans of Guinness and a few whiskeys. As often as not he'd fall asleep on the couch, the TV spewing whatever shite was on, and he'd wake in the early hours and stagger to bed.

Routines and rituals, every day much like the last. Which was why, this morning, Dan became aware of being followed along Lupus Street on the way to St. George's Square.

He kept his head down as he walked, his paper tucked under his left arm, his right hand in his coat pocket, holding the two packets of cigarettes. Don't run, he told himself. Then he gave a quiet laugh. Run? At his age, and in his shape? Jesus, he'd collapse before he got ten feet.

Dan paused at the top of Ranelagh Street, looked around to check for cars turning into the corner. He waited for a van to exit the junction. Checked again, saw the man slow down, trying to look casual.

Forty-ish, Dan thought. Tall and dark-haired. Casually dressed, good clothes. He wasn't a paramilitary, he was almost certain. They would never wear good clothes unless it was a disguise. He didn't have that look about him, whoever he was. Maybe a cop? No. Not that either.

He crossed the junction and kept walking, weaving

among the other pedestrians. All suits and designer hand-bags. Pimlico had been a shithole when he moved here thirty years ago, given one of the council flats in Churchill Gardens. Back then it was ordinary people, decent people, who lived and bred and died there. Now it was full of rich bastards pushing out the poor bastards like him. Gentrifica-tion, they called it. There was nothing gentle about it.

Dan found himself getting angry. For a moment, he thought it was at the injustice of losing this neighbourhood to the fuckers with the money. Then he realised he was angry at being followed, at being found. Not that he lived in hiding, but he'd always kept to himself, avoided drawing attention.

His first months in London had been spent in near con-stant fear, so bad that he'd had to go to the doctor with his nerves. Every man on the street had a pistol hidden beneath his coat, every shadow held a watchful spy, every footstep behind was a quickening approach. But he got over that fear. He had to. There was no choice in the end. He changed in that first twelve months, was hardened by it. Neither the cops nor the MI5 people would look out for him. He had to do it for himself.

Now he reached the pedestrian crossing at the stop of Clavenden Street, the green man already flashing, no need to stop. Which was a pity, because it would have been an opportunity to look around, get another gander at the man who followed as he was forced to draw close.

No such luck. He kept going, keeping his space as steady as his age would allow. Short of breath now, but not struggling. Not yet. He felt his heart knock, breathed in deep through his nose, out through his mouth, getting all the oxygen he could.

The crowds thickened towards the crossing at the Square, the church across the way. People heading for Pimlico tube station, the fancy offices on Vauxhall Bridge Road, or across the river. They bunched beneath the lights. Dan turned his head, tried to get one more look at the follower, could only make out a vague shape at the edge of his vision. He was smart, holding back, but not too far, being polite, letting others step in front of him. The light changed, and Dan let a few people stream past him until their annoyed excuse me, pardon me, do you mind, became too much.

Dan crossed knowing that if he stopped right now, in the middle of the road, the follower would probably slam into his back. He considered it for a moment but changed his mind. Don't show your hand too soon, he thought. Fewer people on the pavement leading down the long side of the gardens. Hardly any at all, and now the follower's footsteps rang clear because there were no others to hide them. Dan slowed. The footsteps slowed. He sped up. So did they.

He reached the gate halfway down the gardens, the one that opened onto the path, the path that led to the fountain at the centre, surrounded by benches. That was where Dan most liked to sit, smoking a fag, reading the paper, listening to the flow and bubble of the water.

But not today.

Today was different.

JASON PAUSED AT THE gate as it swung shut behind his father. Yes, it was definitely him. Long Dan McCoubry. Not so long now, slumped with age as he was. That had thrown him when he first saw the old man two days ago. All these years, his father had been fixed in his mind at young middle age, hair still black and thick with Brylcreem, always flopping over his eyes to be pushed away with hard thin fingers. Jason summoned that image. The shirtsleeves rolled up. A cigarette behind his ear. Skin red from working in the sun.

But this old man. His skin was almost as grey as his hair, his face sunken. The pallid, lined face of a smoker, his thinning white hair yellowed at the front by the nicotine.

It had been easier to find him than he'd expected. He'd had all sorts of notions about witness protection programmes, new identities, but in reality they'd just set him up in a flat here thirty years ago and let him get on with it. Jason had gone to an old school friend who was now a detective inspector in the PSNI, given him the full name, date of birth, and the knowledge that his father had gone to London. Less than twenty-four hours later, his friend had come back with two men by that name. A little checking, including a peek at the DVLA database, and the one in

North London was discounted, leaving only the man Jason had followed to these gardens.

Two days he'd been watching. Just to be sure. No, that was a lie he'd been telling himself. It had nothing to do with certainty, it was beyond certainty. The truth was that he was afraid.

Of what, exactly?

That he'd got the wrong man? The worst that could happen would be a shrug, a sorry, you've got the wrong bloke, mate. No, that wasn't the worst. The worst would be if he had the right man, but the right man told him to go, leave him alone. Jason didn't know if he could take that. Didn't know how he might react, tears or rage or both.

Open the gate, Jason told himself. Open it and walk through. Catch up with him. Tap his shoulder. Call his name. Call him Dad. Whatever, just do it.

He pushed the gate open, let it swing closed behind him, and walked along the path, heading back towards the church. His father stepped beneath the shadows of the trees, his pace slowing, as if he knew Jason was there.

Jason quickened his own steps, a light jog, until the old man was within arm's reach, and now he saw just how old he was, how sloped his shoulders, how bent his back. He felt a chill as the shade of the trees covered him. He reached out, a hand on his father's shoulder.

"Da—"

Dan McCoubry turned, quicker than Jason would have

thought possible, his face cold and empty, no recognition. Jason felt something at first cold, then searing hot, by his navel. Pain followed. Then another cold stab, and another, and another. More of them, cold, hot, pain, then something warm spreading across his belly and down his thighs.

"Da—"

His knees folded, and he landed on his hip, then onto his side, his head resting on the path. So very warm here. The ground so soft. He wanted to sleep. Close his eyes and let the earth swallow him. But he needed to say it.

Dad.

The word never left his mouth.

DAN MCCOUBRY TURNED AND walked away, heading to the church, folding the blade and slipping the knife back into his pocket. Not too much blood. He glanced down, saw a spot the size of tuppence coin on his shoe. Pity, he'd have to get rid of them. But not too bad otherwise.

No one had seen. He was sure of that. It had been quick, silent. The bastard had tried to say his name. But Dan had been ready with the knife. He was always ready. Had to be. If he wasn't, he'd have got a bullet between the eyes. Like that time nearly thirty years back, when the man with the Belfast accent had found him taking a drunken piss in an alley. He'd zipped up, turned, heard the man say, "How're ya, Long Dan. The boys back home say hello." The man had raised a revolver, pulled the trigger, and nothing happened, just a dry click. The man's expression dropped and Dan took his chance. A brick did him in. He had run home and washed the pieces of skull and brain off his hands.

This had been no different. Get him before he gets you. Don't think, just do it. If he hadn't, he'd be the one lying with his life bleeding away into the grass.

By the time he'd slipped around the back of the church and out the other side of the gardens, he knew what to do. Walk to the river, get rid of the knife. Get back home, get cleaned up, get rid of the clothes. Maybe some CCTV had got him entering the park, maybe it hadn't. He'd kept his head down like he always did. Nothing to be done about it now.

Dan McCoubry re-joined the crowds, the good people going about their good business, no one watching him, no one recognising him. Whatever happened later, right now, on this pavement, among these people, he was safe.

London safe.

QUEEN OF THE HILL

Cam the Hun set off from his flat on Victoria Street with fear in his heart and heat in his loins. He pulled his coat tight around him. There'd be no snow for Christmas, but it might manage a frost.

Not that he cared much about Christmas this year. If he did this awful thing, if he could actually go through with it, he intended on drinking every last drop of alcohol in the flat. He'd drink until he passed out, and drink some more when he woke up. With any luck he'd stay under right through to Boxing Day.

Davy Pollock told Cam the Hun he could come back to Orangefield. The banishment would be lifted, he could return and see his mother, so long as he did as Davy asked. But Cam the Hun knew he wouldn't be able to face her if he did the job, not on Christmas, no matter how badly he wanted to spend the day at her bedside. He'd been put out of the estate seven years ago for "running with the taigs," as Davy put it. Still and all, Davy didn't mind coming to Cam the Hun when he needed supplies from the other side.

When E's and blow were thin on the ground in Armagh, just like any other town, the unbridgeable divide between Loyalist and Republican narrowed pretty quickly. Cam the Hun had his uses. He had that much to be grateful for.

He crossed towards Barrack Street, the Mall on his right, the old prison on his left. Christmas lights sprawled across the front of the gaol, ridiculous baubles on such a grim, desperate building. The Church of Ireland cathedral loomed up ahead, glowing at the top of the hill, lit up like a stage set. He couldn't see the Queen's house from here, but it stood just beneath the cathedral. It was an old Georgian place, three storeys, and would've cost a fortune before the property crash.

She didn't pay a penny for it. The Queen of the Hill had won her palace in a game of cards.

Anne Mahon and her then-boyfriend had rented a flat on the top floor from Paddy Dolan, a lawyer who laundered cash for the IRA through property investment. She was pregnant, ready to pop at any moment, when Dolan and the boyfriend started a drunken game of poker. When the boyfriend was down to his last ten-pound note, he boasted of Anne's skill, said she could beat any man in the country. Dolan challenged her to a game. She refused, but Dolan wouldn't let it be. He said if she didn't play him, he'd put her and her fuckwit boyfriend out on the street that very night, pregnant or not.

Her water broke just as she laid out the hand that won

the house, and Paddy Dolan's shoes were ruined. Not that it mattered in the end. The cops found him at the bottom of Newry Canal, tied to the driver's seat of his 5-Series BMW, nine days after he handed over the deeds. The boyfriend lasted a week longer. A bullet in the gut did for him, but the 'Ra let Anne keep the house. They said they wouldn't evict a young woman with newborn twins. The talk around town was a Sinn Féin councillor was sweet on her and smoothed things over with the balaclava boys.

Anne Mahon knew how to use men in that way. That's what made her Queen of the Hill. Once she got her claws into you, that was that. You were clean fucked.

Like Cam the Hun.

He kept his head down as he passed the shaven-headed men smoking outside the pub on Barrack Street. They knew who he was, knew he ran with the other sort, and glared as he walked by. One of them wore a Santa hat with a Red Hand of Ulster badge pinned to the brim.

As Cam the Hun began the climb up Scotch Street, the warmth in his groin grew with the terror in his stomach. The two sensations butted against each other somewhere beneath his navel. It was almost a year since he'd last seen her. That long night had left him drained and walking like John Wayne. She'd made him earn it, though. Two likely lads had been dealing right on her doorstep, and he'd sorted them out for her.

Back then he'd have done anything for a taste of the

Queen, but as she took the last of him, his fingers tangled in her dyed crimson hair, he noticed the blood congealing on his swollen knuckles. The image of the two boys' broken faces swamped his mind, and he swore right then he'd never touch her again. She was poison. Like the goods she distributed from her fortress on the hill, too much would kill you, but there was no such thing as enough.

He walked to the far side of the library on Market Street. Metal fencing portioned off a path up the steep slope. The council was wasting more money renovating the town centre, leaving the area between the library and the closed-down cinema covered in rubble. Christmas Eve revellers puffed on cigarettes outside the theatre, girls draped with tinsel, young men shivering in their shirtsleeves. The sight of them caused dark thoughts to pass behind Cam the Hun's eyes. He seized on the resentment, brought it close to his heart. He'd need all the anger and hate he could muster.

He'd phoned the Queen that afternoon and told her it had been too long. He needed her.

"Tonight," she'd said. "Christmas party at my place."

The house came into view as Cam the Hun climbed the slope past the library. Last house on the terrace to his left, facing the theatre across the square, the cathedral towering over it all. Her palace, her fortress. The fear slammed into his belly, and he stopped dead.

Could he do it? He'd done worse things in his life. She was a cancer in Armagh, feeding off the misery she sowed with her powders and potions. The world would be no poorer without her. She'd offloaded her twin sons on their grandmother and rarely saw them. No one depended on her but the dealers she owned, and they'd have Davy Pollock to turn to when she was gone. No, the air in this town could only be sweeter for her passing. The logic of it was insurmountable. Cam the Hun could and would do this thing.

But he loved her.

The sudden weight of it forced the air from his lungs. He knew it was a foolish notion, a symptom of his weakness and her power over him. But the knowledge went no further than his head. His heart and loins knew different.

One or two of the smokers outside the theatre noticed him, this slight figure with his coat wrapped tight around him. If he stood rooted to the spot much longer, they would remember him. When they heard the news the next day, they would recall his face. Cam the Hun thought of the ten grand the job would pay and started walking.

For a moment he considered veering right, into the theatre bar, shouldering his way through the crowd, and ordering a pint of Stella and a shot of Black Bush. Instead, he thought of his debts. And there'd be some left over to pay for a home help for his mother, even if it was only for a month or two. He headed left, towards the Queen's house.

His chest strained as he neared the top of the hill, his breath misting around him. He gripped the railing by her door and willed his heart to slow. Jesus, he needed to get more exercise. That would be his New Year's resolution. Get healthy. He rang the doorbell.

The muffled rumble of Black Sabbath's *Supernaut* came from inside. Cam the Hun listened for movement in the hall. When none came, he hit the doorbell twice more. He watched a shadow move against the ceiling through the glass above the front door. Something obscured the point of light at the peephole. He heard a bar move aside and three locks snap open. Warm air ferried the sweet tang of cannabis and perfume out into the night.

"Campbell Hunter," she said. "It's been a while."

She still wore her hair dyed crimson red with a black streak at her left temple. A black corset top revealed a laced trail from her deep cleavage, along her flat stomach, to the smooth skin above her low-cut jeans. Part of the raven tattoo was just visible above the button fly. He remembered the silken feel against his lips, the scent of her, the firmness of her body. She could afford the best work; the surgeons left little sign of her childbearing, save for the scar that cut the raven in two.

"A year," Cam the Hun said. "Too long."

She stepped back, and he crossed her threshold knowing it would be the last time. She locked the steel-backed door and lowered the bar into place. Neither bullet nor battering ram could break through. He followed her to the living room. Ozzy Osbourne wailed over Tony Iommi's guitar. A black artificial Christmas tree stood in the corner, small skulls, crows and inverted crosses as ornaments among the red tinsel. Men and women lay about on cushions and blankets, their lids drooping over distant eyes. Spoons and foil wraps, needles and rolled-up money, papers and tobaccos, crumbs of resins and wafts of powder.

"Good party," Cam the Hun said, his voice raised above the music.

"You know me," she said as she took a bottle of Gordon's gin and two glasses from the sideboard. "I'm the hostess with mostest. Come on."

As she brushed past him, sparks leaping between their bodies, Cam the Hun caught her perfume through the room's mingled aromas. A white-hot bolt crackled from his brain down to his groin. She headed to the stairs in the hall, stopped, turned on her heel, showed him the maddening undulations of her figure. "Well?" she asked. "What are you waiting for?"

Cam the Hun forced one foot in front of the other and followed her up the stairs. The rhythm of her hips held him spellbound, and he tripped. She looked back over her naked shoulder and smiled down at him. He returned the smile as he thanked God the knife in his coat pocket had a folding blade or he might have sliced himself open. He found his feet and stayed behind her as she climbed the second flight to her bedroom on the top floor.

The décor hadn't changed in a year, blacks and reds, silks and satins. Suspended sheets of shimmering fabric formed a canopy over the wrought-iron bedstead. A huge mound of pillows in all shapes and sizes lay at one end. He wondered if she still had the cuffs, or the—

Cam the Hun stamped on that thought. He had to keep his mind behind his eyes and between his ears, not let it creep down to where it could do him no good.

"Take your coat off," she said. She set the glasses on the dressing table and poured three fingers of neat gin into each.

He hung his coat on her bedpost, careful not to let the knife clang against the iron. She handed him a glass. He sat on the edge of the bed and took a sip. He tried not to cough at the stinging juniper taste. He failed.

Somewhere beneath the gin's cloying odour, and the soft sweetness of her perfume, he caught the hint of another smell. Something lower, meaner, like ripe meat. The alcohol reached his belly. He swallowed again to keep it there.

The Queen of the Hill smiled her crooked smile and sat in the chair facing him. She hooked one leg over its arm, her jeans hinting at secrets he already knew. She took a mouthful of gin, washed it around her teeth, and hissed as it went down.

"I'm glad you called," she said.

"Are you?"

"Of course," she said. She winked and let a finger trace the shape of her left breast. "And not just for that."

Cam the Hun tried to quell the stirring in his trousers by studying the black painted floorboards. "Oh?" he said.

"There's trouble coming," she said. "I'll need your help."

He allowed himself a glance at her. "What kind of trouble?"

"The Davy Pollock kind."

His stomach lurched. He took a deeper swig of gin, forced it down. His eyes burned.

"He's been spreading talk about me," she said. "Says he wants me out of the way. Says he wants my business. Says he'll pay good money to anyone who'll do it for him."

"Is that right?" Cam the Hun said.

"That's right." She let her leg drop from the arm of the chair, her heel like a gunshot on the floor, and sat forward. "But he's got no takers. No one on that side of town wants the fight. They know I've too many friends."

He managed a laugh. "Who'd be that stupid?"

"Exactly," she said.

He drained the glass and coughed. His eyes streamed, and when he sniffed back the scorching tears, he got that ripe meat smell again. His stomach wanted to expel the gin, but he willed it to be quiet.

"So, what do you want me to do?" he asked.

She swallowed the last of her gin and said, "Him."

He dropped his glass. It didn't shatter, but rolled across the floor to stop at her feet. "What?"

"I want you to do him," she said.

He could only blink and open his mouth.

"It'll be all right," she said. "I've cleared it with everyone that matters. His own side have wanted shot of him for years. Davy Pollock is a piece of shit. He steals from his own neighbours, threatens old ladies and children, talks like he's the big man when everyone knows he's an arsewipe. You'd be doing this town a favour."

Cam the Hun shook his head. "I can't," he said.

"Course you can." She smiled at him. "Besides, there's fifteen grand in it for you. And you can go back to Orangefield to see your mother. Picture it. You could have Christmas dinner with your ma tomorrow."

"But I'd have to—"

"Tonight," she said. "That's right."

"But how?"

"How? Sure, everyone knows Cam the Hun's handy with a knife." She drew a line across her throat with her finger. "Just like that. You won't even have to go looking for him. I know where he's resting his pretty wee head right this minute."

"No," he said.

She placed her glass on the floor next to his and rose to her feet, her hands gliding over her thighs, along her body, and up to her hair. Her heels click-clacked on the floorboards as she crossed to him. "Consider it my Christmas present," she said.

He went to stand, but she put a hand on his shoulder.

"But first I'm going to give you yours," she purred. "Do you want it?"

"God," he said.

The Queen of the Hill unlaced her corset top and let it fall away.

"Jesus," he said.

She pulled him to her breasts, let him take in her warmth. He kissed her there while she toyed with his hair. A minute stretched out to eternity before she pushed him back with a gentle hand on his chest. His right mind shrieked in protest as she straddled him, grinding against his body as she got into position, a knee either side of his waist. She leaned forward.

"Close your eyes," she said.

"No," he said, the word dying in his throat before it found his vocal cords.

"Shush," she said. She wiped her hand across his eyelids, sealed out the dim light. Her weight shifted and pillows tumbled around him. Her breasts pressed against his chest, her breath warmed his cheek. Lips met his, an open mouth cold and dry, coarse stubble, a tongue like ripe meat.

Cam the Hun opened one eye and saw a milky white globe an inch from his own, a thick, dark brow above it, pale skin blotched with red.

He screamed.

The Queen of the Hill laughed and pushed Davy Pollock's severed head down, rubbing the dead flesh and stubble against Cam the Hun's face.

Cam the Hun screamed again and threw his arms upward.

The heel of his hand connected with her jaw. She tumbled backwards and spilled onto the floor. The head bounced twice and rolled to a halt at her side. She hooted and cackled as she sprawled there, her legs kicking.

He squealed until his voice broke. He wiped his mouth and cheeks with his hands and sleeves until the chill of dead flesh was replaced by raw burning. He rolled on his side and vomited, the gin and foulness soaking her black satin sheets. He retched until his stomach felt like it had turned itself inside-out.

All the time, her laughter tore at him, ripping his sanity away shred by shred.

"Shut up," he wanted to shout, but it came out a thin whine.

"Shut up." He managed a weak croak this time. He reached for his coat, fumbled for the pocket, found the knife. He tried to stand, couldn't, tried again. He grabbed the iron bedpost with his left hand for balance. The blade snapped open in his right.

Her laughter stopped, leaving only the rushing in his ears. She looked up at him, grinning, a trickle of blood running to her chin.

"What are you?" he asked.

She giggled.

"What are you?" A tear rolled down his cheek, leaving a hot trail behind it.

"I'm the Queen of the Hill." Her tongue flicked out,

smeared the blood across her lips. "I'm the goddess. I'm the death of you and any man who crosses me."

"No," he said, "not me." He raised the knife and stepped towards her.

She reached for Davy Pollock's head, grabbed it by the hair.

Cam the Hun took another step and opened his mouth to roar. He held the knife high, ready to bring it down on her exposed heart.

He saw it coming, but it was too late. Davy Pollock's cranium shattered Cam the Hun's nose, and he fell into feathery darkness.

He awoke choking on his own blood and bile. He coughed and spat. A deep, searing pain radiated from beneath his eyes to encompass the entire world. The Queen of the Hill cradled his head in her lap. He went to speak, but could only gargle and sputter.

"Shush, now," she said.

He tried to raise himself up, pushing with the last of his strength. She clucked and gathered him to her bosom. He stained her breasts red.

"We could've been good together, you and me," she said.

His mouth opened and closed, but the words couldn't force their way past the coppery warm liquid. He wanted to weep, but the pain blocked his tears.

"You could've been my king," she said. She rocked him and kissed his forehead. "This could've been our palace on the hill. But that's all gone. Now there's only this."

She brought the knife into his vision, the blade so bright and pretty. "Close your eyes," she said.

He did as he was told. Her fingers were warm and soft as she loosened his collar and pulled the fabric away from his throat.

The cathedral bells rang out. He counted the chimes, just like he'd done as a child, listening to his mother's old clock as he waited for Santa Claus. Twelve and it would be Christmas.

It didn't hurt for long.

THE NIGHT HAG

She is awake. This is certain. She sees the room in the half-light, the nightstand, the lamp, the mobile phone. Someone is here. They embrace her, pinning her arms to her side. A leg wrapped around hers, pressing it down onto the mattress. She wants to lift her head, but a hand forces it into the pillow.

It is a woman, she is almost sure of that. Although she cannot see her, she knows her skin is blackened as if smeared with soot and ash.

She thinks, who's there?

Lips against her ear. A low, breathy giggle.

She wants to scream. No one is here to help her, but she wants to call for help anyway. She tries. The hand slips down around her jaw, closes it tight. Her tongue is locked in place. Her voice churns in her chest and throat but can't escape her mouth. She cries with every exhalation, pulling air through her nose, in and out, in and out, more frantic with each breath.

Help me.

God someone help me.

Help.

Then she's gone.

CATHERINE WOKE AGAIN, A second return to the room and the half-light, the nightstand, the lamp, the mobile phone. Her breath rasped in and out of her, her heart knocking in her chest, feeling like it could come untethered.

Calm, she told herself. Be calm.

She closed her eyes and turned her face into the pillow, smothered a low groan. Her hands grasped the bedsheets, her feet kicking against the mattress as if she were trying to climb it.

"God," she said, the vowel drawing out long and thin, the consonants swallowed by the pillow.

She turned onto her back, saw the flame-retardant tiles on the ceiling, the ones she'd wanted to tear down ever since she'd moved into this house.

"Oh, God," she said, a whisper this time, because it was a blasphemy, and fear was no excuse for taking the Lord's name in vain.

Catherine sat upright, letting the duvet slip away, feeling the early morning chill creep under her nightdress.

Might as well get up and go downstairs, she thought.

Have a cup of tea.

CATHERINE WAS AT THE library before opening time, waiting for them to unlock the doors. She had driven her ten-year-old Skoda Fabia into town and enjoyed a scone and a milky coffee at the little café next door, pretending to read one of the newspapers they kept in a rack for the customers.

That had kept her occupied until ten minutes to ten, and she had been waiting out here in the cold since then.

Helen, the manager, let her in at three minutes to the hour.

"Morning, Catherine," she said, wearing a layer of cheer over the fluster. "Sorry to keep you waiting, Tanya's off sick and I'm single-manning today."

"Not to worry," Catherine said, her own cheer masking her impatience.

She entered the library and walked straight to the row of computers along the side wall.

"Were you looking to use the internet?" Helen asked. "The network's on a timer, so it won't come on until ten. It'll be another minute or two to get everything switched on and booted up."

"No hurry," Catherine said, keeping her voice warm and smooth.

She sat down at the first computer and waited for what seemed an unreasonably long time.

As Helen fussed at something in her little office at the back, she called out, "Would you like a cup of tea? A coffee, maybe?"

Catherine almost said, yes, a coffee, please, but then she remembered the one she'd just had with a scone. She wasn't in the habit of drinking coffee, finding it made her jittery. Along with the three cups of tea she'd had that morning already, she decided against any more caffeine.

"No, thank you," she said.

A small red light blinked into life on the front of the computer terminal before her. She pressed the power button and waited while the machine booted up, her nails digging into her palms as she watched hourglasses and spinning wheels.

Finally, at last, the login dialogue appeared. Catherine knew her membership number and password by heart, and she typed them in, one stabbing forefinger at a time, clunk-clunk-clunk-clunk. Now the desktop and the scattering of icons. She chose the one for the web-browser, click-click.

Catherine knew how to do a Google search, having attended a class on using the internet at this very library. She typed once more, forefingers seeking out the keys, jabbing at them as if they were getting a scolding.

Woman holds me down on bed.

A few seconds of spinning wheels, then a list of results.

"Goodness," she said. "Oh, my goodness."

This wasn't what she expected to see. Not at all. She scanned the list, the lurid descriptions, thinking, surely the library would block this sort of thing?

"Everything all right, Catherine?"

Helen's voice from behind, coming towards her. Catherine grabbed the mouse, couldn't see the pointer on the screen, jiggled the mouse around until she found it.

Helen, right behind her.

"No," Catherine whispered, and her finger reflexively hit the left button, clicking a link to who knows what.

A page loaded on the screen.

Erotic Stories for Couples, it said.

And there was a photograph. Not entirely pornographic, but certainly not appropriate for a Tuesday morning at the library.

"What are you . . ."

Helen's voiced tailed off, her question answering itself.

"You might want to keep that sort of thing for home," Helen said. "I'm not judging, mind, just saying. There's a time and a—"

"I didn't mean to search for that," Catherine said, rather too forcefully.

Helen reached around her and took the mouse, guided the pointer up to the top of the browser window, and miraculously made the Google home page appear in its place.

"Then what did you mean to search for?"

Catherine felt herself stiffen, unused to sharing details of her life with people, even those she knew passably well.

"A . . . a dream I keep having. At least, I think it's a dream. It doesn't feel like one when it's happening."

Helen took the seat next to her. "What kind of dream?"

Catherine took a breath, clutched her hands together in her lap. "No. No, it's all right, I don't want to trouble you with my old nonsense."

"Tell me," Helen said, placing a hand on her forearm.

Catherine remained still and silent until Helen squeezed her arm.

"I wake up," she said. "That's the thing, you see, I'm wide awake when it happens. I know I am. I can see everything around me, I can hear everything. And I know there's someone with me. A woman. It's always the same woman. It's like she's holding me."

Catherine wrapped her arms around herself, tight.

"And I try to ask, who's there? But she holds my mouth shut. I try to turn my head, but she's holding it in place. I can't move my arms or my legs, she's got me pinned down, and she's so strong. So, so strong. But she's gentle, too, she doesn't hurt me. Not really. And then she starts whispering to me. That's when I try to scream, but I can't. She's holding my jaw too tight, and my tongue won't work."

She realised she'd been digging her nails into her upper arms. A small angry sting remained there when she took her hands away.

"And then she's gone," Catherine said. "She just . . . dissolves away, and I can move again."

Helen sat with her chin resting on her hand, her elbow on the desk. "How often does this happen? When did it start?"

"The first time was about six months ago, then it happened again a couple of weeks later. And a couple of weeks after that. But it's happening more often now. Twice this week. It's getting to be so I'm afraid to go to sleep in case she comes again."

Helen remained quiet, watching.

"I suppose you think I've gone mad," Catherine said.

Helen smiled. "Not at all. It's called sleep paralysis. I've never had it myself, but my husband has had it a few times."

"Sleep paralysis," Catherine echoed.

"From what I've read, the brain sends out a hormone that stops you from moving while you dream, but sometimes it overlaps with waking. You're awake but you're dreaming, and that hormone has you paralysed. It's sometimes accompanied by hallucinations, very often an old woman. The Night Hag."

"The Night Hag?"

"My husband saw her at the foot of the bed, then she'd climb on top of him and hold him down. Scared the life out of him."

Catherine nodded. "It is . . . frightening."

Bloody terrifying, she thought.

Helen stood. "Wait here."

Catherine watched as she crossed the library and browsed the nonfiction section, running her fingertip first along one row of spines, then another. Eventually she found what she was looking for, pulling a large book with a colourful cover from the shelf. She carried it back to Catherine and set it on the desk with a thump.

"Let's see," Helen said, fanning through the pages. "Here."

She turned the book so Catherine could read the title at the top of the page.

A Terrifying Nocturnal Visitor: The Night Hag.

Below the title, a reproduction of an old painting, a grotesque image. A woman lay on her back, her head and shoulders falling back off the bed, her breasts indecently close to spilling out of her nightclothes. And perched on her stomach, a squat devil of a creature, grey skin, long red tongue hanging from its gaping mouth.

"Well, she doesn't look like that," Catherine said.

"Read the text," Helen said. "It might help you understand what's happening."

"Maybe," Catherine said, but she suspected it wouldn't.

"You said it started six months ago," Helen said.

"That's right."

"Wasn't that around the time your mother . . . the accident?"

Catherine looked at the creature on the woman's chest. Its gnarled features, its wicked gaze.

"Around then, yes," she said.

"Perhaps it's related. Grief can do strange things to a person's mind."

Catherine didn't respond, having been given an answer to a question she hadn't wanted to ask. Of course it had occurred to her that the appearance of the woman in her bed coincided with her mother's death—in fact, the woman had first visited the night of her mother's funeral—but she had refused to link the two in any way.

"You okay, Catherine?"

Helen's words pulled her from the idea, the ridiculous notion dissolving in her mind like steamy breath on a morning breeze.

"Yes, I'm fine," she said, but she really wasn't.

Not at all.

CATHERINE TOOK THE BOOK home and read the piece six times. The book was about dreams, their meanings and interpretations. She leafed through it, mostly hokum about symbolism, the names Freud and Jung appearing here and there, along with a host of other shysters and heathens. But the section on the Night Hag felt true and real.

For some, the Hag stood in a corner, watching. For others, she sat on her victim's chest. And for many, like Catherine, she held her prey down. Sometimes she wasn't a she at all.

Catherine read it again after her dinner of a fishcake and boiled potatoes. She read the hysterical accounts of old crones and their watching and sitting and holding. But the most important passage of all, the one she read over and over, was that the Night Hag was not real. Not real at all, only a dream for the waking, a malfunction of the brain.

"Not real," she said aloud several times as she fetched herself a cup of hot chocolate and two digestive biscuits. She said it again, numerous times, as she dressed for bed, even as she brushed her teeth, spitting toothpaste onto the mirror over the washbasin.

She said it one last time as she pulled the bedclothes up to her chin and closed her eyes.

"Not real," she said, and believed it to be true.

SHE IS AWAKE. THIS is certain. *She sees the room in the half-light, the nightstand, the lamp, the mobile phone. Someone is here. They embrace her, pinning her arms to her side. A leg wrapped around hers, pressing it down onto the mattress. She wants to lift her head, but a hand forces it into the pillow.*

The woman is back. The Night Hag.

Catherine wants to tell her to go away, to leave her alone, but the hand has closed around her jaw, sealing it shut.

The lips against her ear, the hot breath.

Oh God, oh Jesus, make it stop.

Catherine can't see the blackened hand, but she can feel it, the fingertips seeking her lips, pressing between, penetrating, the jagged nail against her teeth, scratching her gums.

The woman giggles.

I know what you did, *she says.*

Now Catherine must scream. She must, but she can't. Her throat won't open to let it out. Her cries gurgle there, drowning.

I know what you did.

Now, at last, Catherine can open her mouth. She screams, a high wailing cry, and her arms and legs are free. Turning in the bed, rolling over, she sees the shape of a woman crawl away, sinking down the side of the bed, out of view.

Catherine cries out once more, a formless howl.

I know what you did.

CATHERINE OPENED HER DOOR to Pastor John Lipton exactly one hour after she'd called him. She had offered to walk to the church, but he said no need, he would come to her. A panicked sixty minutes later, she had tidied and hoovered every room that he might possibly enter, including her small kitchen, to which she brought him.

"I like what you've done with the place," he said as he took a seat at the fold-out table.

"Thank you," she said, even though she hadn't done anything to the house she'd been renting for half a year. The same tired off-white paint and avocado tiles covered the walls, the same linoleum flooring underfoot as when she'd moved in. "Tea? Coffee?"

"Tea would be lovely," Pastor John said.

Catherine had boiled the kettle in preparation only a few minutes before and it hissed and bubbled immediately when she flicked the switch. Two matching mugs sat ready, along with a caddy full of teabags and a sealed jar of instant coffee. A sheet of clingfilm covered a plate of biscuits. They talked as she prepared the tea.

"You seem to have found your feet," Pastor John said. "After everything that happened, it's good to see you soldiering on."

"I've you and everyone at the church to thank," Catherine said, "the way you all rallied round me."

"Well, that's the whole point of the church, isn't it? It's not just a building. It's a community. Have you thought any more about getting out and about? A little job somewhere, maybe? Even volunteering. It does you no good to stay cooped up here all the time."

"Maybe in a month or two," Catherine said. "I seem to be able to fill my days without too much trouble. Sugar?"

"One, please," he said. "It's not just a matter of filling time, though, is it? It's also about connecting with people."

Catherine placed the two steaming mugs on the table, removed the clingfilm from the plate of biscuits.

"I see people," she said. "When I go to the shops, and there's Helen at the library, and everyone at church."

"You need more than that," he said. "You were a carer for your mother for . . . how long?"

"Nearly thirty years," Catherine said, sitting down.

"And now she's gone, what do you do with yourself?"

"Like I said, church, the library. The shops once or twice a week. I keep busy."

"Okay, but think about it. There's lots you could contribute. Don't shut yourself away. Anyway, what was it you wanted to talk about?"

Catherine dropped her gaze to her tea, still untouched on the table in front of her. She had been certain of the question she wanted to ask when she called Pastor John an hour ago, but now the certainty cracked.

Pastor John reached out, touched his fingertips—

to her teeth

—to her forearm.

"Catherine, what's wrong?"

"You believe in heaven," she said, her voice small and trembling.

"Of course."

"And hell?"

"I don't know if it's a fiery lake or not, but yes, I believe there is a place that is apart from God."

"Is there another place?" she asked, unable to look at him.

A pause, and then he asked, "What do you mean?"

"Is there a place that's neither heaven nor hell? Somewhere different?"

"Do you mean somewhere like purgatory? That's not something I believe in."

She scratched the side of her index finger with her thumbnail, peeling skin away.

"Catherine, what is this about?"

She looked at him, saw the concern on his face, and she felt a shameful wave of foolishness.

"Has something happened?" he asked.

She shook her head, no.

"I've just remembered," she said. "I'm sorry, I have an appointment. I need to go."

THE WIND BLEW HARD across the municipal cemetery, no trees to break it, no structures other than the maintenance buildings down by the gates. Miserable drizzle came with the wind, dragged from the low grey cloud and into Catherine's cheeks and ears. She pulled up her coat's collar and wished she'd worn the new anorak she'd bought herself for Christmas.

Dead flowers lay scattered on her mother's grave, the vase having long tipped over. It had been six weeks since she'd last visited. At first, she'd come every day, then every few days, then once a week. Then a month. That's how these things go, she supposed. A fresh grave is like a new toy to a child, a thing that loses its shine as days go by. All of the plots in this row appeared neglected, old leaves clustered in the gravel, ornaments toppled.

Catherine felt no guilt. Instead, she felt relief. She wasn't sure what she had expected to find other than the modest headstone and a rectangle of white gravel hemmed in by a low wall of granite. Some sign of disturbance, perhaps. A corner of the concrete cap broken away, earth pushed aside.

"You're dead in there," she said. "You're nothing but bones and old skin and you can't hurt me. Not anymore."

At Pastor John's insistence, Catherine had gone to a grief counsellor after her mother had perished. An effeminate young man whom Catherine assumed to be *one of those*, as her mother would have put it.

"I only need this one appointment," she had told him as he sat in the opposite armchair in his inoffensive little office.

"Oh?" he had replied, smiling gently and raising his eyebrows.

"You see, I'm not grieving. I'm glad she's dead."

He said nothing. She felt a mild disappointment that he didn't express some surprise.

"I prayed she would die," Catherine continued,

unbidden. "I've been praying for a long time. I didn't love her. She didn't love me. She made bloody sure I had nothing resembling a life, I was nothing more than a servant to her, and now she's gone and I'm glad. The night she died, I thanked the Lord Jesus for freeing me of her."

He remained quiet for a moment, then said, "Catherine, when we lose someone so suddenly, and in such circumstances, it can be difficult to process how we—"

"Oh, pish-posh. I've visited her grave every day for the last fortnight, and do you know what I've done each time? I've spat on it."

Now she stood there, rolling saliva around her tongue. When she had a good mouthful, she leaned over and propelled it as hard and as far as she could. Had it not been for the wind, it would have reached the headstone.

"And stay dead," she said.

SHE IS AWAKE. THIS is certain. She sees the room in the half-light, the nightstand, the lamp, the mobile phone. Someone is here. They embrace her, pinning her arms to her side. A leg wrapped around hers, pressing it down onto the mattress. She wants to lift her head, but a hand forces it into the pillow.

And something else.

A high repetitive shrieking. Not her, not the Hag, but something else.

The smoke alarm in the hall downstairs.

There is a fire.

Oh God, no, please, not that.

Lips against her ear, a breathy giggle. Fingers creeping to her lips, between, nails scratching at her teeth and gums.

I know what you did.

Catherine screams with every breath, but each one is trapped in her throat, drowned out by the smoke alarm and the voice in her ear.

I know what you did.

CATHERINE FELL OUT OF bed, landed hard on her shoulder, her legs following, still tangled in the duvet. She kicked herself free and scrambled to her feet, reaching for the door. The floor tilted beneath her, and she fell again, the carpet tearing at her chin. She used the handle to haul herself upright, opened the door, and stumbled out onto the small landing. A moment of disorientation as she navigated the darkness, thinking of her mother's house, the place she had lived for fifty years. The upstairs landing in that house, while it stood, had been long and wide, not the small square of the place she now rented. The top of the stairs in that house was more than a few feet away, and she gasped with shock as her toes reached into cool and smoky air. She grabbed for the handrail, but it was not there, not in this house, and her knuckles slammed into hard plaster and coarse wallpaper.

Weightless, arms wheeling, she cried out. She barely saw the stairs as they raced up towards her, slammed into her chest, punched her thighs, her shoulders, her head. An age seemed to pass before her back hit the hall floor, the rear of her skull cracking on the laminated wood flooring.

Her vision funnelled, time stretching like half-dried glue. She saw the smoke alarm on the ceiling above, the small bright red light in the far distance, its high shriek penetrating the thunder behind her eyes. Then she was gone.

HAMMERING ON THE DOOR. A voice calling through the letterbox.

"Catherine? Catherine, are you there? Are you all right?"

A man's voice. Young, familiar.

"Catherine, I'm going to call the police. Or the fire brigade. I don't know, one of them. Are you there?"

The young man from next door, the semidetached next to hers. He always smiled at her when they passed on the driveway they shared. What was his name?

Catherine lifted her head from the floor and gasped at the pain in her neck, then once more at stabbing in her left side. The smoke alarm still beeped its incessant beeping, the sound of it cutting into her brain like—

a fingernail against her gum

—a dulled blade. She wanted to cry out, but she held it in. With a grinding effort, she rolled onto her side, registering new pains, both sharp and dull, around her body.

"I'm all right," she called.

"Are you sure? Do you need help?"

She couldn't see the front door from here, so he could not see her lying on the floor.

"I'm all right," she repeated. "Everything's fine."

"Are you sure? Can you come to the door?"

She caught the scent of smoke, bitter, acrid, and she coughed. A wave of pain passed through her body, from her head to her feet, before centring on her side.

"No," she said, with more urgency than was necessary. "I'm not dressed. I just . . . I just burnt some toast, that's all."

A pause, then, in an uncertain voice, he said, "Okay, if you're sure. Do you think you can do anything about the alarm? It woke me up."

She pushed herself up onto one elbow, then onto her knees. That stabbing in her left side again. She gave a low groan and took a shallow breath before answering.

"Yes, I'll get it to stop. Just give me a few minutes."

"Okay. Goodnight."

The letterbox snapped shut.

A cracked rib, she thought. A strain in her neck. Lucky that was all. She braced her forearms on the telephone table and pushed herself upright. As she got to her feet, she turned her head, testing the range of her movement. A spasm fired in the muscles between her shoulder and neck. Her knees buckled and she had to support herself on the telephone table until the spasm passed, taking thin breaths so her side wouldn't protest.

That smell, dark and gritty in her nose and throat. The alarm still screeching.

She opened the kitchen door and black cloud billowed out around her, stealing the breath from her lungs, stinging her eyes. Her rib sparked and flared as she coughed. She reached for the light switch and saw a dark blanket covered the ceiling, thinning as it neared her eye level. Crouching down, she pulled the neckline of her nightdress up to cover her nose and mouth, then hurried to the back door, grabbing her keys from the bowl by the sink on the way. Once the door was open, she staggered out into the clean night air. A fresh peal of coughing erupted from her chest, and she clutched at her left side, fearing that it might burst open. Then she vomited onto the paving stones, the foulness splashing onto her bare feet.

Catherine leaned against the windowsill and rested for a time, keeping her breath as shallow as she could. When the thunder in her head had subsided enough for her to think, she peered into her kitchen. The smoke had mostly cleared, and there, on the hob, she saw the charred remains of something. After a few moments, she realised it was the tea towel she had hung on the handle of the oven door before going to bed. The ceramic ring still gave off wisps. From here, she could see the dial on the front of the cooker had been turned up full. Parts of the towel had fallen to the floor, causing the linoleum to blacken and bubble, while others had spilled into the open metal bin she used for her recycling materials.

Newspapers, cardboard. Some of it had caught light and burned out.

"Thank God," she whispered.

What if it had spread? What if there had been more paper and cardboard stacked up around the recycling bin? After all, she knew how dangerous such a thing could be. Hadn't that done for her mother? A stack of old newspapers and boxes piled up beside the cooker, spreading onto the work-top alongside it. When the tea towel in her mother's kitchen had caught alight on the hob, there had been the makings of a bonfire all around it.

Catherine hadn't put the newspapers and cardboard by her mother's cooker, she was quite sure of that. But she hadn't cleared them away either. It was purely accidental that she had knocked some of the newspapers over, and they had spread towards the hob, and the tea towel that had been carelessly left there on the electric ring.

None of it on purpose, oh no.

When she had put her mother to bed that night, endur-ing her moaning and complaining about every bloody fucking thing that she had done wrong that day, Catherine had absolutely not intended to turn the ring up full before heading out for a late trip to the big supermarket in town, the one that stayed open all night.

Catherine hadn't intended for any of that to happen. And yet it had. An accident, pure and simple and fatal and tragic.

And now it had almost happened again.

Except she couldn't remember leaving the tea towel there on the hob before going to bed, nor turning up the ring.

But who had? The doors were locked. No one had broken in.

"Do you think you could sort out the alarm?"

Catherine cried out at the voice. She turned her head to its source and her neck spasmed, causing her to cry out once more. She placed her hand there to calm the muscle.

The young man from next door, peering over the fence at her. She remembered he was quite short, so he must have stood on something.

"Sorry, I didn't mean to scare you," he said. "Do you think you could sort it? It's quite loud. Or I could do it for you."

Catherine coughed, grimaced at the pain, and said, "I'll do it now."

She covered her mouth and nose again and went inside, through the kitchen, and out to the hall. She closed the door behind her and went to the bottom of the stairs, mounted the first step, and waved her hands at the alarm, trying to disperse the smoke and shut it up. The attempt was unsuccessful.

There was a cardigan drying over the hall radiator. She fetched it and waved it beneath the alarm. Still, it shrieked.

"Bastard," she said. "Bloody bastard."

A moment of shock at her own language passed, and she went to the closet where she kept the vacuum cleaner and other such items. She grabbed the broom, went back to the stairs, and stabbed the alarm with the end of the handle.

After three strikes, the alarm came loose and fell to the floor, scattering white plastic on the laminated wood.

It did not quiet.

She inverted the broom and brought the handle down on the alarm with all the strength she had, ignoring the pain it triggered.

The alarm's casing split open and the battery spun away to clatter against the wall.

Silence.

"And stay dead," she said.

HER MOBILE PHONE RANG as she steered the Skoda into the petrol station. She pulled up to the pump, took the phone from the cup holder, and got out of the car, grunting as her rib reminded her of its cracked presence. She checked the phone's display as she walked towards the items stacked at the front of the shop.

Georgina, the display said.

Her sister, three years older, had lived in South Africa for twenty years now. A lecturer at the University of Cape Town. *Hasn't she done well for herself*, people would say. *You must be proud.*

Yes, very, Catherine would say, smiling.

She pressed the answer button.

"Morning," she said.

"Catherine, sweetheart, how are you?"

Georgina soaked up accents like a sponge. She sounded like she'd been born native Afrikaans. Catherine fought the urge the drop the phone and grind it into the ground with her heel.

"I'm fine," she said. "How are you?"

In front of the shop stood bags of coal, firelighters, peat briquettes. She lifted a five-litre jerry can from the stack and walked back towards the pump, her gait stiff from last night's fall. She held the can between her knees as she unscrewed the cap, then set it down.

"I'm good, darling. When are you going to fly down and see us? I have a room just waiting for you."

"Soon, I promise. I just need to renew my passport."

"You've been saying that ever since Mum died."

"I'll get the forms from the Post Office this week."

"Promise?"

"Yes."

"Good."

Catherine removed the nozzle from the pump and inserted it into the can. She squeezed the trigger and the pump hummed.

"Listen, I got a call from that pastor yesterday evening. The one who spoke at Mum's funeral."

"Pastor John," Catherine said.

"That's him. He said he was worried about you, that you weren't yourself. Is everything all right?"

"Everything's fine. I told him yesterday."

"He's concerned that you're isolating yourself," Georgina said, her voice taking on that babyish tone, the one she used when she pretended to care about anyone but herself. "He thinks you need to get out more, do more, see other people."

"I do see people," Catherine said, feeling her anger rise. "The church, the library, the shops. In fact, I could do with seeing fewer people."

Petrol spilled over the top of the jerry can before she could release the trigger. It splashed onto her shoes.

"Oh, goodness. Oh, you bloody bastard."

"What?"

"Nothing," Catherine said.

"Did I just hear my sister use a profanity?"

That sneer in her voice.

"Yes," Catherine said. "Yes you bloody did. And what f— . . . What fff— . . . What bloody fucking of it?"

Silence for a moment, thousands of miles of it.

"Catherine, do you think you should talk to someone?"

"I *am* talking to someone. I'm talking to you, aren't I?"

"You know what I mean."

"Can't you just leave me alone? You and everyone else. Can't you just bloody well leave me in peace?"

Another few seconds of quiet, then Georgina said, "It wasn't your fault."

"I need to go," Catherine said.

"What happened to Mum was an accident. The police, the fire investigators, they all said so. It wasn't your fault."

Catherine smiled.

"Oh, Georgina, for all your education, you really are stupid, aren't you?"

She hung up and tucked the phone into her coat pocket. As she walked back to the shop with the jerry can, screwing the lid on tight, she felt the phone vibrate. She ignored it as she paid for the jerry can and the petrol, thanking the cashier as she took her change.

When she opened the Skoda's boot to put the—

fingers in her mouth

—jerry can inside, she saw three others lined up. She tested their weight. All full. Twenty litres of petrol all together.

She did not remember buying the others.

"How odd," she said.

FOR DINNER, CATHERINE TREATED herself to a small honey-glazed gammon joint she'd bought from Marks & Spencer, along with mashed potato. The whole meal cooked in less than an hour with little effort on her part. She even had a glass of white wine with it, though she wasn't overly keen on the taste of wine. After the second glass began to make her feel ill, she poured the rest down the sink.

As she turned away, she noticed how the recycling had built up. A stack of it next to the cooker. So many newspapers. So much cardboard. It had begun to topple and spread around the floor, and onto the work surface by the cooker. And there, that book Helen at the library had found for her, the one about dreams. It lay open, face down, its pages stretching across the hob.

"Goodness," she said aloud.

I should move that, she thought. That and the recycling. It's dangerous.

As she climbed the stairs to ready herself for bed, she found the carpet damp beneath her slippers. And a strange smell. Sweet, chemical, cloying. It made her lightheaded. In the bathroom, she changed into her nightdress, washed her face, brushed her teeth.

In her bedroom, she noticed the same dampness on her bare soles, the same smell that seemed to make her head float above her shoulders. She climbed into bed and shivered. The sheet beneath her body clung to her back, as if she'd had an accident, like her mother had been prone to, and the liquid had crept across the mattress.

As she lay in the darkness, she found the sweet chemical smell had become almost comforting. When she inhaled through her nose, the odour seemed to reach deep inside her head, and she began to drift on its currents and soothing waves.

How nice, she thought.

SHE IS AWAKE. THIS is certain. She sees the room in the half-light, the nightstand, the lamp, the mobile phone. Someone is here. They embrace her, pinning her arms to her side. A leg wrapped around hers, pressing it down onto the mattress. She wants to lift her head, but a hand forces it into the pillow.

She wants to speak, to say, I know it's you, *but the hand clasps over her mouth, sealing her jaw shut. The fingers find her lips, and this time she does not resist. She welcomes their intrusion. If she could open her jaw she would allow her tongue to greet them.*

She feels no desire to scream. Even as the bright glowing orange crackling dancers enter the room and climb the walls, even as they advance towards her bed, she is calm and quiet.

The breathy giggle in her ear.

I know what you did.

So do I, *she wants to say, but she can't.*

She closes her eyes and kisses the hand that holds her still.

BLACK BEAUTY

"Play something."

"I can't."

"You should," he says.

The guitar sits there on the floor between us, nestled in its case, inky black. Light from the bedsit's bare bulb reflects on its curved face.

"I can't."

I cough, spitting blood through broken teeth.

"Why not?"

He hunkers down next to me. Sixty, I guess. Strong. Big shoulders. Scarred face. He takes a pair of wire cutters from his pocket. Snip, snip.

I'm trying not to cry.

"I can't," I say.

"Then why did you take it?"

"I thought I could sell it," I say.

He points. "Do you know what that is?"

I shake my head.

"Course you don't," he says. "That's a 1957 Gibson Les

Paul Custom. All original. They call it the Black Beauty. I can't tell you what it's worth now, that doesn't matter, but I can tell you I worked my arse off to buy it for my boy. And it was worth every drop of blood and sweat to see him play it, to see him make his living off it, so he didn't have to do the things I've done."

"I'm sorry," I say, but I know it's too late.

"Sorry? Sorry you robbed it off him? Or sorry for putting him in hospital?"

"Just . . . sorry."

"Then show me."

"Show you what?"

Closer now. I feel his breath.

"Show me how bad you wanted it. Show me how much you wanted to play it. Look at it. It's beautiful, isn't it?"

I look at the guitar. I look at my fingers. I look at the wire cutters in his hand.

Snip, snip, snip.

"Pick it up and play it," he says. "Play it well, or . . ."

Snip.

I reach for the guitar, touch the strings with my fingertips.

The last thing they'll ever feel.

PART II:
OLD FRIENDS

FOLLOWERS

Maybe if he had one more drink they'd leave him alone. Gerry Fegan told himself that lie before every swallow. He chased the whiskey's burn with a cool, black mouthful of Guinness and placed the glass back on the table. Look up and they'll be gone, he thought.

No. They were still there, still staring. Twelve of them if he counted the baby. Even its small blue eyes were fixed on him.

He was good and drunk, now. Tom the barman would see him to the door soon, and the twelve would follow Fegan through the streets of Belfast, into his house, up his stairs, and into his bedroom. If he was lucky, and drunk enough, he might pass out before their screaming got too loud to bear. That was the only time they made a sound: when he was alone and on the edge of sleep. When the baby started crying, that was the worst of it. He feared that less than the gun under his bed, but not by much. One day that balance might shift. One day he might taste the gun's cold, hard snout before a fiery sun bloomed in his skull. Maybe tonight. Maybe not. The whiskey would decide.

Fegan raised the empty glass to get Tom's attention. "Haven't you had enough, Gerry?" asked Tom. "Is it not home time yet? Everyone's gone."

"One more," said Fegan, trying not to slur. He knew Tom would not refuse. Fegan was still a respected man in West Belfast, despite the drink.

Sure enough, Tom sighed and raised a glass to the optic. He brought the whiskey over and counted change from the table.

Fegan held the glass up and made a toast to his twelve companions. One of the five soldiers among them smiled and nodded in return. The rest just stared.

"Fuck you," said Fegan. "Fuck the lot of you."

None of the twelve reacted, but Tom looked back over his shoulder. He shook his head and continued walking to the bar.

Fegan looked at each of his companions in turn. Of the five soldiers three were Brits and two were Ulster Defence Regiment. Another of the followers was a cop, his Royal Ulster Constabulary uniform neat and stiff, and two more were loyalists, both Ulster Freedom Fighters. The remaining four were civilians who had been in the wrong place at the wrong time. He remembered doing all of them, but he'd met only three face-to-face.

The woman and her baby in the doorway to the butcher's shop where he'd left the package. He'd held the door for her as she wheeled the pram in. They'd smiled at each other.

He'd felt the heat of the blast as he jumped into the already moving car.

The other was the boy. Fegan could still remember the look in his eyes when he saw the pistol. Now the boy sat across the table from him, those same eyes boring into him as they had done for nearly seven years. When Fegan saw the tears pooling on the tabletop he brought his fingers to the hollows of his face and realised he'd been weeping.

"Jesus," he said.

A hand on his shoulder startled him, and he cried out.

"Time you were going, Gerry," said Michael McGinty. Tom must have called him. He was smartly dressed in a jacket and trousers, a far cry from the teenager Fegan had known thirty years ago. Wealth looked good on him.

"I'm just finishing," said Fegan.

"Well, drink up and I'll run you home." McGinty smiled down at him, his teeth white and even. He'd had them fixed before winning his seat at Westminster two elections ago. He'd never taken the seat; that was against party policy. He did take his seat at Stormont, though, and his place on Northern Ireland's Executive. That had also been against party policy at one time. But times change, even if people don't.

The boy was behind McGinty now, and Fegan watched as he made a gun with his fingers and pointed at the politician's head. He mimed firing it, his hand thrown upwards by the recoil. His mouth made a plosive movement, but no sound came.

"Do you remember that kid, Michael?" asked Fegan.

"Don't, Gerry." McGinty's voice carried a warning.

"He hadn't done anything. Not really. He didn't tell the cops anything they didn't know already. He didn't deserve that. Jesus, he was fifteen."

One hard hand gripped Fegan's face, the other his thinning hair, and the animal inside McGinty showed itself. "Shut your fucking mouth," he hissed. "Remember who you're talking to."

Fegan remembered only too well. As he looked into those fierce eyes he remembered every detail. This was the face he knew, not the one on television, but the face that twisted in white-hot pleasure as McGinty set about the boy with a claw hammer, the face that was dotted with red when he handed Fegan the .22 pistol to finish it.

The smile returned to McGinty's mouth as he released his grip, but not to his eyes. "Come on," he said. "My car's outside. I'll run you home."

The twelve followed them out to the street, the boy staying close to McGinty. The Mercedes gleamed in the orange streetlights. It was empty and no other cars were parked nearby. McGinty had come out with no escort to guard him. Fegan knew the Merc was armoured, bullet- and bomb-proof, and McGinty probably felt safe as he unlocked it, unaware of the followers.

They spent the journey in silence. McGinty never spoke as he drove, knowing his car was almost certainly bugged by

the Brits. Fegan closed his eyes and savoured the few minutes away from the followers, knowing they'd be waiting at
his house.

He remembered the first time he saw them. It was in the
Maze prison and he'd just been given his release date. They
were there when he looked up from the letter.

He told one of the prison psychologists about it. Dr.
Brady said it was guilt (a manifestation, he called it) and
he should try apologising to them. Out loud. Then they
might go away. Later that day, when it was just him and
them in his cell, Fegan tried it. He decided to start with
the woman and her baby. He picked his words carefully
before he spoke. He inhaled, ready to tell her face-to-face
how sorry he was. Even now, years later, he could still feel
the burning sting of her palm on his cheek, the one time
any of them touched him.

McGinty pulled the Mercedes into the kerb outside
Fegan's small terraced house. The followers stood on the
pavement, waiting.

"Can I come in for a second?" McGinty's smile sparkled
in the car's interior lighting. "Just for a quick chat."

Fegan shrugged and climbed out.

The twelve parted to let him approach his door. He
unlocked it and went inside, McGinty following, the twelve
slipping in between. Fegan headed straight for the sideboard
where a bottle of Jameson's and a jug of water waited for
him. He showed McGinty the bottle.

"No thanks," said McGinty. "Maybe you shouldn't, either."

Fegan ignored him, pouring two fingers of whiskey into a glass and the same of water. He took a deep swallow, then pointed to a chair.

"No, I'm all right," said McGinty.

The twelve milled around the room, studying each man intently. The boy lingered by McGinty's side.

"What'd you want to chat about?" Fegan lowered himself into a chair.

McGinty pointed to the drink in Fegan's hand. "About that. It's got to stop, Gerry."

Fegan held the politician's eyes as he drained the glass.

"People round here look up to you. You're a republican hero. The young fellas need a role model, someone they can respect."

"Respect? What are you talking about?" Fegan put the glass on the coffee table and held his hands up. "I can't get the blood off. I never will, no matter how much I scrub them. There's no respecting what I did."

McGinty's face flushed with anger. "You did your time. You were a political prisoner for twelve years. A dozen years of your life given up for the cause. Any republican should respect that." His expression softened. "But you're pissing it away, Gerry. People are starting to notice. Every night you're at the bar, drunk off your face, talking to yourself."

"I'm not talking to myself." Fegan pointed to the followers. "I'm talking to them."

"Who?" McGinty made a show of casting his eyes around the room.

"The ones I killed. The ones we killed."

"Watch your mouth, Gerry. I never killed anybody."

"No, you were always too smart to do it yourself. You used mugs like me instead." Fegan stood up. "I need a piss."

"Don't be long," said McGinty.

Fegan made his way up the stairs and into the bathroom. He closed and bolted the door, but as always, the followers found their way in. Except the boy. Fegan paid it little mind, instead concentrating on keeping upright while he emptied his bladder. He had long since gotten used to the twelve witnessing his most undignified moments.

He flushed, rinsed his hands under the tap, and opened the door. The boy was there, on the landing, Fegan's gun in his hand. He had taken the Walther P99 from under the bed and brought it out here. Fegan knew it was loaded.

The boy held it out to him, grip first. Fegan didn't understand. He shook his head. The boy stepped closer, lifted Fegan's right hand, and placed the pistol in it. He mimed the act of pulling back the slide assembly to chamber the first round.

Fegan looked from the boy to the pistol and back again. The boy nodded. Fegan drew back the slide, released it, hearing the *snick-snick* of oiled parts moving together.

The boy smiled and descended the stairs. He stopped,

looked back over his shoulder, and indicated that Fegan should follow.

Feeling an adrenaline rush that stirred dark memories, his legs shaking, Fegan began the slow climb downward. The others came behind, sharing glances with one another. As he reached the bottom, he saw McGinty's back. The politician was leafing through the pile of unopened bills and letters on the sideboard.

The boy crossed the room and again made the shape of a pistol with his fingers, again mimed the execution of the man who had taken him apart with a claw hammer almost twenty years ago.

Fegan's breath was ragged, his heartbeat thunderous. Surely McGinty would hear.

The boy looked to him and smiled.

Fegan asked, "If I do it, will you leave me alone?"

The boy nodded.

"What?" McGinty turned to the voice and froze when he saw the gun aimed at his forehead.

"I promised myself I'd never do this again," said Fegan, his vision blurred by tears. "But I have to."

"Jesus, Gerry." McGinty gave a short, nervous laugh as he held his hands up. "What're you at?"

"I'm sorry, Michael. I have to."

McGinty's smile fell away. "Christ, think about what you're doing, Gerry. The boys won't let it go, ceasefire or not. They'll come after you."

"Doesn't matter."

"Thirty years, Gerry. We've known each other thirty—"

The Walther barked once, throwing red and grey against the wall. McGinty fell back against the sideboard, then slid to the floor. Fegan walked over and put one in his heart, just to be sure.

He wiped the tears from his eyes and looked around the room. The followers jostled for position, looking from Fegan to the body, from the body to Fegan.

The boy wasn't among them.

One down.

Eleven to go.

FAITH

The day I lost my belief was the same day Mrs. Garrick asked me to help kill her husband.

Not the same moment, mind. The moment God left me was during my Sunday morning sermon. I'd prepared it two days before, read it through a dozen times, like I always did. I recall looking up from the handwritten notes—the church didn't have a computer back then, let alone a printer—and took in the scattering of faces.

The sad, grey, slack faces. Farmers, most of them, scrubbed-up for their weekly duty. Broad-backed wives, thick-fingered children. Boys who could drive tractors before the age of five; girls who longed for the monthly socials and the chance to spin around in the arms of some pimply lad.

I'd been dreading this service. The first since I'd done the shameful thing. I'd felt certain they would see the sin on my face, know where my hands had been. And they would point and hiss, and call me hypocrite, how dare I preach to them after I'd taken her into my bed, after my weakness had betrayed them all.

But as I spoke, my voice riding the swells of the sermon, I realised something startling.

I didn't care.

I didn't care because there is no sin. There is no sin because there is no God. There is no God because there is only us and our impulses, our sordid little desires that drive us through our days until we are too old to desire anything anymore.

The realisation hit me so hard and so clear that I froze there in the pulpit, my mouth open, staring at the people before me. The only words my mind could form were: It's all a lie. But I couldn't let those words find my tongue, or all would be lost. I don't know how long I stood there amid the sound of weight shifting on pews, the clearing of throats.

Mrs. Garrick knew.

From the end of the second to last row, she gave me that half smile, the one that she gave me four days earlier, the one that said: I know you, I know what lives inside you.

Mrs. Garrick got to her feet and went to the door, sly and silent as a cat. She gave me one look as she exited, and moments later I felt the wash of cold air that had travelled all the way from her to me.

As I found my place once more, as the sermon recommenced, I knew where I would see Mrs. Garrick next.

But I was wrong. When I returned to the small house across the churchyard, I expected to find her in the drawing room, waiting for me on the couch where she had first taken my hands and brought them to her body. The want and the terror left me as I stood on the threshold, looking at the empty room, replaced by a painful disappointment.

For a man whose purpose had evaporated half an hour earlier, I was strangely at ease. I knew what I desired at that moment, felt no guilt or shame in the yearning, and my mind had no room for questions of eternity.

It was shortly after her husband, a sergeant of the Royal Ulster Constabulary, survived the bomb attack that Mrs. Garrick began calling on me. The device had been attached by a magnet to the underside of his car, beneath the driver's seat. He lost one leg in its entirety, the other below the knee, and the damage to his lower body was such that he would never lie with his wife again.

Six months ago, she wept as she told me, as if the shame of her husband's unmanning was hers alone to bear. When they brought him home, I went to his bedside, held what remained of his hand in mine while we prayed.

Just words, I know now, meaningless noises that never left that room to drift heavenward.

I called often at the Garricks' home and said many prayers. Sometimes Mrs. Garrick would come to the church, sometimes to my house. Always proper. Always polite.

Then once, when she doubled over with tears, I took her in my arms. I had no sense of crossing a border, passing from a place of sanity and reason to one of lust and folly. It only seemed a human thing to do, a Christian thing, even as her red hair twined in my fingers.

My own wife had died five years earlier. I used to say the Lord took her to his kingdom, back when I believed such things. The truth is she had a brain haemorrhage, a random malfunction of her body. God had no part in it.

I hadn't looked at another woman in that way until Mrs. Garrick fell into my embrace, when I felt her body lean into mine. And I prayed to the Lord for strength, fully believing He was there to listen, that I wasn't talking to myself in my cold and empty bed.

I backed out of my living room, into the hall. I stopped at the foot of the staircase, saw something from the corner of my eye. There, resting on the bottom steps, her coat. My gaze followed the flow of the stairs, and halfway up, a blouse. At the top of the first flight, a pair of shoes. I swallowed and climbed, the trail of clothes leading me to my bedroom, the door open like an eager mouth.

She said nothing as I entered the room and walked to the bed where she lay. For a moment, I considered at least attempting to convince her to get dressed and go, to stop this madness. Instead, I pulled the white collar from my black shirt and claimed the madness for my own.

When we were done, my heart still hammering, the sweat still warm where our skin met, she asked, "Will you help me kill him?"

I said, "Yes, I will."

She had no need to convince me. I had seen enough of her and her husband's lives to understand the logic of it. And without God in my heart, with no soul at risk, then why not?

I went to their house after the evening service. A fifteen-minute stroll from the village, out into the dark of the countryside. I didn't see a single car as I walked, keeping to the grass verge, feeling branches of hedgerow touch my arm as I passed.

The lights of their home came into view. A short gravel driveway. A wall to one side still bearing the scars of the blast. Mr. Garrick had been reversing his Ford Granada when the mercury tilted and the device exploded. He should have checked beneath the car as he was trained to do, but it had been a dark snowy January morning, and he didn't feel like kneeling in the slush with a torch.

I heard it go off. It was not the rolling thunderous rumble of the kind of bomb they'd use to destroy a town centre or a government building, but rather a percussive thump that rattled my windows. In my mind, as I went to my front door, I made a list of parishioners who were possible targets. Mr. Garrick was the first in line.

Mrs. Garrick answered the door, and we exchanged the polite greetings one would expect between a man of the cloth and a member of his congregation. The Garricks hadn't a neighbour to hear within half a mile, but still.

She brought me to her kitchen where we had prayed

countless times over countless mugs of tea and trays of biscuits. Pots and pans sat on the hob, plates and cutlery in the sink, the detritus of her husband's last meal.

"Shepherd's pie," she said. "His favourite."

We both stood in silence for a time, me still in my coat, Mrs. Garrick still in her apron. Eventually, she said, "It's the right thing to do."

I suppose I should have argued, made some plea for her husband's life, but all day my mind had been focused on the place beyond. The place where she and I would be together, the widow and the widower, made as one by their tragic losses.

"Yes," I said. "It is."

"And he has his faith," she said. "Even if he knew what was going to happen, he'd be at peace with it. He'd be sure of where he's going. After, I mean. To heaven."

"There is no heaven," I said.

She looked at me as a child looks at a father revealed in his weakness. "What?"

"I don't believe," I said. "Not anymore."

"Will you leave the church?" she asked.

"I don't know," I said, truthfully.

"Either way," she said, "what we're doing is a merciful thing. Why make him suffer like that? We're kinder to dogs, for God's sake."

"You don't have to talk me into it," I said.

"I'd do it myself if I could," she said. "Whether you believe or not, you're doing a Christian thing."

"You don't have to talk me into it," I said again. "Just make me one promise."

"What?" she asked.

"That afterwards, when it's done, and everything's settled. Promise me we'll be together. The only way I can do this is if I know what's on the other side. Promise we'll be together."

She blinked, and a tear rolled down her cheek.

She said, "I promise."

I nodded, removed my coat, and asked, "How do I do it?"

She brought me to the table where a pestle and mortar sat alongside a scattering of torn sachets.

"Morphine granules," she said. "They're supposed to be taken whole, he's not allowed to chew them, otherwise the morphine will release too quickly. One sachet mixed with yogurt will keep him comfortable through the night."

Her fingertips brushed the rim of the mortar.

"I've put ten sachets in here. I've crushed them up so the morphine will go straight into his system. He should just fall asleep."

She tilted the mortar up, tipped the powder into an open carton of strawberry yogurt and stirred the mixture.

"He can't hold the spoon himself. You'll have to feed it to him."

She handed me the carton, the spoon standing in it.

I wish I could say I had a moment of doubt, that I hesitated. But no. I simply took the carton from her hand, left the kitchen, and walked along the hall to the downstairs room that had been converted into a care unit for her ruined husband.

I knocked and waited. No answer came, so I opened the door and entered. Mr. Garrick lay sleeping, his mouth open, drool shining on his scarred chin. A wisp of a moustache, neatly trimmed. His hair cut as well as could be managed.

A mercy, I told myself.

I went to the chair at his bedside and sat down.

"Mr. Garrick," I said.

His eyelids fluttered open, revealing the blue beneath. Confusion on his face, then recognition that appeared like the sun from behind a cloud. He smiled, showing his remaining teeth.

"Good to see you," he said, his voice metallic with disuse.

I showed him the yogurt and the spoon.

"Mrs. Garrick sent me up with this," I said. "There's something in it for the pain."

"My medicine," he said. "Helps me sleep."

He lifted the gnarled remains of his hands. Two fingers and a thumb on one, three fingers and no thumb on the other.

"I can do it for you," I said.

He smiled again. "Thank you," he said.

I dipped the spoon in, scooped up a generous mouthful of yogurt, and brought it to his lips. He took it all, held it in his mouth, and swallowed. I watched the movement of his throat.

"Like a baby," he said, his voice weak.

I gave him another spoonful.

"If I didn't have my faith, I couldn't survive this," he said.

Another spoonful.

"If the Lord wanted me dead, then I'd be dead. But He let me live, if you can call this living. Must have been a reason. He must want me alive for something. Don't you think so?"

And another.

"I know so," I said, the lie heavy on my tongue. "There are no accidents in this world. Not a leaf falls against His will."

"That's right," Mr. Garrick said, the S soft, the final T blunt.

One last spoonful.

"Every . . . everything . . . happens . . . for . . . for . . . a . . ."

His eyelids fell and rose again, his pupils like tiny dots of ink.

And then he went away. He snored once, a guttural, grating noise from deep in his throat, then his breathing became a wheeze, and then nothing at all.

I watched him for a short time, feeling nothing, least of all like a sinner, before I stood and walked back towards the kitchen. My only thought was of Mrs. Garrick, and tomorrow, and the day after, and how soon we could come out to the world and—

I found her at the kitchen table, leaning back, limbs loose, head lolling, sputum foaming around her open mouth. More torn sachets around the table, an empty glass in front of her, lined with a powdery residue.

I dropped the carton and the spoon, metal ringing against tile.

I fell to my knees and wished I had a God to forgive me.

THE CRAFTSMAN

Albert Ryan watched his long fingers in the mirror as he buttoned his shirt collar. They showed no signs of bending to age, moving with the same deft grace they always had. Last winter, an ache had settled in the ring and little fingers of his left hand. It had neither worsened nor improved since then; it lingered like a dinner guest oblivious to the hour.

He hitched up his tie knot, Double Windsor, smoothed the collar's wings, and ran his hands down his breast. The tie's silk whispered on his fingers. A Taoiseach had given it to him. He couldn't remember which. Either Haughey or Fitzgerald, they swapped office like a game of musical chairs back in the eighties. Albert only remembered the presentation box—Italian, the politician had said—and Celia's eyes when he showed it to her. She had kissed him like he was the only man in the world. It had been a Saturday night. They made love. She clawed the back of his neck and bit his chest. She insisted he wear it to Mass the next morning.

Now he admired it in the dressing table mirror. It was a fine thing, black with navy and silver detail. A craftsman's work if ever he'd seen it. Twenty-odd years old and it looked like it had been woven yesterday.

Celia's voice drifted from the grand old bed like paper on a breeze. "Bertie?"

He stood, smoothed his Gieves & Hawkes shirt over his stomach, still flat and hard after all these years. His hands travelled to the small of his back, made sure the holster was secure. "Yes, sweetheart?"

"Why are you all dressed up?" she asked.

Albert watched her in the mirror. She smiled in the glass. Today was a good day, all things considered. Yesterday had been bad. She had soiled herself, and they had both wept as he cleaned her. But this afternoon she could see him, know him, talk to him. He hoped she didn't remember the day before.

"I'm heading out for a wee while," he said.

"Into town?" she asked.

"No, love," he said. "Into Dublin."

"Oh? What for?"

He turned from the mirror. Her head tilted on the pillow, and her eyes glittered like a girl's. He so wanted to press that pillow into her face. Spare her from the bad weeks and months ahead. She frowned, seeing his heart like she always did.

"Such a saggy face," she said, pouting.

He had been jowly since his early thirties, despite his athletic build. He looked like a forlorn bloodhound by the time he met her at a party in Mallahide, when he was thirty-six and she a decade younger. Still now, he had no idea how he'd won her, only that she had stroked his cheek and called him "saggy face."

"Go back to sleep," he said. He approached the bed. Portraits of Christ and the Virgin hung over it; smaller images of her favoured Saints stood on the bedside locker; her Rosary lay pooled on the blankets. Celia had gathered God close to her since the diagnosis. Sometimes she cried out for forgiveness in her sleep.

He touched his fingertips to her lips. She dutifully pursed them, but there was no moisture, no warmth. Only the gesture, and that was enough.

In a way, she was still as beautiful as that day in Mallahide when she'd made him blush by letting her hip brush his groin as she slipped past. There had only ever been Celia. She was the all and everything he knew about women. Still as beautiful, yes, but now cut from wax, a hollow mannequin modelled on the woman who had claimed him wholly thirty years ago.

"What are you going into Dublin for?" she asked. She stretched under the bedclothes, a long and languorous wave along her body, as if this were any lazy day. Only the crease on her forehead betrayed the pain it caused her.

"To see a man about a dog," he said, feeling a small but rapturous peal of mischief in the teasing.

She smiled, showing her missing teeth. "My daddy used

to say that. When he was keeping secrets. What secrets are you keeping, Albert Ryan?"

He sat on the edge of the mattress, leaned down, and kissed her forehead. Her skin felt so thin and dry he imagined his lips pressed against her bare skull. Still, he kept his mouth there, letting his fingers tangle in her hair.

"No secrets from you, sweetheart," he said. "Never have, never will."

And wasn't that his great mistake?

She knew. All along, she knew what he did. He trusted her because she loved him, and he loved her. He would never have believed a vulgar sickness could render love and trust meaningless.

"The doctor," he said. "I'm going to see him."

"Why?" Her head turned so that the loose skin on her cheek wrinkled against the pillow.

"To kill him," he said.

"But why?"

Such sadness in her eyes. He turned away. "You said things."

"What things?" she asked.

"About what I do—what I did—for a living," he said.

"I didn't," she said. "Did I?"

"You did, sweetheart." He placed his fingers against her cheek. He felt her remaining teeth through the thin curtain of flesh.

"I didn't mean to," she said.

He smiled down at her. "I know."

"You mustn't," she said, her mouth pinched with regret. "He's good."

"I must." Albert stood. "Sleep now. I'll be home soon."

HE WALKED THE TEN minutes to the DART station in Dun Laoghaire, overlooking the bay. The pistol nestled snug in the hollow at the small of his back. It was an excellent weapon, small, designed for concealment, and handmade to order by an Austrian gunsmith. A first-rate artisan, now dead some ten years, and the work hadn't been cheap. The pistol's chamber held one .22 calibre round. Albert had loaded it with a hollow-point. The same Austrian had made the round, also an exquisite thing. The bullet was soft lead, cast in a fluted jacket that would allow it to split into pieces on penetration, each fragment taking its own trajectory through flesh and organs. The pistol had a low velocity, so close range was preferable. A clear shot to the temple would be best.

When Albert boarded the train, a kind young fellow vacated a seat for him. He considered protesting—even at sixty-six he was probably fitter than this youngster—but it would serve his purpose better to play the weak old man. He sat down and thanked the boy.

The weapon did not rub or bulge. A soft buckskin holster held it secure. A fine craftsman from Walsall, near Birmingham, had made it. The best leatherwork in the world came from Walsall, as grey and oppressive a town as Albert had ever seen. He remembered collecting it from the workshop, and the warm velvet scent of the place. The holster seemed so insignificant among the saddles and bridles, but the craftsman had dedicated as much care to this small piece as he had the grandest items. It was beautifully stitched, and even bore a delicate brand in a Celtic pattern. Age had given it a deep red lustre, and he always admired it for a moment or two before inserting the pistol and sliding it down behind his waistband, affixing the loop to hold it in place.

Albert Ryan admired nothing more than craftsmanship, for he too was a craftsman. Skill and care in one's work gave a glimpse of the divine to anyone with the eyes to see it. He had owned many beautiful things in his life. The Aston Martin V8 had been the most treasured among them. He remembered Celia giggling and gripping his arm as he pushed it hard along a coast road in Antrim, across the border in the North, hedgerows whipping by on one side, the North Atlantic disappearing to infinity on the other. She had not asked questions when he left their hotel alone that night, or when he returned two hours later. And she did not protest when he forbade her to listen to the news the following morning. For all her girlishness, which she never lost as the years burnt away, Celia had flint at her centre. He loved her for it.

He caught himself smiling and brought his hand to his mouth. A young woman smiled back at him from the seat opposite. He considered ignoring her, but for some reason he said, "Good memories."

Her smile broadened for a moment, lighting sparks in his stomach, before she returned her eyes to her paperback.

Fool, he thought. This was why no one hired him anymore. He had softened in his later years. That was why the money had dried up and he had to sell the damn car. That was why he had to sell their home with the sea view, the home Celia loved more than anything, and take a miserable flat that overlooked nothing but other anonymous apartment blocks. Their wonderful things never seemed at home in the new place, so selling them off didn't matter so much. Hardly anything mattered after Celia started bleeding.

He disembarked at the Grand Canal Dock station and walked the short distance to the bus stop. The traffic would be slow to the clinic in Rathgar, but he didn't mind. Time had taken on a strange elasticity these past few years, even more so since Celia fell ill. A few minutes here or there wouldn't matter.

Albert was gambling on the slender doctor, a handsome man wearing well in his young middle age, to leave the clinic at a normal hour. Ideally, Albert would study a subject for days, maybe weeks, before carrying out an action, but this particular matter was urgent.

He considered it as he climbed aboard the bus and took a seat. The doctor would always nod and smile as Celia rambled, as she was prone to do these days. Sometimes she would recount her time in London, working as a secretary in the Irish embassy, or perhaps Paris. She had only been stationed there a few months, but she still found delight in recalling her walks around Montmartre.

On occasion, her memories were more delicate. The visiting nurses blushed as she boasted of her husband's prowess as a lover. "Oh, those hands," she told them. "And he was never selfish. He always put my pleasure before his own. A wonderful thing in a man, that, you'll be lucky to find the same."

Albert had smiled weakly as the nurses tried not to snigger. But this morning had been unfortunate. She had been speaking quite coherently about the importance of discretion when working at a consulate, the doctor giving her his most patronising smile as he examined her, his skilled fingers dancing across her body.

"Of course," she had continued, "discretion has been my greatest talent. All these years, and no one ever suspected anything of him. To think those hands, those giving hands, could have done such things. But he always kept them clean. I never once saw blood on them. Not a drop. Even that time we had to go away. Where was it, Bertie? Lebanon?"

And that had been enough to end the doctor's life, whether he understood the implication of her ramblings or not. Albert knew it only took one loose thread for everything to unravel. It may have seemed random nonsense from a dying woman, but if the doctor picked at it, if he thought about it at night as he waited for sleep, he might just get a hold of that thread and start pulling.

And that could not be. Albert knew the procedure. At the slightest risk of exposure, they would close him down. That's what they called it. Closure, as if he were a shop going out of business. One day, one evening, one morning, he would simply be gone. And then who would take care of Celia? They would send her to some desperate grey place where she would die alone and frightened, in pain, wondering why her Bertie did not come for her.

No. Not while he had strength in his hands and iron in his chest.

"I love her too much to let her die like that."

"Excuse me?" the plump woman next to him said.

He stared at her for endless seconds. Had he said that aloud? Good God.

"I'm sorry," he said, bowing his head respectfully. "I was daydreaming."

She gave him a thin smile and turned her attention to the Dublin suburbs slipping by the window.

He reached beneath his overcoat and pinched the flesh below his ribs, hard. He had to focus, sharpen his mind. Killing must not be a reckless venture. He had learned that early on and taught it to others. Care and skill were second to only one thing: the will to do what other men can't. But will without craft is empty bluster. Many a man forgot that to his cost.

Thank Christ, Albert's stop approached. The fat woman might take exception to the sweating old fool beside her, she might remember him when she saw the news that night, and all would be lost.

Albert hoisted himself from the seat and made his way to the front of the bus. His feet shifted for balance as it slowed and stopped. He thanked the driver and stepped down. The woman did not watch him from the window as the bus pulled away, leaving him in tree shade on this pleasant avenue.

The clinic stood opposite, an old Victorian house converted to provide the best medical care to those who could afford it. It was in that building that a great tube had swallowed Celia while she trembled. This practice had eaten the last of their savings. The doctor's visit this morning had cost a fortnight's rent on their miserable flat. It had cost the doctor much more.

Albert entered the small park opposite the clinic, found a bench with a reasonable view of the building, sat down, and waited.

"MR. RYAN, ARE YOU all right?"

He seized the wrist, claimed the assailant's balance. Light and oxygen screamed into his brain, dragged him from sleep, battering his heart with adrenalin.

Dear God—the doctor, staring down at him.

Asleep.

Albert sucked air in hard through his nose, letting its coldness blast away the murk behind his eyes.

He had fallen asleep.

How long? The sun had moved below the rooftops, no longer warming his face. An hour? Maybe more. He released the doctor's wrist.

Dr. Moran swayed and regained his balance. He blinked down at Albert, his mouth open.

"I'm sorry," Albert said, feigning weakness and confusion. "You startled me."

"That's okay," Dr. Moran said. "I didn't mean to scare you. I was just about to get into my car when I saw you sitting here. Are you all right? Do you need help?"

He went to put his hand back on Albert's shoulder but seemed to think better of it.

"I'm fine," Albert said.

"And Mrs. Ryan? Any change?"

"No," he said. "She's the same."

"So what are you doing here?" The doctor sat down beside Albert. "Did you want to see me?"

Albert pulled back his sleeve, saw his bare wrist. He'd forgotten his watch. "What time is it?" he asked.

"Just gone six," Dr. Moran said.

"Stupid old man," Albert said.

"What's wrong, Mr. Ryan? Why did you come here?"

Albert sighed, leaned forward, and reached inside his overcoat with his right hand. The early evening air chilled his midriff as he pulled the pistol from the holster. It was small enough for his left hand to conceal it from the doctor's view.

"Mr. Ryan?"

He gave the doctor a soft smile. "My wife rambles. I suppose it's those patches for the pain. What are they, morphine?"

"Fentanyl," Dr. Moran said. "Stronger than morphine. I wouldn't prescribe them if they weren't necessary. She's comfortable, isn't she?"

"Oh, yes." Albert nodded. "But it does leave her a little confused. And then she talks. Old memories and such. Sometimes they aren't her own. She can't seem to keep them straight, keep her memories and her fantasies apart."

"It's a common side-effect." The doctor put his hand on Albert's shoulder. "Is that what's bothering you?"

"In a way," Albert said. "Tell me, do you save many? The people you treat. How many do you save?"

"Some," the doctor said. "Not enough."

"You're a good doctor," Albert said. "You're a craftsman, like me. Well, like I used to be."

"What did you do before you retired?" the doctor asked, leaning back in the seat. "I wondered what Mrs. Ryan meant by the blood on your hands. I couldn't decide if you were a vet or a butcher."

A dry laugh rose up from Albert's belly. "Neither," he said.

"Then what? I wondered if you'd been in medicine, a surgeon maybe, but I don't think so. You'd know about Fentanyl, for one thing."

Albert closed his eyes, committed himself, and opened them again. "You're a good man. We have much to thank you for, Celia and I. It makes me so sad to do this."

"Do what?"

Albert brought the small pistol up to the doctor's temple. "This," he said.

It sounded like a snare drum. Birds scattered.

THE BED WAS EMPTY save for a pale yellow stain.

"Celia?" Albert called from the doorway.

He stepped inside. The dressing table drawers stood open, their contents spilling over the edges. Powder and perfume coated the surface beneath the mirror. Panic flared in Albert's breast, a wild fluttering thing. He willed it to be calm.

"Celia?" he called again.

"In here, Bertie."

Her voice came from the en suite bathroom. It was stronger than he'd last heard it, but metallic, like a rusted blade. Albert passed the bed, registered the smell of stale urine, just another odour of the unwell. Steam warmed his face as he looked in.

Celia leaned against the basin, one hand gripping its edge, a stick figure in her scarlet evening gown. Its straps clung to the bones beneath her tracing-paper skin. He'd forgotten how tall she was.

She applied lipstick, running the stub across her mouth, and dropped it to clatter in the basin. She pinched a tissue between her lips, leaving a deep red kiss on the white paper. The tissue fell from her fingers and wafted to the tiled floor. It soaked up a brighter red from the small puddle it settled in.

"Sweetheart, you're bleeding."

"Am I?" She looked down. "Oh."

"Where from?" he asked.

"I don't know," she said, turning her attention back to the mirror. "It doesn't matter."

Albert noticed the pink blotching on her upper arm.

"Where's your patch?" he asked.

"I took it off when you left," she said.

"But the pain," he said.

She eyed him over her naked shoulder. "It doesn't matter," she said. "How do I look?"

"Beautiful," Albert said.

Celia smiled. Lipstick stained her remaining teeth. Love burned in him like an African sun. "Beautiful," he said again. "What are you doing?"

She turned back to her reflection. "Getting ready," she said.

"What for?"

"You killed that nice doctor," she said. It wasn't a question.

"Yes," he said.

"I'm a sick woman, and I cost that young man his life. For nothing. Just some words." Her knees buckled, and she grabbed the basin's edge. She straightened. "I will die," she said.

"Darling, don't."

He took a step towards her, slipped on her blood, steadied himself with a strong hand against the wall.

"I will die and nothing will stop it," she said. "I will only get worse. I will ramble more and more. What about the nurses? What about the cleaner? What about dear Finula from downstairs? When she reads to me, what if I say something to her? Will you kill her too?"

"Of course," he said.

"Why?" Celia asked. "What for? What good could it do?"

"To protect you," he said. He moved closer. "I only had one talent in life. God help me if I can't use it to protect you." He went to put his hands on her shoulders, but she pushed the gown's straps aside, let the dress fall to her waist.

"Look," she said.

"Darling, don't," he said.

"Look." Her reflection stared hard at him. "Look at me."

Albert looked. He studied the greys and purples of her skin, the places where his hands had once found ripe flesh, the sad remains of the breasts that had caused him to gasp when she first revealed them to him three decades ago.

"Don't," he said.

"You're protecting a skeleton," she said. A tear escaped

her. "I'm dead and rotting. I should be in the ground already, not lingering here."

Albert put his hands on her waist. Her hipbones felt like shards of porcelain beneath the fabric of her dress. He kissed her neck and raised the dress back up, slipping the straps over her brittle shoulders.

"Don't," he said.

Celia watched the reflections of his hands. "Oh Bertie, the things you've done with those," she said. "We'll go to hell, you know."

He slipped his arms around her, his nose and mouth pressed to the nape of her neck. He smelt her sweetness through the decay, still there, underlying the rot.

"Don't," he said.

"I'll go to hell," she said. "I will burn forever and nothing can save me. Not even you."

His tears slicked her loose skin. "Don't," he said.

"But did God give you that talent?" she asked. "I used to wonder about that. It used to keep me awake at night. If God gave you that talent, that craft, how can he damn you for using it? I used to tell myself the people you killed must have deserved it. They had to, or you wouldn't have done it. They were criminals. They were murderers and thieves, and they deserved to die, so you used the talent God gave you. And so we wouldn't go to hell."

Albert raised his eyes from her neck, met hers in the mirror. "Come back to bed, love."

"No." She smiled and tilted her head. "Not now that I'm all gussied up."

She winced at the pain the movement had caused her, and Albert gripped her shoulders to steady her.

"Your God-given talent," she said. "That was how I lived with it. But that poor doctor was good. He didn't deserve to die, but you used your talent on him. So now I know I was wrong all those years. It doesn't matter where your talent came from. We're damned, and that's all there is."

"Don't talk this way," Albert said. "Please."

"I won't have anyone else die because of my blathering." She stared hard at him, her eyes clearer than they'd been for a year. "Do you hear me, Bertie? Not a single person. So I have one thing to ask of you."

"What?"

She reached up to lace her fingers with his. "Such beautiful hands; such a terrible craft."

She turned in his arms, using his thick body for support. Her cheek met his. She ran her fingers along his jowls. "Such a saggy face," she said.

"What do you want?" he asked.

Celia pressed her lips to his. He tasted her lipstick and remembered every kiss they'd shared, from every darkened corner to every sun-washed beach. Her lips moved across his face, gathering the tears from his cheeks as if they were salted jewels.

"Such a saggy face," she said. She smiled and rested her forehead against his.

"What do you want?" he asked.

She kissed him again, hard and final. "You know," she said.

He shook his head. "I won't," he said.

She reached for his hands, brought them to her throat. "You will, Bertie," she said.

Her life pulsed against his thumbs.

"No," he said.

"Yes," she said. "It's your talent. I trust you to do it well."

Warmth lurked in the hollows beneath her chin.

"I can't," he said.

"Yes, you can," she said. "You're a craftsman. You can do—"

She went light and loose as a bag of twigs.

He kissed her once.

"I'll see you there," he said.

THE LAST DANCE

Treanor's Bar never tried too hard to be an Irish pub. Maybe that's why on a busy night you could find more Irish people there than any bar in the city. I don't mean white guys trying to adopt some kind of ethnicity to ease their Caucasian guilt, but real honest-to-God children of Eire.

Plenty of bars gave you the shamrock treatment, Guinness on tap and fiddles on the walls, but Treanor's was the real thing. It seethed with that self-righteous jingoism and sense of injustice that only comes from Ireland.

Do I sound bitter? Well, I have good reason to be. That's why I got out, got away, across the ocean from Belfast to Boston. I couldn't stand the hate anymore. But still, at least once a week, I felt drawn to this sorry excuse for a bar.

This one night, the place was empty save for an old duffer counting change on a tabletop, Mickey the barman, and one stranger who occupied a stool two seats down from my favourite spot. The stale smell of old beer filled my head. Mickey raised an eyebrow and grunted as I limped towards the bar. The weather had turned cold and damp, and my left knee didn't like it one bit.

I loosened the collar of my work shirt. The ID laminate clipped to the pocket proudly told the world I had achieved the office of Warehouse Manager. I wasn't quite a regular at Treanor's, not a part of the furniture, but Mickey didn't have to ask what I wanted. A pint of Smithwick's was ready for hoisting to my lips before my ass was even settled on the stool. I grimaced at the creaking in my knee.

"Quiet tonight," I said.

"Yep," said Mickey.

And that was the sum total of our conversation most nights. Tonight was different, though. Mickey leaned forward as he pretended to wipe down the bar. Mickey never wiped down the bar. The beer stains on there were older than my car, and it's a long time since that peace of shit was new.

Mickey inclined his head towards the stranger. "See that guy?" he whispered.

I tried hard not to look to my right where the stranger sat staring at a shot of whiskey and a pint of Guinness.

Mickey rested his chin on his hand, obscuring his mouth as if the stranger might be a deaf lip reader. I should point out that Mickey isn't the brightest. Between you and me, he knows just enough not to eat himself.

"That guy's been here a half hour," he said.

I shrugged. "And?"

"And he hasn't had a sip. He just sits staring at those glasses like they're gonna start doing tricks or something."

By now, the old duffer had finished tallying his wealth and he approached the bar. "I'm a little short, Mickey. Can you stand me the twenty cents?"

His accent, or what was left of it, sounded like Cork to me. I'd seen him here before, always alone. He probably came to America expecting to make his fortune. The sight of him terrified me. Not because he was a scary guy, you understand, but because he looked like my future. I shuddered and put my glass down.

Mickey sighed, pulled a glass from under the bar, and brought it to the tap. "You're always a little short, Frankie. Drink this one up and go home."

Frankie smiled and reached for the glass full of froth. "Thanks, Mickey. You're a good lad."

He gave the stranger a sideways glance and shuffled back to his table. If the stranger noticed, he didn't let on. He just sat there, staring at his drinks, his shoulders rising and falling with his breathing.

The patchy overhead lighting cast this man in glints and shadows, picking out the ridges and valleys of his face, making it look like a skeleton mask. His hands were spread flat on the bar, as if supplicating themselves to the drink, and their lines gave away his age. Mid-forties, I'd say, about my age, maybe a year or two older.

Mickey leaned back in to me. "What'll I do?" he asked.

"He's paid for them, hasn't he?"

"Uh-huh."

"Then what the fuck do you care? He can piss in them if he wants."

Mickey's face creased. "But he's giving me the creeps. He's not right. Look at him. Does he look right to you?"

"No," I said, "but neither do most of your regulars."

"I'm gonna ask him what's wrong." Mickey didn't go anywhere. "Will I ask him? I'll ask him. Should I ask him?"

"Jesus, Mickey, if it'll calm you down, go and ask him."

Mickey looked to the stranger, then back to me, then back to the stranger again. He straightened and moved along the bar.

"You all right, there?"

The stranger didn't respond.

"Mister? Are you all right?"

"Mmm?" The stranger looked up.

"Is something wrong with the drinks?"

"No," said the stranger.

"You haven't touched them."

"I don't drink anymore." The stranger's eyes moved back to the glasses in front of him. His accent, hard and angular, made me study him a little closer. He was West Belfast, like me. My own accent had been buried beneath almost two decades of Boston living, but his was fresh.

A furrow appeared in Mickey's brow and his tongue peeked out from between his teeth like he was figuring out his taxes in his head. "Then why'd you buy 'em?"

"Because I could. Because I can drink them if I want," said the stranger. "But I don't want to. I don't need to."

"I'll have them when you're done, then," I said. I am not a proud man.

The stranger turned towards my voice, the light shifting on his face. The skeleton mask slipped away and I saw him fully for the first time. He said something, but I didn't hear. My heart was thundering so loud it drowned everything else out. I had to fight to control my bladder. My left leg, my bad leg, throbbed with memory.

Sweet Jesus, I knew his face. Some nights, when sleep shunned me, there was nothing in the world but his face. Other nights, when sleep was more forgiving, it was his face that dragged me back to waking.

The stranger's lips moved some more, and now Mickey stared at me. Mickey said something too, but it sounded like blood rushing in my ears.

"I know you," I said.

Mickey looked back to the stranger, whose face had slackened.

"You're Gerry Fegan," I said.

"No," he said. He turned back to his drinks. "You've got me mixed up."

His fingertip traced a line through the beaded condensation on the glass of stout.

"You're Gerry Fegan from Belfast." I lowered myself from the stool and limped the few steps to where he sat. I pointed to my left kneecap. "You're Gerry Fegan and you did this to me."

He kept his eyes forward. "You've got me wrong."

Mickey's mouth hung open as he watched.

I grabbed Fegan's shoulder and he winced. "Look at me, you piece of shit. You smashed my kneecap. You and Eddie Coyle. You would've done the other one only the cops came."

Fegan turned his face to me. It was cut from flint. "I don't know what you're talking about. You're thinking of someone else."

I moved tight to him, his shoulder pressing on my chest. "Do you remember me?"

"No. I don't know you."

"I'm Sean Duffy. You and Eddie Coyle dragged me into an alley behind McKenna's Bar on the Springfield Road because I bought the wrong girl a drink. Remember?"

"You've got the wrong fella."

"She was Michael McKenna's fiancée, but I didn't know that. We had a dance, that's all." I looked down at my leg as the pain flared in my knee, a keepsake from the bad times. "The last dance I ever had. McKenna found out about it and he had you and Coyle do me over. Do you remember, Gerry?"

Fegan reached up and took my hand from his shoulder. "It's not me."

He got off the stool and turned to the exit. I went after him, hopping and limping to catch him up.

"What was it, a crowbar?"

He kept walking. I reached into my pocket and found the handle of the plastic box cutter, the one I used at the warehouse. My thumb settled on the button.

"Whatever it was, it did the trick. I couldn't walk for a year. My father had to carry me to the toilet. You better stop, Gerry."

The box cutter came out of my pocket, the blade sliding out from the orange plastic handle with a stutter of tiny clicks. Fegan reached the door.

"Stop, you bastard."

He looked back over his shoulder and saw the blade in my hand.

"Easy, Sean," Mickey called from somewhere behind me.

Fegan turned his body to face me.

"So, what are you doing here?" I asked. "It was on the news last month. All the old crew, McKenna and McGinty, all that lot. There was a feud. Someone did them in. Is that it, Gerry? Did you run away in case whoever did them came after you? Did it all catch up to you?"

My hand trembled with adrenaline, my voice shook with hate and fear. I had dreamed of this, of taking from Gerry Fegan what he took from me.

"You didn't run far enough," I said.

Fegan took one step forward so the blade quivered beneath his chin. "No," he said. "I can never run far enough."

I felt Mickey's lumbering presence over my shoulder. "Jesus, Sean, take it easy. Put the knife away."

Fegan's eyes locked on mine, cold and shiny and black as oil. No fear leaked from him. One movement of my wrist would open his throat, but the terror was all mine. "He won't do it," he said. "He's not like me."

I brought the blade closer so it reflected light onto his skin. "I will. I'll do it."

"No, you won't. You can't."

What started in my belly as a laugh came out of my mouth as a whimper. "Why not?"

"Because you're better than me," he said.

From the corner of my eye I saw Mickey sidle up to us, a baseball bat gripped in both hands. "Sean, put the knife away. Mister, whoever you are, just turn around and get the fuck out of here."

I felt the tears, then, bubbling up from inside me. Stupid, helpless child's tears. Hot, scalding tears. "But look what he did to me. Just for a dance. I danced with the wrong girl and look what he did to me."

A memory moved behind Fegan's eyes. "McKenna told me to do it. He never said why."

"So?" The words hitched in my throat. My legs threatened to crumble beneath me. "If he'd told you why, would it have made any difference?"

Fegan didn't think about it for long. "No," he said.

My legs had trembled all they could, and now they betrayed me. Fegan caught the hand that held the box cutter and let my body fall into his. The knife left my fingers and Fegan's arms snaked around me. His breath warmed my ear.

"Michael McKenna's dead now," he said. "Him and the others, they're all gone. But it wasn't a feud. They've all paid for what they did. I made sure of it. Everybody pays, sooner or later."

"Not you," I hissed. "You haven't paid."

"I will." His arms tightened on me. "But not tonight."

I had a second or two to wonder where the knife was as Fegan and I danced in the doorway of Treanor's Bar.

He slipped it into my pocket and his lips brushed my ear as he said, "I'm sorry for what I did."

Then he was gone.

Mickey's thick arms took my weight as the door swung closed and the cool night air washed around me. He guided me back to the bar, towards my stool, but I veered to the right, to where the shot of whiskey and pint of Guinness remained untouched. The black beer was still cold as my shaking hands brought it to my mouth.

Like I said, I am not a proud man.

THE CATASTROPHIST

Tom Shields sat quiet in the passenger seat, watching the fields roll past the window. Morning rain made tracks along the glass, water chasing water. Reminded Shields that he was thirsty. There hadn't been time for so much as a cup of tea before they left the house.

Gerry Fegan drove the Ford Granada. Shields could have driven himself, but Paul McGinty had insisted Fegan do it, seeing as Shields didn't have a license. Neither did Fegan, Shields might have argued, but there were certain men you didn't argue with. Just accepted their word, even when you knew they were wrong.

The knock on the door had come late last night, waking Nuala. She had cursed as she reached for her cigarettes, an overflowing ashtray on the bedside locker beside the bottle of Buckfast, a few mouthfuls left at the bottom. She had lit the cigarette and swallowed the last of the wine.

Shields stepped around the empty crib on the way to the window. Five months and she still wouldn't let him take it away. As if Ruairi would somehow reappear there, returned from wherever he'd been. As if he'd never been inside a white box and covered with earth.

They had fought before they went to bed, both of them drunk. Over something so stupid he could barely remember what it was. All he could remember was losing his temper, and unwilling to hit her, he had hit himself, again and again, until his head went light.

He and Nuala had endured the worst tragedy that could befall a person, they had survived it, yet he lost control of himself over something so trivial that it was now lost in the fog. Clearly, it hadn't seemed trivial at the time. It had seemed terrible enough to make him ball his right hand into a fist and strike his own jaw.

Shields looked down to the street below, saw Paul McGinty and Gerry Fegan waiting beside the Granada.

Downstairs in the kitchen, McGinty laid it out for him. Fegan would be back in the morning, six a.m., to bring Shields down to the border. A young lad had been killed, not one of their own, in a barn in County Monaghan. The barn belonged to Bull O'Kane, and a punishment beating had gone too far.

Now the lad's family were threatening to kick up a stink. They knew they risked getting the same treatment as their son, but still they wouldn't quiet down. They wouldn't go to the cops, they weren't that stupid, but they were agitating around the border village, in church, in the pub, in the

GAA club. The locals were getting riled, questioning the Bull's authority.

Time to sort it out, McGinty had said. Head down there, figure out what had happened, straighten everything out. Fegan would be the muscle, Shields the mouthpiece.

Shields didn't like Fegan. Mid-twenties, tall and thin and quiet, a hardness to him that didn't need bluster to back it up. Fegan might have been fifteen years Shields's junior, but there was no question who was really in charge here. There were only three men in the world who had ever truly frightened Shields. One had been his father, ten years in his grave now. The other two were Gerry Fegan and Bull O'Kane, and not long from now, Shields would have to be in a room with both of them.

"Christ," he whispered.

Fegan turned his gaze away from the road for a moment, then back again. He said nothing. Fegan hardly ever said anything.

They had planned a route this morning while Nuala slept upstairs. A Collins road atlas laid out on the kitchen table. A contact in the RUC had supplied a list of police and army checkpoints, and Fegan and Shields had mapped a way around them.

"Not long now," Fegan said as the road markings changed.

They had quietly, secretly crossed the border. Soon Fegan steered onto a single-track lane, the car rocking and rattling over the rough surface. After five minutes they came to a single storey cottage, a few outbuildings surrounding it. A Land Rover stood in the yard, its tyres and doors caked in mud.

"Was it here?" Shields asked as the car slowed in front of the house.

"Yeah," Fegan said, pointing. "That big shed."

Fegan applied the handbrake, shut off the engine.

The front door of the cottage opened, and Bull O'Kane stepped through, his bulk taking up almost all its frame. A flat cap pulled down low and tight on his head to keep the rain off, an overcoat buttoned to the neck. Two men that Shields didn't recognise followed him out of the cottage.

Shields opened the passenger door and climbed out, but he stayed there, one foot inside, the car between him and the Bull. Pushing fifty, Shields reckoned, but the Bull had always seemed older than that. The way powerful men do.

Fegan got out of the Granada, pulling his collar up to keep a little of the rain from his thin neck. Cold rain, hard drops like nails. The kind of January day when it feels like the sun forgot to rise.

"Gerry," the Bull said, his voice deep and soft. "Tom."

Shields returned the greeting with a nod.

"Sorry to hear about the child," the Bull said.

"Yeah," Shields said.

"You know these two?"

Shields shook his head.

The Bull pointed at one, then the other. "Barry McGowan, Fintan Hart. If you ever need to know what a pair of arseholes looks like, just think of these boys."

The men each turned their gaze away, their jaws tight.

The Bull leaned his head in the direction of the same shed Fegan had pointed to a few moments before. A squat structure made from sheets of corrugated iron.

"This way," he said.

The Bull and his two men trudged off towards the outbuildings, Fegan behind them. Shields waited before he followed. He never liked to have a man at his back when he entered a strange place.

The shed's door creaked and groaned as the Bull opened it. He reached inside and a single bulb blinked on, a warm orange glow. A heat lamp like farmers used to keep the freeze out of their barns.

The Bull stood back, extended his long arm, indicated that Fegan and Shields should step through. Fegan did so. Shields said, "After you."

Shields entered last, felt the heat of the lamp on the top of his head. He smelled animal shit. Fat raindrops clanged on the metal roof. Points of light leaked through holes in the walls. Steam rose from their wet shoulders.

One dark stain on the concrete floor.

"This is where you did the young fella?" Shields asked.

The Bull looked to his two colleagues. McGowan and Hart both looked at their feet.

Hart said, "Yeah."

"It shouldn't have happened," the Bull said. "But it can't be helped now."

"What had the young fella done?"

Hart let the air out of his lungs and looked at McGowan.

The Bull's huge right hand lashed out, the palm slamming into the back of Hart's head. Hart's feet left the floor, and he fell face first, his hands and elbows saving him. As he tried to rise, the Bull kicked him in the arse, sending him sprawling again.

"You see this man?" the Bull said, pointing at Shields. "This man has put more boys in the ground than anyone I know. When he asks a question, you fucking answer it."

Hart got to his feet, went to McGowan's side, rubbing his grazed palms.

"There was a fight in the pub," Hart said.

"You and the young fella," Shields said.

Hart exchanged another glance with McGowan. "The both of us."

"Let me guess," Shields said. "Did the young fella get the better of you?"

They didn't answer. They didn't have to.

"So you decided to teach him a lesson." Shields spoke to the Bull. "Did they okay it with you?"

"They were supposed to just have his knees," the Bull said.

"He kept fighting," Hart said. "If he'd just took his punishment, he'd have been—"

"Stop talking," Shields said.

Hart shut his mouth, an audible click as his teeth came together.

"Let me get this straight, then. This young fella beat the two of you in a fair fight, so you thought you'd have his knees. He wouldn't just lie down and take it, so you stoved his head in."

McGowan spoke now. "It wasn't like that."

"No? That's what it sounded like to me. Which one of you actually did it?"

McGowan pointed at Hart, took a step away.

Hart's eyes widened as his gaze flitted from face to face. "It was the both of us. We both did it."

Shields turned to Fegan.

Fegan shrugged and said, "Up to you."

Shields nodded towards Hart.

Fegan reached behind his back, pulled a small semiautomatic pistol from his waistband. He racked the slide to chamber a round, thumbed the safety, and aimed it at Hart's forehead.

"On your knees," Fegan said.

Hart's face went slack. McGowan began to shake.

"I said, get on your knees. Both of you."

Hart lowered himself to the floor, his eyes welling. "No, no, don't, I swear to God, I'm sorry, I didn't mean it."

McGowan backed away as Fegan approached, the pistol still trained on Hart's head.

"You too," Fegan said.

McGowan did as he was told. A dark stain appeared on his crotch, spread down his thighs.

"Hang on," the Bull said. "I didn't agree to this."

"I was told to come down here and sort this mess out," Shields said. "That's what I'm doing."

The Bull stepped between Fegan and Shields. "You don't do my boys without my say so."

"It's not your decision to make," Shields said. "Get out of the way."

"Watch who you're talking to," the Bull said, glaring. "You don't come onto my land and tell me what to do. Not if you ever want to leave it again."

"McGinty gave me authority to fix this any way I see fit. Your boys killed a young fella because they got their arses kicked in a bar fight. The people round here need to know that kind of shit isn't tolerated."

"The people round here need to know who's in charge," the Bull said, stabbing a meaty finger at his own chest, his voice rising. "Me. I'm in charge. And we stand by our own men, no matter what."

"I've been given a job to do," Shields said.

"I don't give a fuck about your job. Gerry, you shoot this boy, you'll have to shoot me too. If you don't, you and Tom will never make it back across the border."

Fegan didn't move, didn't flinch, kept his finger on the trigger.

Gerry Fegan wasn't afraid of anyone. But Shields was. He kept it hidden, kept his face blank, his voice even and calm.

"We have a problem, then."

"Looks like it," the Bull said.

"What do we do about it?"

The tip of the Bull's tongue appeared between his lips, wet them. "How's the wife coping? It's hard, losing a baby."

"That's none of your business," Shields said.

"Maybe not, but you might want to think about how she'll take losing a husband."

Shields said nothing.

"There's a phone box in the village," the Bull said. "Let's go."

SHIELDS SAT IN THE Granada's passenger seat, watching the Bull through the glass of the phone box. Fegan sat on the car's bonnet, watching McGowan and Hart as they waited in the Land Rover.

The phone box stood at the middle of the village's single street, opposite a pub. The same pub where the fight had broken out. Shields imagined it: the raised voices, the calls for calm, we've all had a drink, just leave it. Then the explosion of violence, the fists swinging, glass shattering.

A hundred yards along the street, beyond the last buildings, the border lay. The village in the North, a whole other country visible from where Shields sat. He'd joined up, sworn the oath, to fight for that border to be scrubbed out.

Almost twenty years ago. Thousands dead, but the border survived. Not a single rotten thing that Shields had ever done had made his world any better. That thought kept him awake at night.

The Bull pushed the phone box door open and stepped out, let it swing closed behind him. Shields got out of the car, didn't meet the Bull's stare as he went to the box. He entered, felt the air inside thicken around him. It smelled of piss. A scattering of coins lay on top of the small shelf. The phone's handset dangled by its cable. Shields lifted it, brought it to his ear.

"Well?" he said.

"We've reached a compromise," Paul McGinty said.

Shields swore beneath his breath. "What sort of compromise?"

"Five grand to the parents," McGinty said. "The Bull's going to put that up himself."

"Five grand," Shields echoed, the box giving his voice a hollow resonance.

"It's a decent chunk," McGinty said. "The government will probably give them a pay out too, so they're doing all right out of it."

"They lost their son, for Christ's sake."

"McGowan and Hart," McGinty said. "Take their knees. You can do it yourself, if it makes you feel better. Use Gerry's gun."

Shields felt his anger rise. He swallowed it, breathed in through his nose, out through his mouth.

"That young fella beat them in a fight," he said, "so they took him out to a barn and beat him to death. You think a few quid and a visit to the hospital is a fair price for that?"

McGinty sighed, a distorted rush of air against the mouthpiece.

"You know what you are, Tom? You're a catastrophist. Anything goes wrong, you think it's the worst thing ever. Even with everything you and Nuala suffered over the last few months, you still haven't learned to keep perspective. You have to learn to let some things go. Not everything is a catastrophe, you know? So, some young culchie messes with the wrong boys, gets what's coming to him. And you know what? The world's going to keep turning."

"Not for his parents."

"There you go again. A catastrophe. It doesn't have to be like that. Just give the parents the cash, then sort McGowan and Hart out. Then it'll all be over, you can go home to your wife, and life goes on."

"It's not right," Shields said.

"I never said it was," McGinty said. "I've made my decision. Just do what I've told you."

Shields hung up and said, "Fuck."

HE SET THE FAT envelope on the kitchen table.

The mother's eyes streamed, a constant flow of tears. The father looked defeated, like all the life had been sucked out of him. Her fingers were stained nicotine yellow. He smelled of whiskey. They all sat around the table, the two brothers and three sisters in the other room. Fegan waited outside in the car.

Silence. A deeper quiet than Shields had known since his own child's wake.

"His name was Kevin," the mother said. "Kevin Doherty."

"I'm sorry," Shields said.

"Kevin was a good boy," the mother said. "He didn't deserve it. He was just home from university for the holidays. He was over in England. He took the chance to get out, make a decent life for himself. He never wanted anything to do with your lot."

"I'm sorry," Shields said again, his voice not even a whisper.

"Them two wouldn't leave him alone that night, kept at him, why wouldn't he join up. Why did he run off to England? Did he think he was better than them?"

Shields went to speak, but she raised her hand like she was *his* mother, ready to slap him across the head. He reflexively ducked, as if he was a child, as if this was *his* mother's kitchen and he had done some terrible mischief for which chastisement would surely come.

"Don't you dare say sorry to me again," she said, venom on her tongue. "They picked the fight because they didn't like him, because he was different. And you know what? He *was* better than them. Better than that bastard Bull O'Kane. Better than you. And they couldn't stand it, so they killed him."

Shields cleared his throat and said, "McGowan and Hart will be punished for what they did. I'll see to it myself."

The father paled further, his shoulders slumped, folding in on himself.

"Punishment," the mother said. "You'll break their knees, maybe shoot them in the leg. And they'll go on living while my boy's lying up in Belfast waiting for someone to cut open what's left of him."

For a moment, Shields considered telling her about the baby. He knew what it felt like to lose a child. But your child wasn't murdered, she'd say. And he would have no answer for that. He would have to turn his face away.

Shields pushed the fat envelope across the table to her. She looked at it as if it were some foul thing. Then she reached for the envelope, lifted the flap, looked inside.

"How much?" she asked.

"Five thousand," Shields said. "It'll cover the funeral, and you'll have enough left to maybe take a holiday, or whatever you—"

She threw the envelope. The weight of it smacked against Shields's cheek. It burst. Tens, twenties, fifties, they all scattered and fluttered to the floor.

The mother stood and said, "Get out of my house."

The father slipped from his chair, got down on the floor, gathered up loose bills.

"Leave it," she said.

Shields went to say sorry one more time, but her fierce

stare carried a warning. He got to his feet, left the kitchen, walked along the hall and out through the front door.

Fegan looked up as he approached the Granada. Shields opened the passenger door and lowered himself inside.

"Okay?" Fegan asked.

"Just drive," Shields said.

THEY WAITED IN THE barn. McGowan and Hart in the centre, under the glare of the heat lamp. The Bull with a shotgun slung across his forearm. Four more men, two of them armed with AK47s. Hart stood silent while McGowan trembled and whimpered.

Shields let Fegan enter ahead of him, then followed. He smelled the men, the odour of their sweat cutting through the lingering animal scents.

McGowan burst into tears, snot dripping over his lips.

"Christ almighty," the Bull said. "Pull yourself together, boy, you're getting off lightly."

McGowan wiped his cheeks and mouth on his sleeve, leaving a trail of mucus on the fabric.

"We ready?" Shields asked.

"Aye," the Bull said. "Let's get it over with."

He stood back, let Shields come close to the two men.

Shields took the pistol from Fegan's outstretched hand. A Walther PPK, now that he saw it up close. Compact and light in his grasp. Shields checked the chamber; the cartridge was still in there. He thumbed the safety off.

"It's a small calibre pistol," he said to the two men. ".22 rounds. They won't do too much damage. Now lie down."

McGowan and Hart hesitated, looked to the Bull.

"No getting out of it, lads," the Bull said. "Do what you're told and we'll get you to hospital when it's done."

They both lowered themselves to the concrete floor, lay on their backs. The two unarmed men hunkered down and grabbed their ankles, held the legs steady.

Shields stood over them and thought of the fat envelope hitting his face, the money scattering. He thought of the mother and her vicious tongue, the pain scorched onto her face. The father and his narrow shoulders unable to bear it.

"The Bull's right," he said. "You're getting off lightly."

Shields aimed the muzzle at Hart's left knee, put his finger on the trigger. He imagined the small hole appearing, the gasp and the scream that would follow.

He saw money flutter. Saw a boy boarding a boat to England, maybe a plane. A life ahead of him, away from all this.

He thought of his own son, Ruairi, dead and gone. He thought of how the baby cried. How the noise had been the worst thing in the world, drilling into his head every night until he couldn't think. How he had just wanted him to be quiet.

He hadn't meant it.

Honest to God, he didn't mean for it to happen. But the noise, the constant crying, crying, crying.

The baby weighed almost nothing. Like shaking a doll. Stiff for a moment, then loose like a handful of rags.

Then no more crying.

Shields blinked, cleared his head.

"The young fella's name was Kevin Doherty," he said, "and you killed him for no good reason."

Before anyone could stop him, he moved his aim to the centre of Hart's chest. Pulled the trigger twice. Saw Hart's eyes widen in the fraction of a second it took to shift his aim to McGowan.

McGowan's tongue went to the back of his front teeth as if making an N sound, as if he were going to scream no, don't, don't kill me. But he never got the chance.

A ringing in Shields's ears, a billow of smoke in the air above the two dead and dying men.

He tossed the pistol away. It clattered across the concrete, into the shadows.

The two men who held McGowan's and Hart's ankles let go and stood. The other two raised the AK47s and aimed them at Shields.

"Jesus, Tom, I wish you hadn't done that," Bull O'Kane said.

"I had to," Shields said.

The Bull let the air out of his lungs, shook his head. He turned his attention to Fegan, who lingered by the door.

Fegan stood with his weight on both feet, his hands out from his sides, ready to fight.

"Go on home, Gerry," the Bull said. "I'll deal with this."

Fegan met Shields's gaze. Shields knew then that Fegan would fight for him if he asked it. But he would not.

"Yeah, go home, Gerry. It'll be fine."

Fegan stared for a moment longer, then turned to the door.

"Gerry," Shields called after him.

Fegan stopped in the doorway, looked back into the shed.

"Tell Nuala I love her," Shields said. "Tell her I'm sorry."

Fegan nodded and pulled the door closed behind him.

Shields got to his knees, closed his eyes, and waited for the world to end.

THE TRAVELLER

A Novella

1

The Traveller let himself free of the shadow and walked into the feeble light. His footsteps on the grimy tiled floor sounded like those of a child, soft and unsure. The air around him was weighted by the odour of stale beer, just as it had been the last time he'd walked across this dim room.

Tommy the barman stood at the till counting change. Smoke ribboned from the cigarette he held pinched between his lips. The coins clattered in their compartments, metal on plastic. The visitor's eyelids twitched at the noise. The Traveller drew closer to the bar until his fingertips felt the thick tacky varnish on the wood.

How long?

Days? Weeks? Centuries?

The Traveller couldn't be sure. Time had come to seem like warm water to him, a thing he could feel but could not grasp. Gaps in his memory, hours lost to blackness, his awareness coming and going. His mind disappearing then coming back, finding himself in places he had no recollection of arriving at.

Like here. Like now.

Tommy stopped breathing. The cigarette fell from his lips into the open till drawer. His eyes met the visitor's in the mirror behind the stacked glasses and suspended optics.

"Hello, Tommy," the Traveller said.

Tommy dropped his gaze and took a shuddering breath.

"No, no, no," he whispered.

The Traveller said, "I want a drink."

Tommy shook his head. "No. Not real. Not real." He brought his hands to his face, covered his eyes. "You're not real," he said.

"Tommy, I want a drink."

Tommy spun, threw a bag of coins at the Traveller's chest. The bag burst. Ten-pence pieces scattered, jangling, glittering, rolling. The sound went on forever.

The Traveller said, "I want a whiskey."

"You're not real," Tommy said, the first tear beading on his cheek. "You're dead."

"So they say," the Traveller said. "But I still want that drink."

"Get the fuck out," Tommy said, no force behind the words. "Get out. Now."

The Traveller ran his gaze along the row of optics. He found a bottle made of green glass, the amber fire held within, a cream-coloured label. He pointed.

"There," he said. "Jameson's."

"Please go."

"Give me a Jameson's."

Save for the slightest shake of his head, Tom stood still.

"A Jameson's," the Traveller said.

Tom swallowed. He took a glass from under the bar and went to the optic. A round bubble floated up through the bottle as the glass filled with whiskey. He brought it back to the bar and set it on the wood. He stepped back.

The Traveller reached for the glass.

"It's been a while," he said.

Tom kept his gaze down. "Drink it and go."

The warm scent of earth and spices filled the Traveller's head, and caramel, sparking a memory of a small boy that might have once been him. The whiskey warmed his lips and tongue. The heat crept down his throat to his chest. It glowed in him like his burning soul.

He set the glass back on the bar.

Then he noticed his fingers.

He splayed them on the bar top, one long, thin hand beside the other. The lines and the scars. He thought about bringing his fingertips to his face, but something told him no, he would only feel madness there. Or he could look into the mirror behind the bar and know himself.

But the Traveller wanted no such thing.

"I told you to go," Tom said.

The Traveller heard the words, sounds in the air around him, but they held no meaning. He kept his gaze on his hands. The memory of touch prickled his skin. He felt the bone, the flesh, the blood, broken and spilt so many times. Had he done those things?

"What time is it?" he asked.

Tom said, "Please go."

The Traveller turned his head from side to side, saw the dingy bar all around him. "How did I get here?"

He felt air move. Before a further thought had formed in his mind, he raised his left forearm, met Tom's wrist. The baseball bat waved uselessly above the visitor's head. He reached up with his right hand, plucked the bat from Tom's grip.

Tom backed away until he bumped against the till's open drawer. The Traveller held the bat in front of himself, felt the weight of it, the chill of the metal.

"I've no cash for the drink," he said.

"Just go," Tom said, tears dropping from his cheeks.

"No," the Traveller said. He dropped the baseball bat to the floor. It rang hollow against the tiles. "I came here for something. What did I come here for?"

"How should I know?" Tommy asked. "I've nothing for you."

The memory came back to him. The job he came to do.

"I need some things," he said.

"I can't do anything for you," Tommy said, anger growing within the fear.

"Yes, you can," the Traveller said.

"I can't."

The Traveller remembered it all now. Who he was, why he was here, what he needed.

"I need weapons," he said. "And I need information."

"Please just go," Tommy said.

"Not on your fucking life," the Traveller said.

2

Ellen McKenna pressed herself into the farthest corner of the seat, her shoulder against the window, becoming as small as possible. She upped the volume on her phone, pushing more sound into her earbuds, letting the abrasive noise of Morbid Angel drown out everything else, even the rumble of the bus's engine. Her school bag acted as a shield, held tight across her body.

No one spoke to her. No one looked at her. Not today, anyway. There were other times when they did. When they called her Freak McKenna, when they accidentally clipped her with an elbow or a foot, when they pushed her down one of the staircases at Ballycastle Grammar. She had learned how to hide in plain sight, to go unnoticed. It was the only way.

She had tried fighting back once, like her father had told her. The other girl had shoved her into a corner, held her there, and spat in her face. For a dare, probably. Ellen had used a move her father had taught her, jamming her fingertips hard into the base of the girl's throat. The girl had staggered back, coughing, clutching at herself. Ellen should have left it at that, walked away. Instead, she punched the girl with as much force as she could channel into her fist. The girl went down, blood spouting from her nose, spilling on the floor. The other kids gasped, some screamed.

That was when the name Freak took hold. At least they didn't come at her so often now. A stupid name was a price worth paying. Her father had stopped asking her about friends.

The bus journey from Ballycastle to Cushendun took thirty-eight minutes. By car, it was only twenty, but her father slept in the afternoons. In the mornings, when he came home from his night shifts at whatever security job he was working, he would sometimes drive her to school before returning home, getting drunk, and going to bed by noon.

They'd been up here on the coast for seven years now. Her memories of living in Belfast, and her mother, had grown more vague with each year that passed. Over time, they had become tangled with the darker shadows that she tried to forget. Her father had told her they were leaving all that behind when they moved here. Those terrors could not follow them out of the city. A new start, he had said, a new life. Ellen had seen more human cruelty in those few years than most do in a lifetime, was too well acquainted with death. Coming here was supposed to be an escape, but she knew now there was no such thing.

She had loved it when she was small. Living so close to the beach. Her father took her paddling in the waves almost every day back then. Sometimes down to the caves, through the echoes and darkness, to the strange gate at the end. Nuns had lived in the house on the other side, he'd told her, cut off from the world. The house was a shell now, waiting for demolition, but the idea of it remained. A place so separate from everything.

She thought she would like that. Not to be a nun, but to be isolated by the sea, a passage through the cliffs the only way in or out. An iron gate between her and everyone else.

Except she was never really alone, was she?

She never had been. They were always there with her, the Others. She had forced them into the background over the last few years, their faces becoming indistinct, their presence more shadow than light. By force of will, she had silenced them, but they had never truly left her.

Ellen and her father had stopped talking about the Others years ago. He didn't want to know, as if acknowledging the reality of them would shift the balance of his world. And she couldn't blame him. These days, they didn't talk about much of anything at all.

Through the bus window, the pine forest gave way to scrubland, churning hills of coarse grass yellowed by wind and rain. Sheep dotted the slopes, foraging. She had thought this place beautiful at one time, a landscape where adventures could be had. But now it appeared desolate, the sky forever grey, rain constant and insistent, like a headache that won't lift.

In the longest hours of the night, when she was alone—but not alone—in their small house while her father patrolled some housing development, Ellen considered the possibility that she might never leave this place. In only a couple of years, she could do whatever she wanted, move away to a different town, a different country. But her father would still be here, digging his grave a little deeper each day. She knew if she wasn't here with him, he might not be alive to grunt at her across the table as he ate the dinner she'd made for him.

Sometimes she hated him for it. At times she wished his heart would give out, or that he'd happen upon a thief with a knife, or he'd take a corner too fast as he drove home. Something quick so she could bury him and be gone from here. And every time she wished for these things, she scolded herself, ashamed of her selfishness.

Ellen closed her eyes and rested her head against the glass, listening to the grinding guitars and hammering drums, the growling vocals. Time passes more quickly when you can't see it. She kept them closed until she felt the bus sway at the turn into the northern end of the village. Opening them, she saw the caravan park, the rows of trailers lined up, waiting for the sun to return along with their owners. The sea came into view, the bay sweeping from Tornamoney in the north to the small harbour in the south, the cliffs rising above, the caves beyond.

She looked out across the water, shining dark as slate,

the horizon barely distinguishable where it met the sky. Gulls circled and swooped. The Sea of Moyle stretched from here to Scotland, less than fourteen miles away, a border between the Atlantic and the Irish Sea. On a clear day, the Mull of Kintyre was visible in the distance, houses like pinpoints on the hillsides. But not today. Nothing out there but waves and pregnant cloud. The bus approached the clusters of low whitewashed buildings that made up the village of Cushendun. This side of the river was a designated conservation area, and property developers had been kept out, leaving these old houses intact, not intruded upon by holiday homes.

The bus steered right, then left, into the centre of the village. It pulled up at the stop by the post office, and Ellen climbed out of her seat, keeping her gaze on the floor as she made her way down the aisle. She couldn't hear them, but she knew they called, *See ya, Freak*, and worse. As the bus pulled away, leaving her there with the late autumn breeze chilling her skin, she did not look at them.

A few minutes' walk took her out the other side of the village to the bridge over the river mouth. A gull stood on the wall, picking at some food it had scavenged, undeterred by her passing. She crossed to where the road curved back inland. Their house stood in a pair of semidetached homes, the other better kept, even though it remained empty most of the year. A weekend getaway for a middle-class couple from Belfast. She did not know their names.

Ellen let herself in and stood for a moment at the foot

of the stairs, listening. There, her father's snoring, deep and drunken. It was how she knew he was alive. She pulled her phone from her jacket pocket to check the time: just gone four. Time to do her homework, then take something from the freezer to put in the oven. The door to the kitchen was closed, and she knew what she would find when she opened it: empty beer cans, maybe a plate with crumbs of toast on it. She would clear the mess away before spreading her schoolwork over the small table.

As she reached for the door handle, something stopped her. A desire to flee, to leave the house and never come back. She was used to such feelings, of being bidden by unknown voices, but this had a clarity that rang through her. Her hand dropped to her side and she studied the door.

Wood, nothing more. Hinges and handle. A thing between her and the room on the other side, that's all.

"Stupid," she said aloud, and turned the handle, letting the door swing inward.

She saw the blood first. Red arcs across the walls and window, over the sink, trails of it running down the cupboards.

Then she saw him. The thin man.

He had once had a name, but she had pushed the memory of him so deep down in her mind that she could not recall it. She had once held his hand, hard and bony. He had been eaten by the same fire that had taken her mother, in a house far away from here. She only saw it in dreams, black smoke and orange flames, devouring everything.

The thin man sat at the table, those hard hands laid flat on its surface, fingers spread. He stared at her, eyes wide.

Not real, she thought.

None of it is real.

Yet she felt him there, the presence of him, the weight of him. She dropped her bag at her feet and stepped into the kitchen.

What was his name?

The towel draped over the edge of the sink caught fire. Flames spread, the blood as fuel. Now it was all around. Fire and smoke. But no heat. Only cold.

The thin man's lips moved, but she could not hear him.

What was his name?

He spoke in silence, his eyes wide.

What was his name?

Gerry. His name was Gerry. She had once held his hand and walked with him.

And now he was here in fire and blood.

"He's coming," Gerry said, the flames licking at his clothes, the skin on his hands blistering.

Ellen tried to ask, *who?*

"He's coming," Gerry said. "Run."

The flames crept across the floor to her, carried by the blood. They touched her legs, and now she felt them, the burning, the devouring. She screamed.

Gerry got to his feet, screamed at her in return.

"Run!"

Everything burning.

"Run!"

Ellen fell into darkness.

When she woke, her father held her, cradling her on the kitchen floor.

No blood. No fire.

"What happened?" Jack Lennon asked.

"He's coming," Ellen said.

3

Another gap in his consciousness. They were becoming more frequent, and the Traveller supposed he should see a doctor about them. And the headaches, thunderous, hammering pain that pulsed from the front of his skull to the back. He hated doctors, but sometimes they couldn't be avoided. Like when he'd had the surgery to make him look more human. They'd done the best they could, and with a hoodie shrouding his face, he could walk along the street without drawing too much attention. But if anyone looked twice, they would see.

He should have died. Spared himself the pain. But he was a stubborn bastard, so he'd crawled out of that house near Drogheda even as it collapsed in flames, got himself out of there and away. The days and weeks after were hellish. All because of an old man's anger and a cop who should have stayed out of it. It hurt so bad he lost his mind, but he survived out of pure bloody spite. He hadn't been back in Ireland since then, but now he was here, ready for work.

The Traveller sat in the ten-year-old BMW 3-series he'd

sourced through an old contact in the motor trade. A private sale to a woman who didn't exist anymore, at least not above ground. By the time the Driver & Vehicle Agency figured out it had been registered to a ghost, the car would have been burnt out in a field somewhere across the border.

How long had the gap been? He checked his watch. Nearly thirty minutes. He might have missed his target. The lane leading to the home of Detective Superintendent Dan Hewitt stood thirty yards along the road. This layby off the motorway was as close as he could park up and still get a view. Not that it mattered now. Those missing thirty minutes had wasted an evening's waiting and watching. His decision now was call it a night and come back in the morning, or approach the property on foot.

The first choice was clearly the more logical. He took the second.

When there was no sign of traffic in either direction, he got out of the BMW, locked it, and jogged across the road. He carried no weapons and no identification. Better to be without should he be caught. If he got lucky and an opportunity arose to take care of Hewitt tonight, he was more than capable of doing that with his hands.

A low barrier ran alongside the hard shoulder, which he stepped over, and into the trees. A minute or so of pushing through and under low branches took him to the lane that led to the house. He followed it, staying within the treeline. Full dark out now, but there was enough moonlight to go by. It didn't take long to arrive opposite the gates, electric, lights and a camera above a numeric keypad. He stayed far enough back to remain out of the camera's reach.

Hewitt was a senior cop, and a dirty one at that. The security around the place would be tight. More lights and cameras around the property, he could bank on that. Maybe a dog. Hewitt didn't seem like the kind of man who'd keep a pet, but he might have the sense to own a German Shepherd or a Doberman to deter visitors.

Through the gates, he could see the driveway, and the glow of the house. A big spread. A wall stretched in each direction from the gate, three feet high, topped by an iron fence bringing the barrier to maybe six feet. Remaining hidden in the trees, he made his way to the far end, then ducked across the lane, his footsteps softened by fallen leaves. The neighbouring property was older, less well kept, fronted only by hedgerow with a wire fence. He forced his way past the end of the hedge where it met Hewitt's wall and pushed aside the metal post that the wire fence had been tied to. It offered barely any resistance.

A tall wooden fence made a border between this property and Hewitt's, no more than two or three years old. He made his way along it, keeping the neighbour's house to his left. A rusting Nissan Note sat in the driveway, an old person's car. As he drew nearer the house, he saw the living room window's curtains were open. An elderly man sat dozing in an armchair, the light from the television reflecting blue on his face. A calico cat watched him from the windowsill, showing only a casual interest in the intruder.

The Traveller moved farther along the fence until he was out of view of the window, then stood still and listened. Only the sound of trees whispering, distant traffic. An aeroplane somewhere high above. He gripped the top of the fence and pulled himself up just enough to see into Hewitt's property.

The cop's car sat in front of the double garage. He cursed, knowing his mind's absence had caused him to miss Hewitt's return home. But still, at least he had an idea of what time it had been. He considered returning to his BMW and coming back in the morning, but now that he was out here, exploring, he might as well get a better look at the place.

Dan Hewitt, wicked bastard that he was, had done well for himself. Nice car, nice house. Maybe just affordable enough between his and his wife's income that he wouldn't have to answer too many questions. But a man can't be so wicked for so long without making enemies.

The contract had been taken out by Laima Strazdienė.

He had met her a week ago in an industrial estate on the outskirts of Brussels. It had been before dawn when he parked up between two warehouses, both of them deserted. He had been there for only a matter of seconds before a black Range Rover pulled up alongside his hire car. Two large men in good suits climbed down from the SUV. While one turned in a circle, examining the world of concrete and metal around them, the other indicated that the Traveller should get out of his car. The Traveller did so, and the large man searched him, arms and legs, torso, collar, belt, his pockets. When he was satisfied, the large man opened the Range Rover's rear door.

"In," he said.

The Traveller did as he was instructed, hoisting himself up into the vehicle. The leather seat seemed to swallow him whole. As the door closed, he turned to see the other occupant.

There was hardly anything of her. She had clearly been a small woman, and even more so now that she had been diminished by illness. Her elegant clothes appeared almost empty, as if they had been arranged loosely on the seat, her head suspended above them. Her features might have been elfin at one time, but now her skin was stretched across her skull, her makeup unable to hide her pallor. The tubes of a nasal cannula fed into her nostrils, the hose snaking up over her ears. A small canister of oxygen stood in a wheeled trolley on the floor. Her breath sounded like tearing paper, and the odour of sickness tainted the car's air.

But her eyes, sharp and hard like black diamonds. He could barely look at them.

"I want three people to die," she said.

"Who?" the Traveller asked.

"Two men and a young woman," she said. "The two men you know. This is why I have chosen you."

The Traveller knew their names, but he would not say them until she did.

"They killed my sons, my two boys. Tomas had his throat cut in a whorehouse. Two days later, Arturas was shot like a dog by the roadside. I will die soon, but the truth is, I have been dying since that winter. They should have been great men, but their lives were squandered because of these three people. Two of them are in Ireland, both policemen, Dan Hewitt and Jack Lennon. You have dealt with them before. The young woman, I have been seeking her for years. I am close to finding her, she is somewhere in Kyiv, but I can't wait any longer. When my people have tracked her down, I will pass her information on to you. In the meantime, you will take care of the others."

"All right," the Traveller said. "You know my rates. It'll be done as soon as I get the first payment."

"The money will be transferred today. May I ask one question?"

"You can ask. Doesn't mean I'll answer."

"You have reason to kill Lennon yourself," she said. "After so many years, why haven't you?"

He looked at the frail shadow of a woman and wondered how long she had left. Death lingered over her, biding its time. Her sins were legend and she was perhaps only weeks away from discovering if heaven and hell were fairy tales or reality.

Why had he allowed Lennon to live this long? The Traveller had asked himself that question many times. Even though he could barely face it himself, he told her the truth.

Now he was here, back in Ireland, across the border in the Black North, ready to take Laima Strazdienė's revenge for her sons. One of them had been executed on a roadside near the airport, the other had his throat cut. He wondered if Dan Hewitt had pulled the trigger. Hewitt didn't seem the type to cut a man's throat, but a bullet in the head? Sounded right.

A shallow, sluggish stream ran along the rear of the neighbour's property, and Hewitt's. Only a foot or so of sodden ground provided a path along Hewitt's fence. The Traveller followed it until he reached a gate. It would be secured, of course, but he tried it anyway, reaching through the hole to feel the padlock on the other side.

Without warning, the rear of the house became illuminated, the trees all around lit up. He drew back his hand, wondering if he'd tripped a motion sensor. Then he heard a door close, and a voice.

"I know . . . I know . . . Don't worry about it. If they had anything solid, your client would've been charged by now. They're just fishing . . . Honestly, stop panicking . . . Yes, it's easy for me to say because it's the truth . . . Just tell him to calm down, don't do anything stupid, and let me take care of things from my end."

The Traveller bent down and peered through the hole

in the gate. Hewitt paced a circle around the garden as he talked, came close to where the watcher crouched, then turned his back, walking to a darker part of the lawn, shaded from the lights by a shed.

Leave now or take the opportunity?

The Traveller gripped the top of the gate, wedged his foot into the hole, and pulled.

"Yes, the usual," Hewitt said, pausing. "I'll expect the transfer by the morning."

Hewitt hung up and cursed under his breath. Didn't hear a thing as the Traveller approached across the grass. He sealed Hewitt's mouth with one hand, reached for the holster at the cop's hip with the other. Hewitt's hand clamped onto the Traveller's, tried to pull it away from the pistol's grip. They danced there in the darkness behind the shed, feet slipping on wet grass, heels digging into the earth.

Finally, the Traveller released the weapon from its holster, and he forced his hand up, bringing Hewitt's with it. With the muzzle pressed against Hewitt's cheekbone, he whispered into his ear.

"Take your hand away or I'll blow your fucking face off."

Hewitt complied, holding both his hands out.

"You make a sound and I'll go in there and kill your wife and both your kids. Do you understand?"

Hewitt struggled. The Traveller pushed the cop away, into the side of the shed, and aimed the Glock at his chest.

"Do you remember me?"

Hewitt stared, shook his head, his hands raised.

The Traveller took a step back, into the light, drew back the hood, showing what they'd saved of his face.

"You remember, you piece of shit whore's son?"

Hewitt took a step closer. "You died," the cop said.

"Fake news," the Traveller said, "isn't that what they call it these days? I know I look a little different than the last time you saw me. Actually, thinking about it, you couldn't see me then, could you? I seem to remember giving you a face full of pepper spray."

"And you broke my nose," Hewitt said, squaring his stance but unable to mask the fear in his voice.

"Did I? Jesus, I don't remember that."

"I did what was agreed on. I got you out of that cell. I've no quarrel with you, so what do you want?"

"To talk, first of all. I've got a couple of questions before we get down to business."

"Talk? Where? My family are—"

"Here's fine," he said. "Your missus comes out looking for you, then we'll just have to deal with that, won't we?"

Hewitt was trembling now, close to panic.

"Calm yourself," the Traveller said. "You just answer my questions, and everything will be fine. I'll be on my way, you won't see me again."

Hewitt gave a whine of an exhalation. "What do you want to know?"

"Where's Jack Lennon?" he asked.

Hewitt almost smiled with relief. "Jesus, you want him? You could have just asked me and I'd have told you."

"Go on, then," the Traveller said.

"He got out of the job on a medical pension a few years ago. He has a place in Cushendun, up on the northeast coast. I don't know the address, but it's near the bridge over the river. Him and his daughter live there."

The Traveller remembered the little girl, no more than six when he'd spoken with her in a prayer room at the Royal Victoria Hospital, in Belfast. A teenager by now. She had terrified him then, the way she seemed to see right into the very soul of him.

"He works for a security firm now," Hewitt said, his words quickening as he gave away his old friend. "Watching over building sites, patrolling warehouses, that sort of thing. He's a wreck, from what I've been told. Working nights, drinking in the day. He'll be no trouble. You won't hurt the girl, though, will you? She didn't do any—"

Before Hewitt could move, the Traveller was on him, pushing him back into the wall of the shed, in the darkness. He pressed the Glock's muzzle against Hewitt's lips.

"Open your mouth," the Traveller said.

Hewitt tried to say no, but the metal jammed against his teeth and gums.

"Open," the Traveller said.

Hewitt did as he was commanded, and the Traveller

angled the muzzle up against the roof of his mouth. He heard the patter of fluid on shoe leather.

"You remember Tomas Strazdas? Arturas Strazdas?"

Hewitt choked in reply.

"Their mother sent me. Laima Strazdienė. She wanted you to know that."

Hewitt tried to scream.

The Traveller pulled the trigger.

4

Jack Lennon walked his sixth tour of the site since coming on shift at ten the night before. He left the portacabin that served as the site office on the hour, every hour, and walked every path through the housing development. They were all roofed and glazed now, wired and plumbed, white goods ready to be installed. Turnkey homes waiting for their young, affluent owners, all built shoulder-to-shoulder so one kitchen overlooked another, with hardly any gardens to them. The developer had squeezed as many houses as could possibly fit onto the land, starting at £129,000 for a three-bed semi. Families would start moving in within the next fortnight and Lennon would move on to another job.

Sites like this were easy pickings for a thief. The building materials, before they were assembled, were always good for selling on to another developer. And now the houses had washing machines, tumble dryers, dishwashers, fridge-freezers and ovens, not yet fitted, all sitting on pallets and wrapped in plastic. Two men with a hand truck and a van could make thousands in a couple of hours. Thank God, or Lennon would be out of work.

Not that he'd be any use if a van full of thieves did show up. He was in no shape to tackle anyone, and he certainly couldn't give chase with the limp that had been with him since he'd been shot in the short stay car park of the International Airport a few years back. Weeks in hospital, months of treatments and physiotherapy, all to get a young woman on a flight to Poland and safety, and he still felt like that leg wasn't his own. Even if he could pursue a thief, he doubted his heart would stand it. But most thieves are cowards, so even a useless lump like him proved enough of a deterrent.

It took Lennon thirty minutes to make his way around the entire site, thirty-five if his hip and knee were giving him trouble. Tonight's thin drizzle made it all the more miserable. The kind of rain that finds its way into your collar and your cuffs, down the back of your neck. The comparative warmth of the portacabin called, tempting him to cut short this round, but he would do his job. He didn't have much pride left, but Jesus, he could still limp his way around a building site.

At 4:35 A.M., he finally arrived back at the portacabin, light glowing from inside. He let himself in with the key on the ring chained to his belt. The radio still played, and the electric heater still hummed. He wiped his boots on the sheets of newspaper that covered the floor and slumped into the chair. Placing his hand on his chest, he listened to his own thumping heartbeat. Even the modest exertion of walking around the site seemed to strain the muscle in his chest, stealing the air from his lungs. The sensation of floating washed through his head, and he breathed deep and slow to bring everything back into balance. There was still coffee in the thermos, but caffeine at this time was a bad idea. He had promised himself he would not open a beer when he got home and instead go to bed straight after leaving Ellen to school. Deep down, he knew he wouldn't keep that promise, but he didn't have to admit that just yet.

As the radio played inoffensively soft rock music, he set a timer on his phone for twenty minutes and folded his forearms on the desk. He rested his head there and closed his eyes. As his mind drifted, he thought of Ellen, and what had happened the afternoon before.

Her cry had pulled him from the depths of sleep, and he had clambered out of bed, tripping over the sheets. Downstairs, he found her on the threshold to the kitchen, staring at the ceiling, eyes wild.

She had come back to herself with a gasp and said, "He's coming."

Ellen couldn't, wouldn't tell him who. Lennon pressed her on what had happened, what she'd seen, but she had said nothing, nothing, and ran upstairs to her room. Sleep still blurring his mind and vision, he had looked around the kitchen, seeking some sign of what had left her on the floor. The place was a mess, but no more than usual.

It had been at least two, maybe three years since Ellen had experienced such an episode. She had learned to keep these things to herself—feelings, visions, visitations, whatever anyone wanted to call them—mostly because he didn't want to hear about them. The idea of it unsettled him in a way that he had no desire to confront. The notion of things lurking beyond his sight was patently ridiculous. He would not consider such nonsense.

It didn't matter that to acknowledge the things Ellen experienced would be to acknowledge his own fear. He simply didn't think about that.

But this, hearing her cry out, finding her on the floor, could not be ignored. He had gone upstairs and knocked on her bedroom door.

"What?" she had called, as if he had knocked a hundred times already.

"You okay, love?"

A pause, then, "Yeah."

"Do you want to talk?"

No answer.

"I think we should talk about it," he said.

"I just slipped," she said. "The floor must have been wet or something."

"You said, he's coming. Who's coming?"

Music erupted from inside. Some death metal band or other, hard and grinding. Loud enough that he'd have to open the door if he wanted to be heard. But it was her space, the noise creating the shield she needed. He rested his head against the door frame and mourned for the little girl he had first brought to this house. The girl who squealed as the waves splashed against her legs, who kicked saltwater at him and giggled.

Lennon missed that little girl.

THE TIMER ON HIS phone sounded, twenty minutes up, jerking him awake from a thin and queasy sleep. He lifted his head and reached for the phone, fumbling for the icon to stop the abrasive jangle. Close to five in the morning now. The first workmen would be on site by seven and he could go home. Maybe Ellen would feel more like talking when he drove her to school. But probably not.

A craving for a cigarette dried his throat even though he hadn't smoked in years. Instead, he fetched a blister strip of painkillers from his pocket. Not prescription strength, but enough to dull the edges. He swallowed three with the dregs of a bottle of water while Toto played on the radio. A fanfare signalled the hourly news bulletin, a syndicated report from an English station. He listened with half an ear: more turmoil in Westminster with a paralysed government in stalemate with an impotent opposition, a general election just days away; America dealing with the latest fallout from its leader's Twitter addiction; more atrocities in the Middle East.

And reports of the death by gunshot of a senior police officer in Northern Ireland. Although official reports have given little information, a source close to the family has suggested a possible suicide at the property outside Belfast. More to follow.

Lennon reached for the radio and switched to a local station.

More of the same sketchy details, no name, no exact location. Could be anybody. So why did the news cause an alarm in his mind, a chill that rippled out from his centre?

He told himself to forget it, to get on with his next round. But as he toured the nearly finished homes with their stickered windows and empty rooms, as his heart lumbered in his chest, he couldn't shake the certainty that the reported death was the start of something.

AS LENNON DROVE HOME in the early light, he gambled on his old friend Alan Uprichard being up and about. The former Chief Superintendent had retired not long after Lennon had quit the force, and they had stayed in touch, albeit infrequently. Uprichard was the closest thing he had to a real friend. Lennon called up the number on his contact list and pressed the phone to his ear. The Bluetooth on his ageing car had stopped working long ago. Uprichard answered almost immediately.

"Jack," he said, "I thought you might call."

"Who was it?" Lennon asked.

"Hewitt."

The phone almost slipped from his fingers. He pulled into a bus stop and applied the handbrake.

"You there, Jack?"

"Yeah, I'm here."

"How do you feel about it?" Uprichard asked.

"I don't know," Lennon said. "God knows, I've wanted to piss on his grave plenty of times. But now it's real."

"Hmm. Death has a funny way of clarifying how you feel about a man. You hated him, I know, but he was your friend at one time. One doesn't cancel out the other."

Bloody Uprichard, Lennon thought, always too wise for his own good.

"He got Marie killed," he said. "My little girl doesn't have a mother because of him."

That was only one of Hewitt's sins. The bastard had once paid another cop, a young Detective Sergeant in need of money, to kill Lennon, and the hit had almost succeeded. Lennon had a limp, no spleen, and regular nightmares as reminders of the incident.

"I wouldn't be surprised if you got a visit from some of our former colleagues," Uprichard said, "asking you to account for your whereabouts yesterday evening."

"Don't worry," Lennon said, "it wasn't me. Even if I'd wanted to, or I was fit for it, I'm not that stupid. The news report said something about suicide."

"No," Uprichard said, "that was some relative running their mouth off. His wife called it in as self-inflicted, it was his own weapon after all, but there was a set of footprints at the scene. Someone came in over the back fence and left the same way. Just dropped the pistol and ran. Still, whoever did it made it look self-inflicted enough that the first responders weren't as careful about preserving evidence as they should have been."

"Have they anyone in mind for it?" Lennon asked.

"No one in particular. It happened in a blind spot behind a shed. No one checked the CCTV until they found the footprints, but all it got was a glimpse of someone going over the fence. I'm sure forensics will turn up more."

Lennon remained still and quiet, thinking of Dan Hewitt and all the times he'd wanted to choke the life from him.

"Listen, Jack."

"Yeah?"

"He had it coming. You and I both know he was a wrong 'un, into all sorts of bad doings. You've nothing to feel guilty about."

"I know," Lennon said. "Thanks."

"Anyway, how's your girl getting on?"

"I need to go," Lennon said.

He hung up and pulled out of the bus stop.

5

Ellen knew the questions would come. She had hoped her father would be late home so she could go for the bus, but no luck. He ignored her suggestion of getting some rest while she made her own way to school. There was no avoiding it. They had barely left the house before it started.

"So, you want to tell me what happened yesterday?" Lennon asked.

"I told you already," Ellen said. "It was nothing. I just slipped and fell."

"Didn't sound like nothing."

"Can we just leave it?"

"No, we can't," he said, his voice hardening like it did when he wanted to show his authority. Not that he had any.

"I just . . . I maybe hit my head when I fell, that's all."

"Did you see something?"

Ellen concentrated on her fingers, twined in her lap.

"What did you see?"

"I don't do that anymore," she said. "Like you said, it was never real. It was just my imagination playing tricks."

"All right, then, what did you imagine you saw?"

Ellen turned her gaze out the passenger window. The yellowed grass, the endless sloping hills, the bleary sky. Rain streaked the glass. She wanted to tell him to shut up, to mind his own business, but she didn't have the will to endure the fight that would follow.

"Don't get upset about it," she said. "Don't get angry."

"I won't," he said.

Ellen knew there was no point in asking her father to promise. Jack Lennon was not a man who kept promises.

She took a breath and said, "The thin man."

If he reacted, she couldn't see. She kept her eyes turned to the passing hills.

"It's been a while," he said, eventually.

"His name was Gerry, wasn't it?"

"Gerry Fegan," Lennon said. "He was a killer. I don't know what drew your mother to him."

"I remember holding his hand," Ellen said, feeling the dry skin against hers, the bones within the flesh.

"He died a long time ago," Lennon said. "Same time as your mother."

"He helped us," Ellen said. "Didn't he? He was a friend. I remember that."

A few moments passed, then Lennon said, "Your mother shouldn't have got mixed up with him."

Ellen had little memory of the fire, the house that burned, or what brought her and her mother there. She knew Marie

McKenna more as a photograph, a still image, than as a living person. And she recalled the thin man as a dream, a visitor in the night who used to speak softly to her when she was small and afraid. His presence had always been a soothing one, not the fearful vision she saw the day before.

"There was blood," she said. "Yesterday, when I saw him. On the walls. On the floor. Everywhere. Then it caught fire and I was burning."

"Did he say anything?"

"He said, he's coming. He said, run."

She looked to her father now, and he stared at the road ahead. His hands tight on the steering wheel, the muscles in his jaw working. His breathing seemed more strained than usual.

"It was just a dream," she said.

"Yeah," he said. "Just a dream."

They didn't speak for the rest of the journey to Ballycastle. Total silence, not even the radio to break it. Lennon normally kept it on one of the news stations, but not this morning. When they pulled up outside the school, double-parked, she undid her seatbelt and opened the passenger door. His hand on her arm made her pause.

"Listen, I'll maybe pick you up today. Save you going for the bus."

"Why?"

"Just . . . because."

"I can get the bus, it's fine."

"No, I'll lift you. I want to."

"Then you can't drink this morning."

"I wasn't going to."

Ellen examined her father's face, searching for the lie. She found none, and it frightened her.

"All right," she said.

"And if you see anyone hanging around today, outside the school or wherever, anyone you don't know, anyone paying attention to you, you call me right away, okay? Don't worry about waking me."

"Dad, what's going on?"

"Nothing," he said. "You need to get going or you'll be late."

Ellen climbed out of the car and walked towards the school gates. She looked back over her shoulder to see her father watching from the car, still double-parked, no sign of moving even though he blocked traffic. Her shoulder brushed a tall man coming the opposite way, and she mumbled sorry. She gave her father one more glance. He did not pull away until she was inside the gates. She paused there and watched him pass. Neither of them waved.

She took the earbuds from her blazer pocket and inserted them, chose a Cannibal Corpse album, and jacked up the volume. Her head down, she walked along the drive to the main school building, avoiding the gazes of the other kids filtering in. Above the guitars and blast beats, she heard *Freak, Freak, Freeeaaaaak*, shouted after her. She ignored it as she always did. Instead, she focused on her phone, where she called up the web browser and opened the local BBC news page. The first headline made her stop in the school doorway.

Slain PSNI Officer Named: Detective Superintendent Daniel Hewitt Murdered at Home.

Shoulders and elbows buffeted her, and one boy leaned in close, shouted, "Get out of the fucking way, Freak."

Ellen got moving, found her way to the girls' toilets. She locked herself in a cubicle, removed the earbuds, lowered the toilet seat, and sat down to read.

A senior officer of the Police Service of Northern Ireland found dead at the rear of his property outside Belfast has been named as Detective Superintendent Daniel Hewitt of the Intelligence Branch, based at Ladas Drive station.

PSNI sources have confirmed that it has now become a murder inquiry. It is reported that sometime after 8:00 P.M., DSI Hewitt's wife heard a gunshot from the family's back garden. When Mrs. Hewitt went out to investigate, she found her husband's body with his personal protection weapon by his side. It is understood that Mrs. Hewitt made a panicked 999 call stating her husband had taken his own life, but sources say that evidence at the scene indicates another party was involved. The killer is believed to have entered the property by scaling a fence at the rear, used DSI Hewitt's own weapon against him, and escaped the same way.

Sources have not ruled out paramilitary involvement in the killing, but say multiple avenues are being explored.

This is a breaking news item and more information will be added as it becomes available.

Ellen read the story again, and a third time.

Daniel Hewitt. Dan.

The name was familiar, but she couldn't think why. She didn't know any of her father's old colleagues in the police. He hardly ever talked about his time as a cop, and when he did, it was without fondness. Either way, this had to be the reason for her father's edginess this morning. But what did it have to do with what she saw yesterday?

The bell rang. Registration first, then double maths.

Ellen made her way to the form room and took the farthest seat back she could find, close to the window. Christ, there was Tim Cochrane, gawping at her again. He was into metal too and thought that gave them some sort of bond. His clumsy attempts to befriend her had seemed sweet at first but had now become an annoyance. He thought she owed him something just because he didn't join in the taunting, didn't call her Freak. But like most boys, he was incapable of reading the signals that she wasn't interested, no matter how clearly she sent them. She didn't want to be caught looking back, so instead she turned her gaze to the window.

The driveway leading to the front gates, and the road

beyond, was visible from here. She watched the traffic, some cars stopping to drop off latecomers, the rest speeding by.

It took a moment to notice the man walking past the gates. Tall, hunched over, moving as if he was in discomfort. The same man she had brushed against earlier. He turned his head to glance towards the school buildings.

Ellen remembered her father's warning, to call him if she saw anyone.

No, he was just a man, out for a walk. Maybe going to the shops down the road for a paper or cigarettes. The sort of man she wouldn't have noticed any other morning.

The form teacher called her name, and she replied, *here*.

Just a man walking, she thought. Nothing to do with me. Nothing at all.

6

Lennon dropped his keys on the kitchen table and went to the fridge. A four-pack of Stella in there, and a few bottles of supermarket own-brand pale ale. Vodka in the freezer. This had become his daily ritual: coming home from the school run, drinking till noon, then going to bed until eight in the evening. But not today. He had told Ellen he wouldn't.

"Shit," he said, and closed the fridge.

He needed something else to occupy his hands, to take into his body. Anything to keep his mind in one place. He searched through the drawers, digging though old cutlery, dead batteries, unopened mail. Then the top cupboard, where the pills and medicines were kept. He pulled out a plastic box, overflowing with co-codamol packets, and reached to the back, feeling for . . . there. A rectangular package, no branding, just warnings of death and disease. Five cigarettes inside, probably stale, but they would do. He reached up into the cupboard again, his fingers seeking out the farthest corners, and found a disposable lighter.

And the A4-sized manila envelope that he kept there.

A few minutes later, he sat on a folding chair on the tiny patch of concrete that passed for a back garden. On the picnic table, a glass of water and a now empty blister strip of painkillers. It wouldn't take long for the codeine to begin fizzing in his brain. In the meantime, he lit one of the cigarettes and drew deep on it. The nicotine hit hard, making his head float, then he coughed up blue smoke that drifted away on the breeze. Lennon cursed, rested his spinning head in his hands, waited for his heart to settle.

Dan Hewitt, dead. The idea should have gladdened him. Lennon had been no angel when he was on the job, but Hewitt was as dirty as a cop could be. Ruthless, greedy, arrogant. The world would get along fine without him. But still, an alarm had sounded inside Lennon when he first heard the news report in the early hours, and it had only grown more insistent since then.

Hewitt had sold him out years ago, betrayed him to a contract killer known as the Traveller, leading to the death of Ellen's mother. Lennon hadn't been the Traveller's target back then, but his life had been blown apart by the collateral damage. The following two years on the force had been a grind, Hewitt pulling strings wherever he could to make Lennon's life difficult, hoping he could push him into quitting the job. Then the botched attempt on Lennon's life had finished it. Although he remained a police officer for more than a year after, Lennon had ceased being a cop the moment he had to kill another to save himself. All Hewitt's doing.

Lennon had no grief to spare for him, but it didn't sit right. Trouble was coming. He could feel it in his aching joints.

He took another drag on the cigarette, felt the heat of it in his throat, and reached for the envelope on the table. Inside, one open card, and seven other envelopes, all sealed. The first was a Christmas card, a glittery winter scene on the front, a banal greeting printed inside. And beneath that, in a childish hand, two lines intersecting to form the letter T.

When the card came Lennon had been in a private hospital ward, out of danger from his wounds, but still tethered by wires and tubes to the equipment that hummed and beeped around him. Uprichard had brought the card to him. Lennon didn't open it till he'd gone. He'd never told anyone about them as they arrived year after year. He would stash them away, unopened. That was the creeping fear of it, knowing that the Traveller was still out there; but he kept it to himself because deep down he was ashamed of that fear.

Lennon leafed through the sealed envelopes, each of them addressed to him at Ladas Drive station. The address was computer printed on some of them, handwritten on others, each in a different script. Each was posted from a different city in Europe.

One more lungful of smoke, and he opened one. Another Christmas card, another insipid message of seasonal cheer, another letter T in its childish, slashing scrawl. He opened another, and another, until the tabletop was covered in cards and ripped envelopes.

A waste of time, he realised. He had always known what was in them. It would have been more useful to go back into the house, upstairs, and open the lower drawer in his bedside locker. There, wrapped in an old T-shirt, was the pistol he had bought years ago, a handshake deal in a graveyard in Belfast. At least two years since he had cleaned it, checked its operation.

And why would he do that?

The world was the same shape and size as it had been this time yesterday, save for one dead crooked cop. In all likelihood, Hewitt had got himself into some dirty deal or other and it had come back to bite him. Nothing to do with Lennon.

Except, he knew. And so did Ellen.

He took one last draw on the cigarette, ground it out with his heel, then gathered up the cards and torn envelopes. Inside the kitchen, he kicked the door closed and dumped the card and paper in the bin. Best thing he could do now was get some sleep. Ellen would be safe in school. No one would try anything in daylight, anyway.

As Lennon exited the kitchen into the hall, he saw the silhouette of a man through the frosted glass in the front door.

He froze there, on the same spot where Ellen had fallen the day before.

The man brought his nose to the glass, hands cupped around his eyes, peering through. Lennon could make out none of his features, and he was certain the man could not see him. His heart rattled in him and he feared it would choke itself on the adrenalin that flooded his system. He dragged air in through his nose, held it, out through his mouth, counting, forcing himself to remain calm, not to panic, not do anything stupid.

The doorbell rang, and Lennon felt it as a shock of electricity. Then the man rapped his knuckles on the glass. Lennon edged into the space beneath the stairs, ducking his head low, watching the door. The man bent down, and fingers intruded through the letterbox. Lennon pressed himself into the darkness and listened until he heard the letterbox snap shut. He leaned out and saw the man step back from the glass. Then the silhouette moved to the side, out of Lennon's vision.

He seized the opportunity to move to the stairs, as quickly and quietly as he could manage with his limp. In his bedroom, he opened the drawer, pushed detritus out of the way, and pulled the T-shirt from the back. He shook the pistol loose, popped the cylinder, checked it was loaded. Snapping the cylinder back, he crossed to the bedroom door and the small landing, where—

That noise.

Lennon held his breath, listening through the rushing in his ears.

He hadn't locked the back door. Closed it all right, but he hadn't locked it.

The noise had been it opening. Now he heard it closing again.

The man was downstairs in his house.

Lennon swallowed a curse and brought his thumb to the pistol's hammer. He drew it back until it locked into place. Edging to the top of the stairs, he peered down, keeping his body behind the bannister.

A click and a creak as the door to the kitchen opened. A shadow stretched along the hall.

A voice, deep and calm.

"I know you're there, Mr. Lennon. I'd like a word."

7

The Traveller had Google Maps open on the laptop he'd bought from a repair store. Although he couldn't make sense of a string of words, he knew enough to enter the name of a town.

C-U-S-H-E-N-D-U-N.

A bloody marvel, it was. A phone call to Tom at McKenna's bar had gotten him Lennon's address, and right here on the screen was his house. He'd barely have to scope the place out at all.

A chime alerted him to an incoming Skype message. He opened the app, and the computer's screen-reader recited the words in its flat tone: "Call me."

He clicked on the contact, the only one on this laptop, and initiated a call, the musical ringtone bubbling along as he waited for an answer. The headache that had been threatening for the last couple of hours began to show itself. He massaged his temples with the heels of his hands. The headaches were becoming more frequent, along with the gaps in his consciousness. He supposed he should be worried about that.

At last, she answered.

"Yes," Laima Strazdienė said.

"I saw your man last night," the Traveller said. "I gave him the message."

"I know," she said. "What about the second message?"

"I'll deliver that soon, don't worry. Tonight or tomorrow night. I've got the location, I just need to figure out a delivery time. It's in hand."

"I have the third message for you to deliver," Strazdienė said.

"Yeah? The woman?"

"In Kyiv, as we discussed," she said. "I'm sending an attachment."

The screen-reader said, "User TZK345689 wants to send a file attachment. Do you want to accept it?"

He clicked the green button.

"Take care of your business in Ireland," Strazdienė said, "then travel to Kyiv. It's taken years to find her. Now I want her dealt with. When you deliver the message, take your time. If you can, deliver the message to her brother first. They share the same apartment in Kyiv. Let her see it delivered. There will be a bonus if you do that for me. Record it if you can."

"Why this one?"

The Traveller knew just as well as Strazdienė that they should be cautious in what they said, but curiosity is a powerful driver.

"She started it all," Strazdienė said. "She was a whore working from an apartment near Belfast. She killed my Tomas. She cut his throat with a piece of broken mirror. When you find them, do the same to her brother. Then her."

Static silence for a few moments, both of them knowing she'd said too much.

"I'll take care of it," the Traveller said.

The call ended, and he double-clicked on the attachment.

"A password is required to access this document," the screen-reader said.

He peered at the keyboard, picking out the six letters, jabbing each key in turn.

A scan of a passport, a pretty young woman, blonde, fine-featured. A driver's license, a near identical image of her face. A series of photographs taken from a distance, coming and going from an apartment building, shopping in a supermarket. One in a café with a young man, darker hair, otherwise similar features. The brother, he guessed.

At the end of the document, a page of text, laid out in bullet points as per his usual request, brief so he could make sense of it. The screen-reader recited the points, line by line, as he listened.

Current name: Katina Goreva

Birth name: Galya Petrova

The screen-reader recited the address of her apartment, and of the night school where she worked as a teacher of English.

Easy job, the Traveller thought, even with the brother. A soft target, and a trip to Kyiv, where he hadn't been for some years. But first things first. He returned his attention to the map of Cushendun and the image of Jack Lennon's house.

8

The bell went, and Ellen shoved her books into her bag and made for the door, pretending she didn't hear Tim Cochrane call her name as she shoved the earbuds in as tight as they could go. Double English Lit next, which she didn't mind so much. The class was working through Macbeth, but she'd read it from start to finish already, taking pleasure in the venality of it all. The greed of the protagonist's wife, his weakness as she drove him on, the inevitability of his downfall. While the teacher had the kids take it in turns to read passages aloud, she could zone out for an hour.

She climbed the stairs to the next floor, avoiding eye contact with everyone. No music played in her earbuds, they were for show, but no one called her Freak. That particular taunt was mostly reserved for when there were no teachers around, the beginning and end of the day, and the break for lunch, which came next. She planned to spend the break in the toilets, locked in a cubicle.

Ellen moved with the flow of bodies up the second flight of stairs and onto the landing that led to the humanities rooms, the languages, religion, and English. Her class was at the far end, so again she focused on the floor, ignoring everyone. She studied the cracks between the vinyl tiles, the scuff marks from years of kids tramping up and down this corridor.

Something made her look up.

She wasn't sure what, at first. A disturbance in the flow of pupils, an island between the rivers of coming and going. It took a moment to make sense of what she saw, of who stood there, waiting.

The thin man.

Gerry.

He stared at her, his eyes blazing. She froze in place, staring back. Elbows and shoulders and bags shoved her side-to-side, but she stayed in place. Blood on the ceiling, the windows, the walls, the floor.

A memory came to her, clear and bright. A bathroom in an old house. Gerry sitting on the edge of the bath. Tears in his eyes. She asked, *Where's the baby?*

Heaven, he said.

Ellen didn't know the meaning of the question, nor the answer. Only that the moment could have been the one before this, so hard and real it was in her mind.

The other pupils walked past the thin man, oblivious, not seeing, not touching him. Someone pushed Ellen hard from behind and she stumbled, landed on her hands and knees, her bag sliding away. She looked up as his lips moved.

"He's coming," Gerry said.

Part of her mind noted that she couldn't possibly have heard him so clearly over the chatter and laughter in the corridor, above the calls of Freak, what are you doing down there, Freak? But still his voice rang loud, cutting through everything else.

The blood caught fire, the flames chasing the red arcs all around.

They'll burn, she thought. Everyone will burn.

"Run," he said.

The flames rushed towards her, hungry, devouring.

No, she thought, they won't burn. Only me.

As the fire consumed her, Gerry screamed, "Run!"

She screamed too.

9

The visitor had introduced himself as Preston Montgomery, MI6. Lennon had snorted with laughter, then the man showed him his identification. Lennon had uncocked and lowered the pistol, but kept it in his hand, pointed the man towards the kitchen where they now sat either side of the table. Montgomery wore dark jeans and a gilet over a black sweater. He had sand on his boots, leaving gritty trails on the floor.

"So talk," Lennon said, the pistol laid flat on the table, his hand resting upon it.

Montgomery paid no attention to the gun, hadn't even glanced it, as if it was of no consequence.

"We have a mutual interest," he said.

"Dan Hewitt," Lennon said.

"Not Hewitt, though he has been of interest to me, but rather the man who killed him last night."

Montgomery must have been pushing sixty, shoulders broad and strong, his face marked by scars. Former military, Lennon guessed, had seen some action before going to the dark side.

"Who do think killed him?" Lennon asked.

"I think you know the answer," Montgomery said.

Lennon watched him for a moment, unsure how much to give away, before he realised he was too tired to play games with this man.

"He called himself the Traveller," he said. "I arrested him once, but the identity he gave us was stolen. I never found out who he really was. Do you know?"

"In all honesty, I don't," Montgomery said. "I've been keeping tabs on him ever since he locked horns with you, found out as much as I could. I probably know more about him than any man alive, and that's precious little. I'm not actually sure how much he knows about himself. It's hard to keep secrets these days, no matter who you are, unless you've none to keep in the first place."

"Then tell me what you *do* know," Lennon said.

"Fair enough," Montgomery said. He pointed to the kettle on the countertop. "Mind if I make a cup of tea?"

Lennon waved at him to help himself. Montgomery got to his feet and set about filling the kettle. As he worked, Lennon felt a pang of shame at the state of the place, at the dishes in the sink, at the mess on the worktops. If Montgomery noticed, or cared, he didn't let on.

"What I do know, for a start, is he isn't an Irish traveller, never was. It's just a persona he adopted years ago. I'd heard of him before your little run in with him, but I'd never seen his handiwork before that. At the time, I was more interested in your friend Gerry Fegan. Where are the mugs?"

Lennon pointed. "Top cupboard, above the microwave. Fegan wasn't my friend. I needed his help, that was all."

Montgomery took down two mugs, placed a teabag in each from the caddy by the kettle.

"Gerry was a piece of work. You remember that mess down at the border about ten, twelve years ago? Bunch of republicans wiped each other out on an old farm there."

"My daughter got caught up in it along with her mother."

"I lost a good operative. Davy Campbell was his name, former Black Watch, I was his handler. I had him planted at a high level, such a valuable asset, then along comes Gerry Fegan and blows it all apart. When Fegan started picking off top republicans, there was a real risk of him destroying all the progress that had been made in Belfast. We couldn't have that, so I sent Davy Campbell to try and put a stop to it. I didn't know it would cost Campbell his life. For whatever insane reason, Fegan let Bull O'Kane live. If he hadn't, it would've saved us all a lot of trouble. Then, of course, Bull O'Kane sent our friend the Traveller to clean up the mess. That's where you entered the picture."

He poured steaming water into each of the mugs, then found a teaspoon in a drawer.

"You take sugar?"

"No," Lennon said. "I thought the Traveller had died in the fire along with Fegan. Then I got a Christmas card."

"You still have it?" Montgomery asked, putting the milk back in the fridge.

"In there," Lennon said, pointing to the bin by the back door.

Montgomery placed the two mugs on the table then went to the bin. He lifted off the swing lid and fished out a card and an envelope. He studied both for a moment before dropping them back in.

"Hmm. Eloquent as ever, I see."

He came back to the table and sat down.

"I've had one every year since then," Lennon said, "just to remind me he's out there."

"Sadistic fucker," Montgomery said.

"Where's he been, then?" Lennon asked.

"All over the place, as far as I can tell. After he escaped from the fire, he next turned up in Brazil. He stayed there for more than a year, getting treatment for the burns, then plastic surgery. I'd just tracked him down to a clinic outside São Paulo when he disappeared again. About six months later, I start to hear whispers, the Traveller, the Traveller, like children in a playground talking about the bogeyman. He's working again, people are saying, he's here, he's there, he's bloody everywhere. Sure enough, a prosecutor in Istanbul drowns in his own toilet, a journalist in Juárez falls from her apartment balcony, a businessman in Athens gets knifed in a mugging gone wrong."

Montgomery waved his open hand in front of his face, miming a mask.

"Sometimes a man is seen, his face like it was cut from wax, one ear mostly gone. I've been chasing him around the planet like a dog chasing its tail. But at last, I might just be a step ahead of him."

Lennon slumped in his chair, weary. "Because he's coming for me."

"You remember the Strazdas brothers," Montgomery said.

"Of course," Lennon said.

"I have a contact in Brussels who happens to know their mother, Laima Strazdienė. He doesn't quite work for anyone officially, more of a freelancer, but she feeds him information on who comes and goes through her brothels. Lots of EU types, dipping their wicks while they're in the city on business, that sort of thing. Anyway, turns out she's got cancer, terminal, and she wants to settle a few scores before she goes."

"Like Hewitt," Lennon said. "Like me."

"And a young woman, a Ukrainian."

"Galya Petrova," Lennon said, feeling a chill. "Has he got to her yet?"

"Not as far as I know, but she's not my concern. Anyway, Strazdienė's heard of the Traveller, knows he's familiar with her targets here, so she puts out feelers. And it looks like she made contact. Consider yourself lucky he went for Hewitt first. I caught the first flight over this morning when I heard."

"What, you're going to save me from him?"

"If I do, it'll be incidental," Montgomery said. "My one and only reason for being here is to get this bastard. You might just happen to be useful to me in doing that."

Lennon felt a smile crawl across his lips despite there being nothing to smile about.

"I'm taking a wild guess here, but you're planning to use me for bait."

"Of course," Montgomery said, returning the smile, his eyes cold and glassy.

"One problem with that," Lennon said. "I have a daughter."

"Send her to relatives for a few days," Montgomery said, as if it were the easiest thing in the world. "The McKenna clan in Belfast. They'll be glad to have her, I'm sure."

"No," Lennon said. "She stays with me, no matter what. If the Traveller knows she's somewhere else, that's where he'll go. He'll use her to draw me out. I won't put her at that risk."

"She's at risk one way or the other."

"She stays with me," Lennon said.

Before Montgomery could argue, Lennon's phone chimed and hummed in his pocket. Lennon lifted the pistol from the table and held it in his right hand while he reached for the phone with his left.

"Yes?"

"Mr. Lennon? This is Joyce Boland, vice principal at Ballycastle Grammar. We need you to come in right away.

Ellen had a bit of a turn this morning. She seems to have fainted on her way to a class and she was brought to the nurse's office. The nurse left her for just a few minutes, and when she came back, she was gone. She's not on the school grounds and we're very concerned. We're going to contact the police, but wanted to—"

"No," Lennon said. "No police."

Montgomery sat up, watching Lennon.

"Do you think you might know where she's gone?" the vice principal asked.

"I might," Lennon lied. "I'm coming over now."

He hung up, stashed the phone away, and said to Montgomery, "I need to go. So do you."

Montgomery pointed to the pistol. "I assume you're all legal with that."

"I told you to go," Lennon said.

10

Ellen cursed herself as she sat on the wall at the Marine Corner bus stop, feeling the drizzle soak through her blazer, making her shirt cling to the skin of her back. The last bus to Cushendun had been the 10:55 and there wouldn't be another for nearly an hour. There was a coffee shop across the road, in the hotel, but she didn't have enough money for a coffee and a bus ticket. She could trudge back to school, take whatever punishment was waiting for her, but her pride said no. Perhaps she could have called her father, but then she'd have to explain why she walked out in the first place. Thinking about it now, she wasn't sure what reason she would give.

She had come to on the corridor floor, a circle of wide-eyed faces around her, Miss Tunnock, the French teacher, kneeling beside her, asking what happened, was she okay? She felt the coarseness of her throat and knew she must have screamed. They all stared, boys and girls both, all ages, all gawping at her lying in a heap on the floor. She wanted to dig down below the vinyl tiles, bury herself there, hide from them.

Freak, Freak, Freak, she heard, *Freak.*

Miss Tunnock hissed at them to shut up. Another teacher appeared and helped her to her feet. Together they brought her downstairs and across to the office block to deposit her in the nurse's room. The nurse gave her water and insisted that she lie down.

Ellen listened as they fussed outside the door, whispering loud as thunder about what had happened, how Miss Tunnock had heard the screaming and come running. How all the kids had gathered around. How the girl writhed, wild-eyed, on the floor. Eventually, the nurse came back in, asked how she was feeling.

"I'm okay," Ellen said. "Can I go home?"

"Is there anyone there?"

"My dad," Ellen said. "He works nights."

"We'll have to call him and see. I'd like you to go to A&E, though."

"I don't need to."

The nurse put her hand on Ellen's, leaned in close.

"You had a nasty turn. I really think you should go to hospital, just to be safe."

"I just want to go home."

"Let me talk to your dad about that."

The nurse came closer still, so close Ellen could smell faded perfume and antiseptic hand wash. The odour sickened her.

"Is everything okay at home?" the nurse asked. "Is there anything you want to tell me about?"

"I just want to go," Ellen said.

The nurse straightened and said, "All right. I'll talk to the principal. I'll be back in a few minutes."

Alone again, Ellen stared at the ceiling tiles, the fluorescent lights, the green lingering they left behind her eyelids. She thought of the thin man, Gerry, the blood and the fire. She thought of the warning, and she knew she needed to be home. A few seconds of hesitation, and she swung her legs off the bed, grabbed her bag, and went to the door.

No one saw her leave, no one stopped her at the exit, or at the gate. No one paid her any attention as she walked through the drizzle, nearly fifteen minutes to the bus stop by the marina. It should have been a pleasant place to pass the time, overlooking the sea, watching the boats rise and fall at their moorings. Instead, the drizzle mixed with the wind and the sea spray to make cold needles. She turned up her collar, hunched over, folding in on herself.

"Rotten, isn't it?"

The voice stabbed at her, sent her nerves jangling. She turned her head to see the man sitting on the wall, five feet away. How long had he been there? She didn't answer him, returned her attention to the ground.

"Do you know when the next bus is?" the man asked.

His accent was not local. Southern, maybe Cork. Not Dublin, anyway. And it was familiar, stirring something deep in her memory. She thought of that voice in a quiet room, far away from here. Him surrounded by others he could not see. She tried to banish the memory, fearful of where that trail would lead, but she could not. It lingered in her mind like a bitterness on her tongue.

Ellen nodded to the rectangular notice affixed to the lamp post nearby.

"The times are on there," she said.

She reached into her blazer pocket for her earbuds. Pressed them in. Played whatever she'd listened to last, though she barely registered what it was. So long as it blocked his voice.

The man got up from the wall, passed her on his way to the lamp post. He peered at the timetable, almost pressing his nose against it. After a while, he turned back to her, said something. She looked away again, pretended not to notice. He came closer, waved a gloved hand where she couldn't avoid seeing it. She removed one earbud and looked up at him.

Her gaze lingered for longer than it should have. On his skin, the way it appeared too glossy, like a mask. Like it wasn't his skin at all, but someone else's. Impossible to tell his age. He wore a canvas jacket over a hoodie, the hood pulled up. But she could see the patches of glossy pink scalp cutting through his hairline.

"I'm a bit embarrassed, like," he said, the vowels long, the consonants blunt, "but I can't read. Any chance you could look at the times for me?"

Ellen felt her heart quicken, her breathing deepen. Her limbs crackled with energy seeking an outlet.

Just a man, she told herself.

She stood and went to the lamp post, eye level with the timetable. "Where did you want to go?" she asked, failing to keep the tremble from her voice.

"Derry," he said, close behind her.

She didn't turn her head to look at him. "There's no bus to Derry from here," she said. "You'd have to go to Coleraine, I think, and—"

"Where are you going?" he asked, closer still.

"Home," she said.

"And where's that?"

"Not far," she said, navigating her words with care. "My dad's there. He's a policeman."

"Is that right?" he said. "He knows you're out of school, does he?"

"He's coming to pick me up," Ellen said, turning enough to note the man's proximity, too close. She caught the scent of him, a stale and dark odour, then it was carried away by the wind and drizzle. "He'll be here any minute."

"That's handy. If he doesn't turn up, sure, I could give you a lift. My car's just up there a bit."

Ellen looked back to the timetable on the lamp post, dotted with rain drops. "Then why do you need—"

"Tell you what," he said, his voice lowering, "no sense messing about. Why don't you just come on with me now? Save everyone the trouble."

"No, I'll wait for my—"

His hand gripped her upper arm, hard, fingers digging into her flesh.

"Sure, just come on to the car. It's only up here a bit. No sense making a fuss about it."

She tried to pull her arm away, but his grip tightened.

"Come on, now. No call for this to go bad. It's your auld fella I want, not you."

Ellen became still, staring straight ahead.

"Good girl, nice and easy, now just—"

In one movement, she drove her heel into his knee, dragged it down his shin, and forced as much of her weight as she could into the top of his foot. He grunted, hissed through his teeth, and his grip loosened enough for her pull her arm away. Ellen felt her sleeve tighten around her arm as he kept hold of the blazer, but she slipped free of it, left him the blazer hanging between them like the rope in a tug of war. She twisted her body away, pulling the sleeve from his grasp, and stepped into the road, not pausing to look for traffic. The coffee shop was only feet away, full of people and safety.

A car's tyres sputtered on the tarmac somewhere behind her, and she heard a dull thud followed by a wheezing grunt. She ran, her eyes fixed on the door to the coffee shop. An electronic chime sounded as she entered. Customers and staff went to the window to see the hooded man sprawling on the road, the driver running from the car, kneeling beside him.

Ellen went to the back of the shop, as far into the corner as she could press herself. Between the other onlookers, she saw the man get to his feet, shoving the driver away. He went to the wall where she had sat only a few minutes before and lifted her schoolbag, turned to look in her direction, then ran.

She reached into her pocket for her phone, pulled the earbud plug out, and went to dial the most recent number. Before she could, the phone vibrated in her hand. She thumbed the green icon.

"Dad, please, come and get me, please be quick."

11

Lennon slammed his foot onto the brake pedal, and the car shuddered to a halt. He pulled the key from the ignition, climbed out, and ran to the coffee shop, leaving his car in the road. Inside the shop, he found Ellen at a table, a waitress and a suited man attending to her.

"Dad," she said.

He went to her and gathered her in his arms. The first time in years they had embraced.

"I wanted to call the police," the suited man said, "but she refused."

"I am the police," Lennon said, and he knew they didn't believe him.

He brought Ellen outside, guided her to the car, helped her into the passenger seat. As he climbed into the driver's side, he saw the tremors that had seized her.

"I should've run," she said. "I knew who he was straight away, but I just sat there."

"It's not your fault," Lennon said, turning the key in the ignition. "It's nearly ten years since you last saw him."

"But I remember him," Ellen said, her voice quivering. "I remember him at the hospital. In the prayer room. I can see him there. I can hear his voice. And the Others all around him. All the people he'd . . ."

Lennon knew what she wanted to say. The people he'd killed. Shadows that haunted the Traveller and men like him, whether they knew it or not. She didn't want to believe it. Neither did he.

"He's gone now," he said. "You're safe."

As he pulled away, in his peripheral vision, he saw her shaking hands come to her face. A desperate whine sounded from her as she suppressed tears. He felt something split at his centre, something broken that would never be whole again. The knowledge that he could give her no comfort gnawed at him.

"Let's go home," he said.

"WHO'S THAT?" ELLEN ASKED as Lennon pulled into the driveway.

Montgomery sat on the doorstep, waiting.

"No one," Lennon said, shutting off the engine.

They each climbed out of the car. Ellen held back as Lennon approached Montgomery.

"What now?" Lennon asked.

Montgomery got to his feet. "I wanted to continue our conversation."

"I don't," Lennon said.

"You look rattled," Montgomery said. "What happened?"

Lennon unlocked the front door and turned to Ellen. "Go on inside, get yourself something to eat. I'll not be long."

Ellen watched Montgomery as she entered the house, not looking away until she closed the door behind her.

"How much does she know?" Montgomery asked.

"Enough," Lennon said. He moved between Montgomery and the door, blocking the view of Ellen's silhouette through the glass. "The Traveller came at her earlier. He tried to snatch her, but she got away."

"I think it more likely he let her get away," Montgomery said. "He was probably sending you a message. Trying to get you on edge. You know how he operates. Have you thought about what we discussed?"

"No," Lennon said. "I'm not going to be the worm on your hook, and neither is my daughter."

"I don't see that you have much choice, Jack. He's coming for you, no matter what. You know you can't go to the police, they can't be trusted. You can run, but he'll track you down. Anybody you turn to for help, they'll be in danger too. What other options do you have? Are you going to fight him off yourself?"

"I've done it before."

"Yes, with the help of a madman. And how's the blood pressure these days?"

"What do you mean?"

Montgomery's face remained impassive. "You collapsed about, what, eighteen months ago? Had to go to A&E, or so I hear. They took samples for testing, but you never called for the results, did you? You're a wreck."

Lennon stepped close to him, chest to chest, eye to eye. "Yeah, I'm a wreck," he said. "Look at the shape of me. Look at where I live. How I live. All this is because of men like you, toy soldiers and crooks, pulling other people into your schemes. Well, not me. Not this time. You want to get the Traveller, you bloody well go and get him, but leave me out of it."

Montgomery smirked. "Leave you out of it? You're in it whether you want to be or not. Your only choice is do you accept my help, or do you fend for yourself?"

"You know my answer," Lennon said.

Montgomery took a card from his coat pocket and extended towards Lennon. "Fair enough. Call if you change your mind, day or night."

Lennon glanced at the card but did not take it. Montgomery reached around him and pushed it through the letterbox.

"See you, Jack," he said, and left by the driveway gate.

Lennon watched as he walked towards the village, whistling, hands in pockets.

Inside, Ellen waited at the kitchen table. "What did he want?" she asked.

Lennon didn't have an answer for her.

"What do we do?" she asked.

"I don't know," Lennon said.

"Are we going somewhere?"

"I don't know!"

He regretted raising his voice before the last word left his mouth, hated himself for the wounded look on her face. "I'm sorry," he said. "I know I should have the answers, but I don't. We've nowhere to go, but we can't stay here."

"Then why not call the police?" Ellen asked. "You still know people there."

"No one I trust," Lennon said. "Last time I got the police involved, it cost your mother her life. I won't make that mistake again."

Before Ellen could argue, his phone chimed and hummed. He pulled it from his pocket. *Unknown caller*, the display said, and he knew. He thumbed the green icon and said nothing.

Long seconds passed before he heard, "How're ya, Jack."

He didn't reply.

"Who's your man that's been hanging round, Jack? The big lad with the fucked-up face on him."

Lennon's teeth ground against each other, the muscles in his jaws tightening.

"Former military, I'd say. He has that swagger about him. The way he walks, like he's on parade or something. You know the type. What is he, MI5? MI6? Something else?"

Let him run his mouth, Lennon thought, see if he gives

something away. Ellen watched from the other side of the kitchen, her eyes questioning. He realised he'd pressed his hand against his chest, as if to hold his heart in place.

"You think he can help you, Jack? You think he can stop what's coming? I'll tell you now, Jack, he can't. No one can. It's been too long in the making, this fight. Too many old scores to settle. But I'll tell you what, I'm going to offer you a kindness. I'll only offer it now, just this once. Yes or no, your choice."

"Go on," Lennon said, his voice rattling in his throat.

"My client made it clear to me that she'd prefer you to see your little girl suffer before I end it for you. A bonus for her, a few extra quid for me. But it wasn't a deal breaker. I could leave her be, if I wanted to. All you have to do is come to me. You do that, you take what's coming, save me coming after you, and I'll leave her alone. How's that sound? Take it or leave it, Jack. Yes or no. Five seconds to decide. Four, three, two—"

"All right," Lennon said.

"Good man yourself. I'll call you when it's time."

The line went dead.

12

Ellen watched her father as he stared at the phone in his hand.

"That was him, wasn't it?" she asked. "What did he want?"

Lennon stayed quiet for a moment, then said, "Yeah, it was him. Just more threats."

"You agreed to something," she said. "What was it?"

"No," he said, "nothing."

Ellen knew he lied. She weighed whether to push him for the truth or not, decided now was no time for secrets.

"Tell me," she said.

"There's nothing to tell. Look, I need to show you something."

He reached around to the small of his back, pulled something from his waistband, and set it on the table. It gave a heavy clunk as it met the wood. She stared at the object, her mind unable to decipher what her eyes were telling her. Eventually, she knew what it was. A pistol. A revolver, not the other kind. She knew that much.

Her father pushed the gun across the table towards her, pointed at what looked like a small lever near the grip. "That's the safety catch," he said. "It won't fire unless you push that down. Once you've done that, all you have to do is point it and pull the trigger. If it's cocked, it takes less pressure to fire, but you're more likely to have an accidental discharge. But if someone's coming for you, don't think about it, just aim and—"

"No," Ellen said. "I don't want it."

"Doesn't matter what you want," Lennon said. He reached into his jacket pocket and dropped a handful of bullets on the table. "You keep this close, right? Anyone comes to the door, front or back, to the windows, whatever, you shoot first. Do you understand me?"

Ellen backed herself into the corner. The tears that had been threatening since that man had taken her arm at the bus stop began to rise along with her fear. Fear turned to anger as it reached her mouth.

"I wish you'd never come back for me," she said. "I wish I'd stayed with Aunt Bernie."

He tried to hide the sting of her words, but he could not. His gaze remained fixed on the table, a quiver in his voice.

"You deserved a better life than this," he said. "I know that and I'm sorry. But Bernie and her people are poison. They would've . . ."

"Would've what? Made me one of them? I used to wonder why you hate them so much, but it's obvious. It's because they're my mother's family. They remind you of what you did."

She regretted the words as they left her mouth, even if they were true.

"What I did? If your mother hadn't got mixed up with Gerry Fegan, we never would've—"

The regret dissolved.

"If you hadn't run off and left her when she got pregnant, she never would've had anything to do with him. We wouldn't be here now. She'd be alive and we'd have a proper home. We'd have a real life."

Lennon leaned on the back of a chair, gripped it, his knuckles white.

"I would've let her down sooner or later," he said. "Both of you. I'm not a good man. I never have been. I cheated and lied and drove away anybody ever cared for me. I know you'll be out of here as soon as you're old enough, and I can't blame you. But picking over all that won't do us any good now."

"But a gun will?"

He made no reply, and she saw how he slumped against the chair, as if he would collapse to the floor without it. Ellen had seen photographs of him as a younger man, and he had once been handsome in his own coarse way, not the wretched creature who stood before her now, broken by his own sins. Yet the hard vein of pride remained in him.

"Call the police," she said.

"No," he said. "There's no one there I can trust."

"What about that woman? She helped you before."

"Flanagan? I've not spoken to her in years. Uprichard's retired. There's no one left."

"Then just call the closest station, ask them to send someone. Explain what's happening. That man won't come near here if there are police."

"No," Lennon said.

She hated him then, as she had done so many times before. But this time, she felt no shame in it. He would not be helped, sacrificing them both to his pride.

"If you won't call them, I will."

Ellen pulled the mobile from her blazer pocket, thumbed the Emergency icon on the lock screen, confirmed the call.

"Hang up," Lennon said.

She pressed the phone to her ear, listened to the dial tone. Her father crossed the room to her, reaching. She slapped his hand away, turned her back to him. He tried to grab her hand, and she twisted away.

"Nine nine nine, what's your emergency?"

"Police," Ellen said.

"Hold, pl—"

Lennon seized her hand, crushing her fingers against the phone, pulling it away from her ear. He prised her fingers loose and the phone dropped to the tiled floor, its already cracked screen shattering. Before she could retrieve it, he drove his heel down hard, sending sparkling fragments in all directions. He bent down with a grunt, picked the phone up, and threw it against the wall. It splintered into pieces.

Ellen stepped back, staring at him.

"You're insane," she said.

He stood, breathless, unable to return her fiery gaze.

"You want to die," she said.

"No, I—"

She went for the door, the hall beyond, but he took her wrist.

"Ellen, wait, I—"

She slapped him hard, rocking his head on his shoulders, and he staggered back, releasing her. As he recovered, she hauled the door open, ran to the hall, to the front door, and out. She heard him call her name, but she kept her focus on the path ahead, the gate, the road, ignoring the cold. As he limped after her, panting, shouting, she ran.

The cold air seared her lungs, but she knew he would not, could not catch up with her. She left him far behind, no idea where she would go.

Away.

Anywhere, so long as it was away from here.

13

The Traveller stood up to his knees in the water, cold shooting up his legs, cutting through muscle and tendon, until it reached the core of him.

"Jesus," he said between chattering teeth.

He looked back to the shore and tried to recall wading out here. No memory of it, nor of walking to the beach. He had parked the car in the yard of a derelict farmhouse not far from the village, then called Lennon. It had been the dim end of the afternoon then, but now the coming dusk turned the world grey. Around four, he thought. Thirty minutes gone, at least. In that time, he had left the car and walked here to the beach, and out into the waves.

His first thought was that he needed to see a doctor about the blackouts, the gaps in his consciousness. They had become more frequent, along with the headaches. He wondered if there was a cancer there, some dirty tumour eating his brain one cell at a time. Then he remembered he was up to his knees in the winter sea, and his torso almost folded in on itself with the cold.

He waded back to the beach, fighting against the water, wondering if he'd have drowned if he hadn't come back to himself. Probably, he thought. As the water fell below his ankles, he became aware of how the denim of his jeans clung to his lower legs, weighing them down, and slopping in his shoes.

"Fucking arsehole," he whispered. "Stupid fucking bastard."

Anger swelled in him, at himself for losing his place, and at Lennon for bringing him here. He slapped his own cheek, hard, felt the sting on his hand, but nothing but a faint pressure below his eye, the nerve endings long gone. On the sand, barely beyond the reach of the tide, were the two bags. The girl's rucksack, and his own holdall.

Jesus, what if someone had come along? He'd have killed them, yes, but what then?

"Fuck's sake, get a hold of yourself," he said as he picked up each bag. "Stop shaking."

His body would not listen, the shivers seeming to have taken him whole. Lucky he hadn't gone out much farther. Up to his midsection, and he'd have gone into hypothermic shock. He cursed himself again and carried the bags farther along the beach, north, away from the village. Looking back over his shoulder, he saw the clusters of houses, their white-washed walls still visible in the sinking darkness.

When he was far enough away, he dropped the bags in the sand and knelt down, the soaked jeans chafing the skin of his calves. He opened the girl's schoolbag and looked inside. Textbooks, notebooks, a pencil case with strange letters and icons drawn on it with black and blue ink. He couldn't read them, but he guessed they were whatever bands she liked. Nothing he could use, he threw the bag across the sand.

Opening his own bag, he fetched the cheap mobile phone and dialled. He expected an immediate answer, but it didn't come.

"Fuck you, Jack," he said after the tone. "I'll try one more time. If you don't answer, the deal's off. I'll do the girl first while you watch, and I'll take my time about it. Maybe I'll feed some of her to you. How would you like that? Answer your fucking phone."

The Traveller hung up and dropped the phone back into the bag. He slumped down onto the sand, lay back, and gazed up into the sky, which had turned from milky white to slate grey. His feet ached from the cold. He wrapped his arms around himself.

Maybe he should have kept walking into the water, just kept going until it swallowed him up. Breathed in the salty murk, let it fill his lungs. But that would mean allowing Jack Lennon to live, and he could not do that. Yes, the contract from Strazdienė paid well, but the money didn't matter. He had more of that stashed away than he could ever spend. The truth was Lennon had to pay for what he'd done to him, for leaving him to burn. It had been years, and he was finally here, ready to do it. Ready to take what he was owed.

And then what?

He didn't know, and his mind refused to follow that path. There was only this job and contemplating anything beyond felt like falling from a cliff. Part of him knew why he had taken so long to come back to this miserable scrap of a country, why he had only done so when Strazdienė tracked him down. She had asked why he'd allowed Lennon so many years of life, and that had been his answer: because he didn't know what was on the other side. He had an idea, perhaps, but he could not form the thought in his mind, could not hold it to the light. If he did that, he might as well walk back to the sea right now and keep going.

"Fuck it," he said.

He sat up, reached into his bag, and took the phone out once more. The dial tone purred in his ear.

"Yeah," Jack Lennon said.

"You're a lucky man, Jack."

Heavy breathing at the other end, wind against the mouthpiece. The boy Jack was out and about somewhere.

"Just tell me what you want me to do," Lennon said, wheezing.

"I will, don't you worry," the Traveller said. "What are you doing, Jack? Where are you going?"

"Nowhere," Lennon said, gulping air. "I just stepped outside, that's all."

"Don't fuck me around, Jack. You know what I'll do."

"Yeah, I know."

"All right, listen," the Traveller said. "The caves in thirty minutes. You go first, I'll follow you in. You try to act the smartarse, you bring anyone else, you bring a weapon, then it'll go bad for you, and worse for your girl. Do you understand me?"

"Yeah," Lennon said.

"Tell me you understand."

"I understand."

"You know what's going to happen. You know I'm going to kill you. I'll make it quick so long as you don't give me a reason to make it slow."

"I won't," Lennon said, "but I need more time."

"Time? No, you're all out of that, Jack."

"I just need to take care of some things, then you can do whatever you want with me. I'm done. I'm fucking ready to go, believe me, I've had enough of living like this. You'll be doing me a favour. But there's something I need to do."

"No, Jack, sorry. Thirty minutes, that's all. I don't find you in the caves, it's not you I'll go looking for. Just you remember that. See you there, big man."

He hung up.

14

Lennon stared at the phone in his hand, the screen dotted with fine rain drops.

He stood at the centre of the road, the post office to one side, the old red phone box, the bus stop. No one on the street. Not Ellen, not anybody. She had run, and he could not keep up, his lungs heaving, his hip aching. He put his hand to his chest once more, as if he could steady his heartbeat by touch alone. A dizzy wave rocked him on his feet, and he lurched to the footpath and leaned on the low wall that fronted the gardens of the row of cottages. His breath came in gulping swallows, and a dagger of pain stabbed the upper left of his chest, sent a charge down his left arm. The phone slipped from his fingers and clattered on the ground.

"Fuck," he said, the word forced between his teeth.

Black circles floated in his vision. He tried to blink them away, but they remained, pulsing with the thunder in his head.

"You all right there, fella?" a voice said from behind.

Lennon turned, saw a man, tall, the hood of his coat

pulled up against the drizzle. He held a large white dog on a lead. Lennon recognised him as living in the cottage by the bridge, but he didn't know his name.

"I'm fine," he said.

"Are you sure?" The man took a step closer, and the dog sniffed at Lennon's trousers. He bent down and picked up Lennon's phone. "Do you need me to call someone for you?"

He thinks I'm a drunk, Lennon thought. First time in a month he hadn't been. Straightening, he took the phone from the man's hand. Without offering any thanks, he turned his back on him and walked back towards the bridge, struggling to steady his gait. He felt the man's gaze on his back all the way across to the other side. It took longer than it should have to reach his home, and too much effort to fit the key into the lock.

Inside, Lennon found the card on the floor, the one that Montgomery had slipped through the letterbox. He placed one hand on the radiator to steady himself as he bent down to retrieve it. A groan escaped him as he stood upright. He stumbled to the kitchen, his shoulder sliding along the wall, and slumped into a chair. His breathing became no less ragged as he sat with his head in his hands, willing the storm in his head to ease.

He searched for some feeling for what lay ahead but found none. No regret, no fear, no anger. Only a sense of inevitability, as if every choice in his life and been for the purpose of leading him here, to this, to now.

Eventually Lennon realised he could leave it no longer. He retrieved the phone from his pocket and squinted at the card that now lay on the table. The numbers beneath the name were a blurred jumble. He blinked and moved closer until he could read them, then dialled.

Montgomery answered after the first ring.

"Yes, Jack."

"I need your help," Lennon said.

"Of course you do."

"It's Ellen," he said, the words coming in sputters. "She's run off. We argued. She's upset. I can't. Look for her. I have. To go to him."

"What do you mean, go to him?"

"He promised he'd. Let her be. If I went to him."

"He'll kill you," Montgomery said.

"Doesn't matter. Listen. I need you. To find her. Keep her safe. I don't trust him. You find her. First. She has. Family. In Belfast. You get her to them. Keep her safe."

A pause, then, "All right, Jack. I'll find her. What about you? What are you going to do?"

"Go to him," Lennon said, feeling the hateful weight of metal tucked into his waistband. "And I'll kill him. If I can."

"Good luck, Jack."

Lennon dropped the phone to the table and rested his head on his forearm as it swayed in another dizzy wave. God help me, he whispered into the warm space between his arm and his chest. God help me.

FIFTEEN MINUTES LATER, HE limped along the road that ran between the river mouth and the row of apartment blocks that had been built against the cliff face. Before he left his house, he had chewed half a dozen aspirin tablets, and the grit of them remained on his tongue. The hammering in his chest had eased enough to let him breathe, but the world had taken on a sickly shimmer, as if he saw it through a veil.

He passed the holiday cottage on his left, the bay stretching out into the gloaming beyond, then the water pumping station, both low buildings made from stone. The road curved around to his right, seeming to disappear into the cliff face. As he followed it, he saw the two mouths of the caves, the road swallowed by the larger of them. He hesitated, gazing into the black maw. Waves broke on the rocks just feet away, and for a moment he considered throwing himself on them, cracking his head, letting the water take him.

But he couldn't die yet. Not until he was sure.

Lennon got moving, each step causing his hip to grind, the pain cutting through the fog in his head. His heart maintained an erratic rhythm of its own, sometimes hitting hard, sometimes barely there at all. Once again, he pressed his hand to his chest, as if to soothe it. The darkness crept up around him as he entered the cave, and when he heard his breathing echoing between its walls, he realised how desperate and jagged it was.

He limped towards the rear of the cave and the hint of evening light that loomed there. As he walked, his feet barely left the ground, dragging on the stones and sand. At last, he reached the gate at the far end, where the cave opened onto the gardens of the old house, the derelict building not visible from here. The gate was padlocked, with barbed wire protecting the spaces around it, discouraging anyone who might dare to climb. Lennon turned and leaned against it, the iron hard against his back.

A memory flashed in his mind: walking Ellen down here for the first time, her small hand in his. Seven years old then, maybe eight. Her eyes wide as they entered the gloom, staring at the thousands of stones suspended in volcanic rock, her gasping at the echo of her own voice. She had run to this gate, peered through the bars at the banks of crocosmia, orange in their fiery bloom. He told her about the nuns who had lived here, isolated, the Sisters of Mercy. She had insisted on coming back down here every day for a fortnight, clapping her hands so she could hear the sound bounce off the walls. Now all he could hear was the angry crash of the waves, and he couldn't be certain if the noise was real or only existed in his head.

His heart seemed to shift and turn in his chest, like an animal struggling in a trap. The cave floor tilted beneath his feet, and he would have fallen had it not been for the gate. A fresh spear of pain ran from his chest down to his left bicep before dulling to an ache in his wrist. With his right hand, he reached behind his back and found the grip of the pistol. He withdrew it from his waistband and kept it hidden as he pulled the hammer back.

As his heart stuttered, as his breath came and went, Lennon waited.

15

Ellen ran until her thighs ached, until each footfall sent a shock of pain into her shins, until her lungs grabbed at the air. She stopped and turned in a circle, realised she didn't know where she was. A country road, far enough inland that she couldn't see the grey of the sea, the sky above bruising into darkness.

Fear crept in, seeping through the anger, telling her she'd gone too far. Told her she was in danger out here.

Where was out here?

A cottage a little farther along the road, empty, but not derelict. Another holiday home, like so many scattered around here. A ruin of a building the other way. No sight of water, the thing she had learned to navigate by these last years. The great constant. If the water is there, everything else is here. That she could not see it frightened her.

But she could smell it. Hear it, if she held her breath. It was not far away, and that gave her comfort enough to keep her mind from panic.

Ellen's hand went to her blazer pocket, meaning to find

her phone there, open a map, and get her bearings. Then she remembered it lay shattered on the kitchen floor, reduced to plastic and glass and metal.

She had called 999 before her father took the phone from her, had asked for the police. It was a myth that the emergency services could pinpoint a call, she knew, but they could tell the nearest cellular mast. Maybe they would send a patrol out, a police car looking for trouble. Probably not. She couldn't hope for that.

The phone box in the village, a red one, like the olden days. By the post office and the bus stop. She had run past it not long ago. Surely if she turned back, went the way she'd come, she would wind up back there again.

Ellen closed her eyes and listened. The sea rumbled somewhere off to her left, which meant she faced south. She reached her hand out, towards the water, as if she could feel it there. And she could, like it was magnetic, the waves sending signals to her.

She opened her eyes and walked, first past the ruin, then the bend in the road, listening as she went. Hearing the roar, even though the clamour in her own mind tried to drown it out. But she knew where to go, like a migrating bird, chasing some primal instinct.

Soon, she saw the caravan park, the same one she passed every day on the way home from school. And she knew where she had been, the road and the houses seen from a different perspective than before.

There, the sea. Bleak and grey and beautiful and always.

Ellen walked, hard stepping, the terror kept at bay by the purpose of her mission: get to the phone box. Call the police. Get help.

The whitewashed buildings appeared ahead of her now, low blocks in the dim distance, curving around the bay, the ugly scar of the new apartments on the cliffs farthest of all. The caves beyond, burrowed down under the rock. A stone wall ran along the far side of the road, weathered down, like a long row of stumped and blackened teeth. Grass on the other side, dropping down to the beach. Not far to the village, only a few minutes. A phone call, then she could find somewhere to hide.

Ellen crossed to the footpath that skirted the wall, folded her arms across her stomach, put her head down, and walked. The drizzle had soaked her blazer through, her hair clinging wet and heavy to the back of her neck, around her cheeks. She passed the clumps of trees that backed onto the old church, the lane cutting through them. Not once in the seven years she'd lived here had she ever seen the building that lay beyond the trees. A certainty settled on her: that she never would. And she didn't mind. She only cared that she reached the phone box, that she made that call.

As she walked, the village coming closer, she became aware of an engine behind her, a car slowing. The tyres hissing on the tarmac. She did not look around. Would not.

The car levelled with her, and she saw the white paintwork

in her peripheral vision, the neon yellow livery. A police car. She stopped, turned to it. The car stopped. The passenger door opened.

A policewoman inside, a yellow hi-vis jacket wrapped around her tactical vest, equipment everywhere. Light brown hair, tied up and back. Wide, friendly eyes.

"Are you all right there? It's not a good evening to be out."

Ellen could find no words. She saw the driver duck down to look up at her, a young man, an earnest face peering around his partner.

"We had an emergency call," the policewoman said. "It ended before the operator could establish who the caller was, but we traced it to the mast near here. Have you seen anything while you were out and about? Anything that concerned you?"

Ellen stood, quite silent, rainwater dripping from her hair.

The policewoman turned in her seat, placed her booted foot against the kerb.

"Anything wrong, love?"

Ellen opened her mouth.

"Nothing at all," the man said.

The man who had been waiting on the doorstep earlier. The Englishman with the broad shoulders and the scarred face. The man who had no business here. Ellen didn't know where he had come from, only that he was now by her side, leaning down, talking to the policewoman.

"And you are?" the policewoman asked.

"Preston," he said. "Preston Montgomery. I'm a friend of her dad's. She ran off earlier and he asked if I'd keep an eye out. A little family squabble, you know the sort of thing. I'll bring her home now, don't worry."

"No," Ellen said, snatching her elbow away as his fingers closed on it.

"Honestly," he said, "just a little family argument, nothing to worry about."

The policewoman looked to Ellen.

"Is that right, love? Do you know this man?"

"No," Ellen said.

She tried to walk away, but Montgomery took hold of her sleeve.

"Don't be silly, now," he said.

"Sir, do me a favour and let go of her," the policewoman said.

She gripped the car's door and hoisted herself up.

Montgomery pulled something from inside his coat, and it spat at the policewoman. The policewoman's cheek and forehead cracked open. She slumped down like a bag of meat between the kerb and the car. Inside, the policeman scrabbled for something at his hip. Montgomery crouched, bending at the knees, reached towards the open car door. The thing in his hand spat twice more, phut-phut, and the policeman jerked and bucked, his hands reaching for his throat, before he slumped in his seat.

Neither of them had made a sound, not even a gasp or a sigh. Like week-old birthday balloons deflating, sinking.

Ellen wanted to scream, but she closed her mouth, remained still and silent.

"You need to come with me," he said. "Quick, before someone comes along."

She said nothing.

"They would've killed you," he said, coming in close. "You know who your father was up against. You knew they'd come for him. Come on. He told me to take care of you. Your relatives in Belfast. I'll take you there now. Come on."

Ellen looked down at his reaching hand, saw the rough skin, the veins, the dirt under his nails.

"Fuck you," she said.

She pushed past him, towards the village. The phone box still fixed in her mind. Like an island to swim towards, a safe harbour.

"Ellen, stop," he said. "Your father asked me to help you."

She ignored him, shut it all out, kept walking, knowing is she stopped and allowed her mind to grasp what she had just seen, then it would come undone.

His hand closed on her collar, the other clasping tight around her mouth. She thrashed, tried to remember what her father had told her. Make it hard, difficult. Kick, punch, scratch. Become heavy, immovable.

None of it mattered. She was no more than a bag of twigs in his arms, carried away like a leaf on a breeze. He pulled her over the wall, dragged her across the grass, her heels kicking at the clumps of green. Down over the verge, onto the damp sand. He threw her down, kneeled on her belly before she could writhe away.

"Stop it," he hissed. "Be still."

Ellen slapped him, slashed at his face with her nails. With one hand, he pinned her wrists to the sand.

"Fucking stop it," he said. "Stop it or I'll put your fucking lights out."

He leaned down, his nose an inch from hers, and she saw his eyes. Saw him.

Ellen stopped fighting.

After a few seconds, he said, "Good."

They both became still, breathing in time with the waves, his hard hand over her mouth.

"They would've killed you," he said. "The Traveller has them all in his pocket. They would've brought your body to him, showed you to your father. Then he would have killed him too. Do you understand? The Traveller wants your father to see you dead before he finishes him. He's a bastard like that. The longer you live, the longer your father lives. Do you understand? Tell me you understand."

Ellen nodded, her neck straining against the force of his hand.

He sat up, peering across the grass towards the wall and the road beyond. Where the police car still idled, its occupants dead.

"We need to get moving," Montgomery said. "Right now. Go."

He stood, hauled Ellen to her feet. Shoved her hard in the back.

"Move," he said. "We can't stay here."

She looked back over her shoulder, saw him bring a phone to his ear. He pushed her again, and she staggered forward, towards the village.

"Yeah," he said. "It's all right. I've found her."

16

The Traveller heard Lennon before he saw him, his ragged breath echoing through the cave. Jesus, he sounded like he'd run a marathon to get here. As he moved deeper into the darkness, and closer to the pale remains of light at the far end, he saw Lennon slumped against the gate that closed off the house and gardens on the other side. He stopped.

"How're ya, Jack," the Traveller said.

"You're late," Lennon said.

"Time's a funny thing, isn't it? There's never as much of it as you think. But I'm here now, that's what matters, right?"

He peered at Lennon's silhouette, barely the shape of a man. Hunched against the iron, his legs quivering at the effort to keep him upright.

"Fuck me, Jack, you look like shite. You ought to look after yourself better. Not that it matters much now, mind you."

"I think—"

Lennon interrupted himself with a fit of coughing that bent him at the waist, each hack coming from down deep inside of him.

"I think I'm having a heart attack."

The Traveller couldn't stop the bark of laughter that burst from him.

"No, big man," he said, taking a step closer. "No way you get off that easy. You don't get to die of natural causes. No chance."

Now Lennon laughed, but it sounded painful, rattling out of him like broken glass.

"You'd hate that, wouldn't you? You have to make a production out of it. If it was just a matter of killing me, you could have put a bullet in my head any time you wanted. Over and done. But that's not how you want it to go, is it?"

"Ah, you know me too well, big man."

The Traveller slipped the holdall's strap off his shoulder and lowered the bag to the ground. He hunkered down, unzipped it, and sorted through the contents. First, he removed the Glock 19 and the suppressor, screwed the two together. He popped the magazine, checked it was fully loaded, then slapped it back into place. Pulling the slide back, he saw there was a round in the chamber.

Next, he pulled out a roll of white gaffer tape and showed it to Lennon before setting it on the ground. Then a disposable lighter, the kind with a long flexible nozzle, the kind people use to light barbeques. Finally, a large can of lighter fluid. He brought the nozzle to his nose, inhaled the petroleum smell.

"I know I said I'd make it quick for you, big man, but, I

mean, look at the state of my face. Look at the way you left me. Fair's fair."

Lennon coughed again then let out a low groan.

"So what are you waiting for?" he asked, his voice gargling low down in his throat.

"Ah, sure there's no rush."

"I'll ask that a different way," Lennon said. "Who are you waiting for?"

The Traveller stood upright, leaving the items lined up on the ground, all except the pistol which he held along his thigh.

"You tell me, big man."

"Montgomery," Lennon said. "He's with you, isn't he?"

The Traveller smiled. "Is he?"

"I think so," Lennon said, no surprise or anger in his voice, but a flat acceptance. "I think he's out there looking for Ellen. Or maybe he's found her and that's why you showed yourself. That's what we're waiting for, for him to bring her here. I'm right, aren't I?"

"Maybe," the Traveller said. "Maybe not."

Another fit of coughing erupted from Lennon, and he had to push with his legs, force himself back against the gate to keep from crumbling to the ground. He brought his left forearm to his chest, his fingers grabbing at his clothes. His right hand remained down low, out of view.

"What've you got there, big man?" the Traveller asked.

"You want to see?" Lennon asked.

"Yeah, I do."

The Traveller raised the Glock, brought his left hand up to support it, aimed at Lennon's forehead, but Lennon dropped like a sack of wet clothes. A flash from his hand, a roar that filled the cave. Something punched the Traveller's left shoulder, knocked him off his feet. He squeezed the Glock's trigger as he fell, saw the first round spark off the iron gate. The second hit something with a wet thump, and Lennon groaned.

Before the Traveller's back hit the ground, he heard metal against stone, knew that Lennon had lost his grip on the weapon. Gut shot him, he thought. He's dead. But it'll be slow, painful. Good, he thought.

The pain in his shoulder bloomed, and the Traveller screamed at the roof of the cave, the sound of his own voice swelling between the walls along with the fire in his shoulder.

"Cunt bastard fucker bitch whore's son!"

He rolled to his side, propped himself on his right elbow, the Glock scraping against the ground, got his knees under him, then up, hissing through his teeth at the pain. Lennon lay there on his side, his back still against the gate, reaching, reaching, reaching for something.

The Traveller crossed the ten feet between them, the Glock aimed at Lennon's head, his left arm hanging useless by his side. Everything in his being urged him to put the bastard out of his misery right now, just get it done, empty every single round out of the clip into the fucker's head, leave it a mass of pulped brain and bone.

No. Not after all this work. He had imagined this moment for years, how it would go, how much the cop would suffer for what he'd done. No chance the Traveller would throw that all away now purely to satisfy the anger of the moment. He had a deeper, wider anger that demanded it be quenched.

He squinted at the ground, struggling to find Lennon's pistol in the last dregs of light seeping through the gate. There, he put his foot on it, kicked it away.

"I got you," Lennon said. "You killed me, yeah, but I got you a good one, didn't I, you bastard?"

The Traveller raised the Glock once more, his finger squeezing the trigger. Only an ounce more pressure, and he'd be rid of Lennon forever. But it wasn't good enough. Nowhere near good enough. He lowered the Glock and kicked Lennon hard in the stomach.

Lennon screamed, and so did the Traveller. The effort of the kick had made his arm swing, grinding bone against bone.

"Bastard fucker cunt shit bastard!"

A low, creaking laugh came from Lennon, like the cackle of a magpie.

"You still . . . have a way . . . with words, haven't you?"

"Go fuck yourself," the Traveller said. "And let me tell you something, you piece of shite. Yeah, Montgomery's with me. And he phoned me a few minutes ago to tell me he has your girl. You were absolutely fucking right. And you know what?"

He kicked Lennon again, and once more, both of them screamed.

When the tide of pain had ebbed, the Traveller said, "You know what? I'm going to cover that little bitch of yours head-to-toe in lighter fluid, and I'm going to set her on fire. And you're going to fucking lie there, and the last thing you're going see is your daughter burnt alive. And then it's you, you cunt, you're going to burn too, and when you're nothing but a heap of charred meat, I'm going to piss on you, I'm going to—"

"Hey."

The voice from behind. Montgomery's.

"Dad!"

The girl's.

The Traveller closed his eyes, savoured the smouldering pain in his shoulder, the buzzing between his ears. He opened them, smiled down at Lennon.

"Here we go," he said.

17

Lennon tried to lift his head from the cold damp cave floor, but it was too heavy. He could see the forms of two people from here as he peered between the Traveller's ankles. Dark out there, the weakest of light making it this far from the mouth of the cave, a dim sliver from behind him. But he knew who it was: Ellen and, gripping her arm, Montgomery.

His heart sounded in his chest, limping, its gait as crooked as his own. I'm dying, he thought. And he didn't mind. But Ellen. He knew his heart would give up long before the wound in his stomach finished him. It would cease beating, his chest falling silent, before it could pump the last of his blood from the wound.

But Ellen.

"Montgomery," he said.

The Englishman came closer, Ellen with him. Tears in her eyes. And fear.

"Montgomery," Lennon said, louder. "I know you can hear me. What is he paying you?"

The Englishman ignored him, spoke to the Traveller.

"Get it done," Montgomery said. "We need to get out of here."

"What's the rush?" the Traveller asked, still staring down at Lennon.

"Jesus Christ, man, I heard the gunshots from the bridge. There's two cops dead in a patrol car no more than half a mile away from here. This place will be swarming in a few minutes and there's no way out. Unless your getaway plan is swimming to fucking Scotland, we need to get this over with. That poor bastard's dead already. Just finish it and let's go."

Lennon raised his head an entire inch from the ground.

"What's he promised you, Montgomery?"

"For Christ's sake, shoot him," Montgomery said. "They'll be here any minute."

"Let them come," the Traveller said.

"What?"

As Montgomery's face went slack with disbelief, Lennon let his head fall to the cave floor. He felt a surge of spiteful glee as the Englishman realised, finally, who he was dealing with.

"Let them come," the Traveller said again. "I don't care. This is all that matters, having this piece of shit cowering at my feet. And look at it. Isn't it beautiful? Isn't it just fucking gorgeous?"

"You're insane," Montgomery said.

Lennon laughed, then pulled his knees up as his midsection ignited in pain.

"You're only just getting that now?" he asked between gasps.

The Traveller grinned, giggled. "He doesn't know me at all, does he, Jack?"

"Christ," Montgomery said, "you do what you want, I'm going."

He shoved Ellen against the cave wall. She fell, folded in on herself, arms around her knees.

Good girl, Lennon thought. Make yourself small.

The Traveller looked back over his shoulder at Montgomery. "So you don't want paid, then?"

"My contract's with Laima Strazdienė, not you," Montgomery said. "I'll get paid no matter what you do. You stay here if you want, let them come and get you. I've done my job."

He turned and walked back the way he'd come.

Lennon knew what was coming, even if the Englishman didn't.

"Montgomery," the Traveller said.

The Englishman stopped and looked back over his shoulder.

Fool, Lennon thought.

Montgomery's head rocked with the force of the bullet, a dark mist puffing from the wound. He stood for a moment, locked in place, as if his body couldn't fathom what had happened to his brain. Then he folded down into the ground, an empty vessel, spilled onto the stone and sand.

Ellen cried out, fear and sorrow roped together in her voice.

Lennon wished she hadn't seen that. Then he remembered she had seen much worse.

Somewhere far away, above the echoes of the cave, beyond the rumble and crash of the waves, Lennon heard a high wail. A siren, rising and falling. The Traveller tilted his head, the remains of one ear angled back to the cave's mouth. He stood silent for a moment, locked in place by the sound.

Now, Lennon thought.

He kicked out, his foot arcing behind the Traveller's, catching his heels, dragging his feet from under him. The Traveller cursed and cried as he stumbled back, arms wheeling. He landed hard on his back, his head connecting with the floor, a dull thud. The pistol in his hand spat, and grit and stone fell from the cave roof.

Ellen remained on the ground, locked in place. Lennon called her name. She hesitated for a moment, then reacted, scrabbling across the cave floor, reaching for the revolver. As the Traveller cursed, she grabbed it, aimed, cocked the hammer.

"Shoot him," Lennon said. "Do it now."

18

Ellen's finger curled around the trigger. In the dimness of the cave, she could barely make out the Traveller as he rolled onto his right side, grunting as he dragged his useless left arm behind. He pushed himself up into a sitting position, his gun cradled in his lap, and turned his head to look at Ellen.

"What are you going to do with that, love?" he asked.

"I'll shoot you if I have to," Ellen said.

She saw his smooth skin crinkle as he grinned.

"Oh, will you, now?" he said. "If you were going to shoot me, you'd have done it already."

"I don't want to," Ellen said, "but I will."

He looked down to his lap, shook his head.

"Ah, fuck it," he said.

He lifted his pistol, the long barrel of the silencer seeking out her father. She made no conscious thought to pull the trigger, the twitch of her finger causing the revolver to buck in her hands. In the same moment, the Traveller's pistol flashed, and through the ringing in her ears she heard both men cry out. The Traveller fell sideways, onto his good arm, and remained there, coughing, groaning, cursing.

Ellen crawled towards her father, the revolver scraping on the ground as she went. Lennon looked no more than a bundle of rags piled against the foot of the gate. As she reached his side, she saw his eyes open, searching for her. She saw the wounds in his stomach and in his upper chest and knew he was dying. He tried to say something, but she couldn't make out the words above the sound of the Traveller's curses and the approaching sirens. She leaned down, her ear close to his mouth.

"Finish . . ."

"What?" she asked. "What?"

"Finish him."

Ellen turned, saw the Traveller get to his knees, the lighter in his limp left hand, the can of fluid in the other. His thumb worked the trigger on the lighter, but it lacked the strength to strike it. Movement behind him distracted her.

The shadows, rippling, forming. So many of them, heads and legs and arms, raising their hands, pointing. The Others, free now, the proximity of death setting them loose.

"They're coming for you," Ellen said.

The Traveller looked up from the lighter, still trying to spark a flame.

"I don't give a shite about them," he said, each word a guttural cough. "I'll be dead before they can put the handcuffs on. So will you and your bastard of a father."

"Not the police," Ellen said. "The Others."

He looked up from the lighter.

"What are you talking about?"

"Years ago," Ellen said, "when we were in the prayer room in the hospital. I told you about them. You remember."

He shook his head. "No. No, I don't remember. I don't."

"Yes, you do," Ellen said.

The shadows moved closer, more than she could count, all pointing at him.

"Shut up," he said, trying once more to ignite the lighter. "Shut your fucking mouth."

"They're coming for you," Ellen said. "They'll take what they're owed."

Among the shadows, the thin man, taller than the rest, coming closer than them all.

"Shut the fu—"

The lighter caught, and the yellow flame illuminated his grin. His face contorted with the effort of raising the lighter. Behind it, he raised the can of fluid, the nozzle aimed at her.

"Finish him," her father said in a voice so low she couldn't be sure if she heard him at all.

As Ellen brought the revolver up, she saw an arc of orange and blue flare towards her. She pulled the trigger as she fell back against her father, felt the gun buck in her hand, felt the sear of the flame.

Through the heat and pain, she saw the can in the Traveller's hand burst open, and for a moment the air around him turned a glowing blue. Then a small sun blossomed, swallowing him in its furnace.

She saw the Others, their savage pleasure burning as hot as the flame reflected in their faces. Among them, the thin man stared at her.

"Run," he said.

The revolver fell from her fingers as flame danced along her blazer sleeve. She launched herself past the screaming ball of fire, past Montgomery's body, towards the mouth of the cave. As it came into view, the world beyond was lit with pulsating blue, a siren wail drowning out the screams from behind her. She pulled the blazer off, threw it aside.

Ellen hit the ground outside the cave and a car skidded to a halt, feet from where she rolled, trying to smother the flames that ate her shirt sleeve. A policeman came running, pulling his jacket off, throwing it over her, slapping the flames out.

Before the pain fully revealed itself, she heard the screams echo from inside the cave. When the nerves in her seared skin finally forced the signal to her brain, she screamed too, joining the Traveller's final chorus.

19

Lennon watched the fireball writhe, listened to its agony. The burning liquid crawled across the cave floor, inching closer to him. The walls of the cave danced in blue light and he knew they had come, that Ellen was safe.

He wept, mourning himself. Mourning the life Ellen had ahead of her, the years he would miss. The revolver lay an inch from his outstretched fingers. He gritted his teeth against the pain and rolled his body to close the distance.

The Traveller's screams ebbed away, and he became still. The river of fire came closer.

Lennon wrapped his fingers around the revolver's grip. He pulled back the hammer, put the muzzle between his teeth. He closed his eyes and thought of Ellen. As he applied pressure to the trigger, he asked God to forgive his sins.

It hardly hurt at all.

20

Ellen sat at the table in her Aunt Bernie's kitchen, listening to her talk with Father Coyle as if she wasn't there. Her aunt and the priest each had a steaming mug of tea in front of them, a plate of biscuits at the centre of the table.

"We didn't want her to go to the funeral, but she kicked up such a fuss."

The priest gave a placating smile. "He was her father, after all."

"We don't know that for certain," Bernie said. "He never would take the paternity test."

"Whatever a test might have said, one way or the other, he was a father to her."

Bernie bristled. "Was he? She never should've gone to live with him in the first place. You know he put a gun in my face when he took her from me?"

Another pained smile. "I heard about that, yes."

"Nothing but a bastard who turned on his own."

The priest gave Ellen a glance, ashamed for her.

"Maybe we should be mindful of what we say, we don't—"

"I've heard worse," Ellen said.

Bernie shot her a warning look, was about to speak, but the doorbell interrupted her.

"Christ, who's that now?" she said, getting up from the table and going to the hall.

The priest spoke to Ellen now. "How are you holding up?"

Ellen picked at the dressing that covered her hand to her elbow. "Okay. They don't really want me here, but I don't care. I'll leave when I'm old enough."

"Don't want you here? Sure, didn't they fight your father tooth and nail for custody of you? Bernie's your mother's aunt, isn't she? You're her family."

Ellen shook her head. "They wanted to take me from my father, to punish him. They never wanted me."

"I don't believe that for a second," Father Coyle said.

Ellen couldn't keep the smirk from her mouth. "You don't believe that, but you believe all your Jesus bullshit?"

The priest's face paled. "Now, there's no call for that."

"I'm sorry," Ellen said, meaning it.

He leaned in, placed his hand flat on the table in front of her. A gesture of surrender.

"Look, I can't imagine what you've been through these last few weeks. These last years, for that matter. You've seen more than any child should see."

Ellen suppressed a laugh, remorseful, knowing his sincerity.

"I know about your Aunt Bernie's people. The things

they've been involved with. I want you to know my door is always open to you."

"Okay," Ellen said, looking him in the eye. "Thank you."

Bernie returned, and Father Coyle's hand retreated across the table, into the other.

"Bloody canvassers," Bernie said. "As if they didn't know what way we were voting. I'm sure you've lots to do, Father, so I won't be keeping you."

"Oh," Father Coyle said, giving his full mug of tea a wantful look. "Well, yes, I'll be off, then."

He got to his feet, pulled his coat and scarf from the back of the chair. Bernie ushered him out while he was still trying to get them on. They exchanged a few stiff pleasantries in the hall before Ellen heard the front door close. Bernie came back, lifted the mug from the table, and poured the tea down the sink.

"Can I go?" Ellen asked.

"What did he say to you?" Bernie asked. "When I was at the door, what did he say?"

"Nothing," Ellen said.

"Didn't look like nothing."

"Nothing to do with you."

Bernie turned to glare at her. Ellen got up from the table and went to the door.

"Maybe Jack Lennon was your father after all. You've got his mean streak."

"He was a good man," Ellen said.

Bernie snorted. "Good enough to leave you when you were in your mother's belly."

"He died for me," Ellen said.

"And your mother died for him, fool that she was."

"You didn't know him."

"I knew him well enough. I know how he—"

The tremor that rattled through the kitchen silenced her. The lightbulb overhead dimmed and flickered. Bernie's eyes widened, staring at Ellen.

"You didn't know him," Ellen said. "And you don't know me."

She left her there, went to the cramped room they'd given her. She pulled the old iPod from under the pillow, lay on the bed, and pushed the earbuds in. She closed her eyes and fell into the music.

Acknowledgments

Early in my career, another author told me that this job gets more difficult with each book, and they were absolutely correct. Therefore, my gratitude to those who've helped along the way grows deeper every time I write an acknowledgements page. My heartfelt thanks to:

Nat Sobel, Judith Weber, and all at Sobel Weber Associates; Caspian Dennis and all at Abner Stein. The last couple of years have presented several challenges and I couldn't have made it this far without you.

Juliet Grames, Bronwen Hruska, Paul Oliver, and all at Soho Press, for keeping your faith and patience with me. And for indulging me by publishing this collection.

Geoff Mulligan, who will always remain a friend.

My partners in crime, Chris, Doug, Luca, Mark, and Val, who have given me so much over the last couple of years.

My friends in the crime fiction community, both readers and writers, for your constant support. Special thanks to Colin Scott for saving what's left of my sanity.

John Connolly for your unfailing kindness.

Jo, Issy, and Ezra, for giving me a reason to keep trying.

Continue reading for a preview of

THE HOUSE OF ASHES

FIRE

Glass breaks downstairs and she freezes in her bed, the blankets tight around her. Then a low noise, not quite a thump, but she feels it rise up through the floor, into the bedstead. Outside, a car door slams, then its engine rattles and fades.

She lies still for a time, listening, frightened. People come to her door sometimes. Not often, but sometimes. Children from the village, mostly, daring to walk all the way out here and knock on the mad old woman's door and run into the trees. This is different. She can't tell the time, but she knows it's near dawn from the milky grey that covers everything.

She listens. Something hums down below, as if the house has come awake along with her. A crackling, then one of the cats yowls, things knocked down and scattered. She sits up, the blankets falling away, and the damp chill of the air creeps beneath her nightdress. The smell reaches her, the dark, bitter smell, and she looks to the door, sees the glowing red and orange and the black swirling fingers reaching through the gaps.

Oh, no, she whispers. Oh, no, no, no.

Another cat howls, screams, she hears its pain.

Please God and Jesus, no.

She pushes the blankets back and pulls her legs from under them, ignoring the aches that come along with the movement. Lowering her feet to the floor, her lower back spasms, and she whines. The air has thickened now, the milky-grey light giving way to a greater darkness that reaches inside of her, scratching at her lungs.

She gets to her feet, her hips and knees protesting. The floor seems to tilt beneath her and she staggers to the door, reaching for the old ceramic handle. As she turns it, she feels the presence of heat, but too late. The door is already opening inward, pushed by some mighty force, and she falls back as scorching air blasts through.

As the floor connects with the rear of her head, something fiery streaks through the doorway and into the room, screaming, hitting the far wall, leaping, turning, trying to escape the flames that swarm it. She doesn't know which of the cats it is, but she covers her ears, trying to blot out its torment until it falls silent.

A thick black fog now covers the ceiling, like a roiling sky above her. Her eyes sting, and she coughs so hard she sees dark constellations.

Out, she says. Get out.

She rolls onto her stomach. She knows the stairs are aflame and offer no escape, that the landing will soon be engulfed. The heat is already unbearable. The window above the dresser: she gets her knees beneath her and crawls towards it, gasping and coughing. Items scatter from the surface of the dresser as she pulls herself upright. A hairbrush, a Bible, a perfume bottle that has been empty for decades. She reaches for the sash window, tries to pull it up and open. It will not move, and she cries out in anger and sorrow, knowing that she will die here.

No, she will not. Not now, not like this. Not after everything she's lived through. Not while the children still need her.

Oh, the children.

Are they burning with the wood and floors and walls? She can't hear them, only the cats trapped downstairs. But the children never speak, never make a sound, even when she was a girl, playing with them in the shaded corners of the secret room below the house. They were always silent. But will they burn?

She pulls at the window once more, and this time it moves, if only an inch or two. Enough to get her fingers underneath, to haul upwards with what little strength she has. She tastes the air from outside, clean, so clean. Up onto the top of the dresser, her head and shoulders out and through, and she sees the drop. How far to the ground? She can't tell. It might kill her. Better than burning. Anything is better than that.

Then she's falling.

She is not conscious of climbing through the window, of

hanging by her hands from the frame, or the decision to let herself drop. First she is there, dangling by her fingertips, looking down at the ground, the overgrown bushes below the window, the past autumn's leaves, old gravel. Then the ground is rushing up to her and she cries out.

She turns in the air and catches a glimpse of them, the children, watching her fall. Then she lands in the bushes, branches clawing at her, then rolling away into a drift of leaves and twigs, her shoulder hitting the ground, and the pain is immense, exploding from her arm. Things go black for a moment, and when she opens her eyes again, the children are all around, and she sees the worry on their faces. She goes to speak to them, though she knows not what, and instead screams.

The little boy she knows is Matthew, the boy she has known for so many years, kneels down beside her and takes her hand.

Help me, she says.

The bigger children gather around, watching. The pain comes in waves, in torrents, screaming from the bones of her. She screams too.

From inside the house, she hears walls and ceilings collapse. The children wander away from her vision, towards the flames and smoke. She turns her head to see them return to the house, through the collapsed front door, to where they belong, where they have always been, where they will always be.

There, in the doorway, the girl she knows best of all, looking back at her. The girl in the plain white dress, dark hair falling around her shoulders, clutching a tangled bundle of scarlet ribbons to her belly. She does not burn. The flames do not touch her.

Nothing can touch her.

1: SARA

Sara Keane was kneeling on the kitchen floor not long after six thirty in the morning, scrubbing the flagstones, when the old woman hammered on the front door.

The stains. The brownish-red stains that were so faint she couldn't be sure they were there at all. Was this the third or fourth morning she had woken in the house? Time had become diaphanous, slipping by without her noticing. Days became weeks as she looked the other way, weeks turning to months before she knew they'd been lost to her.

She had not slept since they moved in. Not real sleep, not the warm dark that brings light, but the dim hinterland where bitter memories surfaced to torment her. Each morning, the chattering of birds outside the window banished the last hope of sleep before dawn. Each morning, she came downstairs in the milky-blue early light, passing the stacks of unpacked boxes.

The house had stood for more than a hundred and twenty years, so she was told. It rested behind a cluster of ash trees, taking its name from them: The Ashes, carved in one of the stone pillars at the gate. Her father-in-law, Francis—Francie, as he preferred—had found the house. Bought it for a song and gifted it to Sara and her husband Damien. A fire had left the place a shell, but it had been rebuilt. The original stone flooring remained intact, worn smooth by a century and more of footfall, dark and glossy like the skin of some ancient creature. It felt sinful to walk on it with bare feet, and all the better for it, the stone cooling her soles.

The first morning, however many days ago that was, Sara had come down here at dawn and made coffee while Damien snored upstairs. She noticed the stains over by the alcove that used to be a fireplace. An Aga cooker had been fitted where a wood-burning stove had once been. The stone in front of it was mottled with a deep red, as if something had spilled there years before. Clean it, she had thought. Damien would not tolerate mess. She had fetched a surface-cleaning wipe from a packet by the sink and got down on her knees. The stains seemed to fade as she rubbed the stone, though no residue was apparent on the wipe when she was done. Still, they were gone, and she thought no more about them until the following morning, when Damien was eating toast at the island in the centre of the room. She saw the stains, returned, as morning light brightened the kitchen.

"Look," she had said, touching them with her bare toe, seeking a change in texture against her skin but finding none.

"Hmm?" He did not look up from his phone, one thumb scrolling while he sucked melted butter from the other.

"Those stains are back," she said. "I cleaned them yesterday morning, and now they've come back."

"Yeah?" He took another bite of toast, a sip of coffee, kept his eyes on the phone.

"Look," she said, "here."

Damien huffed out an impatient breath and put his slice of toast on the plate, leaned over on his stool, tilting his head one way, then the other.

"*Here*," she said again, tapping the stain with her toe.

"I don't see it. It's just the pattern of the stone, no?"

Damien wore his good Hugo Boss jeans with a striped shirt tucked in at the waist, brown Grenson brogues, his Canali blazer on a hanger, suspended from a cupboard door. He was starting work today, the new in-house architect at his father's property development firm.

Things had come together quickly after what had happened back home—she still thought of it as back home—in Bath. She had been raised there in the West Country of England, had met Damien at the University of Bath, he a postgrad architecture student, she in her second year of studying for a social work degree. She never imagined, even after they married, that she would come to live in the place he never ever called Northern Ireland. Always the North, the North of Ireland, sometimes the Six Counties, but never Northern Ireland. As if to speak its name would shame him.

She accepted his reasons, even if she never fully understood them. Not that it mattered, she had thought, because they would never move there, not to that place. But then things went bad, she had come so close to that most wretched sin, and they had decided to start over. Here, where he came from.

And it all fell into place, just like that, as if some unknown god had been waiting for her to take the overdose, as if the job for Damien had been here all along, as if this house had been biding its time until their arrival.

"It's there, *look*," Sara said.

Damien pulled a sheet of kitchen paper from the roll on the island and wiped his hands clean before balling it up and leaving it by his plate. He reached for his jacket, slipped it on, and came to her side.

Looking down, he said, "No, I don't see it. It's just the colour of the stone."

"No, it's—"

"It's your imagination. I need to get going. You'll get some stuff unpacked, won't you? I don't want Da to be tripping over boxes when he comes round. You don't want the place to be a tip, do you?"

Francie Keane was due to visit this week to see how the work on the house was coming along. The parts the electrician needed hadn't turned up, and half the light switches remained uninstalled, clusters of wires snaking from the holes in the walls, ready to bite.

Damien didn't wait for a response, and Sara heard the front door close as she toed the stain. When the sound of his car had receded, she went to the sink, filled the plastic basin with warm water and washing-up liquid, and took the dish scrubbing brush from the windowsill. On her knees, she cleaned the floor, the deep red blotches fading into the smooth darkness of the stone.

She knew they would come back.

This morning, as the world lightened, she had listened to the birds for a while before finally giving up on sleep. Some of their calls had become familiar, and she wondered what kinds they might be. Maybe she would buy a book, some sort of guide to the different breeds. Another item on the list of things she would do one day, when she got around to it.

Sara wore a light cardigan over her pyjamas when she tiptoed downstairs, always soft in her step so as not to wake Damien. He didn't like being woken early, and he would be sullen and irritable for the rest of the day if she disturbed him. Half-a-dozen boxes remained in the hall, filled with books and DVDs and CDs, waiting for the joiner to shelve out the alcoves around the fireplace in the living room. None of them were hers. The hall's chill was deepened by the darkness there with no switches yet fitted for the lights.

In the kitchen, Sara filled the kettle and flicked it on. When it had boiled, she warmed the cafetière—Damien insisted that it be warmed first—then spooned in the coffee grounds. As she allowed it to stand, she gazed out of the window over the sink, towards the front of the property. She watched the ash trees, looking for the birds she'd been listening to these last few mornings. Brown earth stretched away from either side of the driveway, dotted by green shoots of new grass, freshly seeded a few weeks ago. The early autumn's first fallen leaves drifted and gathered in the sheltered spots. A river lay beyond the trees and the lane, down a steep bank. Perhaps she would go for a walk along there later; she had intended to yesterday but somehow the hours had gotten away from her, as was their habit.

The warm and earthy smell of coffee reminded her it would be ready now. As she went back to the island where the cafetière waited, she glanced at the floor in front of the Aga and stopped.

Those stains, returned. Of course they had.

She got down on her hands and knees, scratched at the largest one with the nail of her forefinger. The nail was bitten blunt, but she thought she might be able to scratch some of the stain away. She rubbed the tip of her finger against her thumb, looking for residue, even a speck of some crumbling matter. There was nothing.

Sara cursed and got to her feet. She went to the door at the opposite side of the kitchen, the one that opened onto a staircase leading down into the dark. Inside, she found the light switch, one of the few that had been fitted. The space below illuminated. She held the railing as she stepped down, ducking beneath the low ceiling.

She did not like this room, finding it oppressive, the darkness of its corners unleavened no matter how many ceiling lights were installed. Not many houses here had basements, Damien had explained, due to the high water table. But this house had one, dug out decades ago and reinforced with wooden beams, reaching under the hall and part way beneath the living room. His father's tradesmen had modernised the basement, put in waterproof membranes, a new floor, and walls all freshly plastered, ready for painting. It had been plumbed and ventilated and fitted with a washer and dryer, along with shelves for cleaning items. She fetched a mop and bucket from one of the dim corners, and a stout brush from a shelf, along with a bottle of floor detergent.

As she climbed the stairs, Sara did not look back, feeling that she might see someone return her gaze. An irrational thought, but Damien said she was given to those.

In the kitchen, she half filled the bucket with hot water, along with a generous splash of the detergent. She brought the bucket to the space in front of the Aga, and once again got to her knees. Sara soaked the bristles of the brush and sloshed water onto the stained floor. She worked the brush hard into the stone, the detergent foaming. Her temples and jaw ached, and she realised how hard she had been grinding her teeth together.

After a few minutes of scrubbing, she wiped the suds away with her hand, showing clean stone, no stains left. Gone, finally.

"Thank—"

Before the second word could form in her mouth, a thunderous hammering boomed through the house, causing her to cry out. She remained on her knees for a moment, her mind scrambling to make sense of the noise, what it was, where it had come from.

Again, the rattling, booming thunder. Again, she startled.

Damien. Don't wake Damien.

As that thought flitted through her head, she realised it was the new front door. Someone banging hard on the PVC. She looked to the window over the sink. The sky still bluish grey, barely dawn. A pealing fear sounded in her. No one knocked on doors at dawn unless they brought terrible news. Sara got to her feet and went to the sink, leaned over it, peered through the window.

There, an elderly woman, impossibly small.

She wore a nightdress, a dressing gown pulled loosely over it, one foot bare, the other with a slipper half on. The woman's eyes darted here and there, across the front of the house, window to window. Her face twisted with fright and confusion. It occurred to Sara that she should go to the door and open it, ask this woman what she was doing here, help her.

Don't wake Damien, she thought, the words pushing to the front of her mind.

As she remained frozen in place, staring, the old woman noticed her. The woman stepped towards the window, limping. Only inches between their faces now, separated by glass, the old woman's eyes wild and piercing. Her mouth moved, and Sara heard her voice, weak and wavering, but she could not discern her words.

The old woman formed her right hand into a fist and hammered on the windowpane, wrenching Sara from her paralysis. Sara stepped back, retreating from the woman's stare. The woman pounded on the glass once more.

Help her, Sara thought. For God's sake, help her.

Finally, she moved, went to the hall and the front door. She pulled the lever handle, but it remained solidly in place. Locked, she remembered, and she ran back to the kitchen, to the bowl on the island, and grabbed the keys. Returning to the hall, she unlocked the door and opened it. The old woman was already there, pushing, pushing, stronger than Sara could have imagined, her voice rising as she forced her way inside, past Sara and into the hall. A trail of bloody footprints followed her. The insane idea to get the mop from the kitchen and clean the floor flashed in Sara's mind.

The woman turned in a circle, her burning gaze moving from floor to wall to doorway to Sara, her voice a panicked shriek.

"Who are you?" the woman asked. "Why are you in my house?"

Sara backed against the wall, her hands up and out, as if to defend herself. "I live here," she said. "We just moved—"

"Get out!" The woman bent double with the force of her own voice. "Get out of my house!"

Sara shook her head. "I don't—"

"Where are the children? What did you do with the children?"

Damien appeared on the stairs, eyes puffy, hair tousled, fastening the belt on his jeans, still wearing the T-shirt he'd slept in. The woman heard his footsteps, turned to stare up at him.

"What are you doing in my house?" she shouted at him.

"Oh, Jesus," he said. He paused for a moment, then rushed down the remaining stairs.

"Damien," Sara said, "what's going—"

Before she could finish the question, the woman turned back to her.

"Get out of my house! Get—"

She fell to the floor like a bundle of twigs. While Sara remained against the wall, her back pressed to it, Damien rushed to the old woman, crouched down beside her. The woman cowered on the stone floor, her hands up to shield herself.

"You're all right, love, let's get you back." He turned to speak to Sara. "Grab my car key from the kitchen."

Sara didn't move. "We need to call the police."

"No police," he said, his voice hardening. "I'll take her back. Just get the key, will you?"

"Take her back where? She's bleeding. She needs a hospital. We should call—"

"Just get the fucking key!"

His anger stirred her into motion, and she knew not to argue any further. She hurried to the kitchen, avoiding the woman's bloody footprints. When she returned with the key, fat and black in her palm, he snatched it from her and hauled the woman to her feet. The woman cried out as he pushed her towards Sara.

"Keep a hold of her," he said as he went to the mat by the front door where his trainers sat beside hers.

Sara took the woman in her arms, felt her quivering, felt the chill of her skin through the dressing gown.

"My God, she's freezing," Sara said, wrapping her open cardigan around the woman, hoping to share some warmth with her. "She needs to go to hospital."

Damien pulled each shoe on, yanking on the toggled cord to fasten them. "The care home can sort that out."

Sara felt anger drag her into the moment, time and reality connecting for the first time in months.

"What care home? Damien, who is she?"

"It's not my home," the woman said. "*This* is my home. Where are the children? They need me. Where are they?"

Sara bent down to the woman's eye level. "What children? What's your name?"

Damien took the woman from Sara's arms, his eyes flashing a warning. She did not drop her gaze.

"Never mind her name, she's away in the head. Just get that floor cleaned."

As he carried her to the front door, still open, the woman said, "Mary. My name's Mary, and this is my house."

Damien slammed the door behind him.

Sara looked down at her bare feet and saw she stood in the woman's blood.

2: MARY

Here, now, till I tell you.

I always lived in the house. I never knew any different. Underneath, in the room down the stairs. In the dark. That's what I remember the most, when we were telt to put the lamps out. They locked the door at the top of the stairs and that was that. Dark until they opened it again. I still don't like the dark.

As far as I know, I was born there. Nobody ever telt me any different, and I don't mind any different. From I was wee, that's all I remembered. Always. Thon room under the house, then the rest of the place when I was allowed up.

The only light down there was the couple of oil lamps they allowed us to have. It was always cold and wet. They'd made a floor out of wooden boards, and a ceiling, with posts to holt it up. The floor was always damp. Sometimes, if it rained hard outside, mucky water would come up through the cracks.

I don't mind what age I was the first time they let me up the stairs by my own self. Five, maybe, or six. Old enough that I could do a lock of wee things about the place. Sweeping up the floors or dunging out the ashes from the fireplaces. Mummy Noreen telt me what to do. Says she, when the Daddies is around, you don't look at them, just you get on with your work. Just you pretend you aren't there, and they'll not bother with you. Unless they *do* bother with you, then you be polite and don't give them any cheek.

So that's what I did. I just bate on with what I had to do, and if Daddy George or Daddy Ivan came in, I just put my head down and said nothing. And that wasn't hard to do, either. I was wild afeart of them. They weren't slow about giving beatings, them boys. Many's a time Mummy Noreen or Mummy Joy would have a black eye or a sore back from a kicking.

Daddy Tam was the worst of them. He was a cribb'd auld skitter, so he was. He'd slap you soon as look at you. And them big hands of his. If he hit you, you knew you were hit.

I mind the first time he hit me. I'd finished sweeping up the ashes around the hearth in the living room. It was the wintertime because it would've foundered you in the house, but I remember the sun was out, and it was shining between the bare branches of the trees outside, and through the windows. Mummy Joy had just cleaned them, and you'd hardly know the glass was there she'd cleaned them that well. And I was there in the room all by myself and the sun was shining in and it felt warm on my arms, so here, didn't I start dancing? I don't know what notion I took, but I started twirling around like I don't know what. Just spinning around and tittering away.

Then something slammed into my head, bang, and I didn't know what it was. I thought the roof had fallen on me. Then here's me on the floor, didn't know what way up I was, and Daddy Tam's standing over me.

Says he, What do you think you're at?

I was that afeart I couldn't answer him. I just stared up at him. Then he kicked me in the backside, awful hard, I'd never felt the like of it. I'd been hurt before, I'd had the odd wee bump or scrape, but no one had ever *hurt* me before. Not like that.

I don't mind too well, but I suppose I must've cried or screamed because Mummy Joy came running in and she got down beside me, between me and Daddy Tam, and says she, Get you away from her.

No one ever talked back to Daddy Tam. Never, never, never. I could see the anger in him. He was always angry, that man, they all were, but this was not the same. He was raging so much he went all quiet. And pale, except for the red blotches on his cheeks. I remember his big hands opening and closing. I remember feeling Mummy Joy starting to shake.

Then he points at me, and says he, Get thon child out of my sight, then you get back up here.

Mummy Joy didn't argue with him. She picked me up and she carried me out into the hall, then into the kitchen, and through the door and down the stairs. She put me on the wee bed I had in the corner and put a blanket around me.

I suppose I must've been crying, and Mummy Joy was too, and says I, Don't go up there, but says she, I have to, and away she went. She left me holding one of the wee dollies I'd made from tying sticks together with twine, the ones I kept hidden under my mattress so Daddy Ivan wouldn't take them from me.

I heard all of it, Daddy Tam shouting and raging, the banging and the thumping, her screaming. It sounded like he was dragging her across the floor, back into the kitchen, and the way she was squealing, I suppose he must've been dragging her by the hair. Then I heard Daddy George telling him to quit it, he was going to kill her if he kept on.

So what if I do, says he.

Then I'll kill you, says Daddy George.

Then them two went at it. Mummy Joy closed the door behind her and came down the stairs in the dark. She found her way to me and got into the bed and we cuddled up in the dark, under the blanket. All the time, from upstairs, banging and thumping and shouting. Then we heard Daddy Ivan come along and that was the end of it. As afeart as I was of Daddy Tam, him and Daddy George were more afeart of Daddy Ivan.

A wee while later, I don't mind how long, Mummy Noreen came down and she lit the lamps and said we should stay down there for the rest of the day, just till things calm down. Things is bad, says she. Daddy Tam's thran, he's in a terrible twist, and he's on the drink again. Don't show yourself, either of yous, not till tomorrow, not till he's sobered up.

What age was I then? I don't know. Six, maybe. I never had a great notion what age I was. Tell you the God's honest truth, I don't know what age I am now.

But that was our days and nights. Up early in the morning, up into the house, cleaning and tidying, Mummy Noreen sometimes doing the cooking for the Daddies, other times Mummy Joy. Then downstairs in the evening to ate whatever leftovers there was. Whoever did the cooking always made sure there was just enough. Then when it was time to go to sleep, one of the Daddies would call down to us to put the lamps out, and he'd close the door and lock us in for the night.

It was always like that. Sure, I never knew any different.

Other Titles in the Soho Crime Series

FRANCINE MATHEWS
(Nantucket)
Death in the Off-Season
Death in Rough Water
Death in a Mood Indigo
Death in a Cold Hard Light
Death on Nantucket
Death on Tuckernuck

SEICHŌ MATSUMOTO
(Japan)
Inspector Imanishi Investigates

MAGDALEN NABB
(Italy)
Death of an Englishman
Death of a Dutchman
Death in Springtime
Death in Autumn
The Marshal and the Murderer
The Marshal and the Madwoman
The Marshal's Own Case
The Marshal Makes His Report
The Marshal at the Villa Torrini
Property of Blood
Some Bitter Taste
The Innocent
Vita Nuova
The Monster of Florence

FUMINORI NAKAMURA
(Japan)
The Thief
Evil and the Mask
Last Winter, We Parted
The Kingdom
The Boy in the Earth
Cult X

STUART NEVILLE
(Northern Ireland)
The Ghosts of Belfast
Collusion
Stolen Souls
The Final Silence
Those We Left Behind
So Say the Fallen
The Traveller & Other Stories

(Dublin)
Ratlines

REBECCA PAWEL
(1930s Spain)
Death of a Nationalist
Law of Return
The Watcher in the Pine
The Summer Snow

KWEI QUARTEY
(Ghana)
Murder at Cape Three Points
Gold of Our Fathers
Death by His Grace
The Missing American
Sleep Well, My Lady

QIU XIAOLONG
(China)
Death of a Red Heroine
A Loyal Character Dancer
When Red Is Black

JAMES SALLIS
(New Orleans)
The Long-Legged Fly
Moth
Black Hornet
Eye of the Cricket
Bluebottle
Ghost of a Flea

Sarah Jane

JOHN STRALEY
(Sitka, Alaska)
The Woman Who Married a Bear
The Curious Eat Themselves
The Music of What Happens
Death and the Language
 of Happiness
The Angels Will Not Care
Cold Water Burning
Baby's First Felony

(Cold Storage, Alaska)
The Big Both Ways
Cold Storage, Alaska
What Is Time to a Pig?

AKIMITSU TAKAGI
(Japan)
The Tattoo Murder Case
Honeymoon to Nowhere

AKIMITSU TAKAGI CONT.
The Informer

HELENE TURSTEN
(Sweden)
Detective Inspector Huss
The Torso
The Glass Devil
Night Rounds
The Golden Calf
The Fire Dance
The Beige Man
The Treacherous Net
Who Watcheth
Protected by the Shadows

Hunting Game
Winter Grave
Snowdrift

An Elderly Lady Is Up
 to No Good

ILARIA TUTI
(Italy)
Flowers over the Inferno
The Sleeping Nymph

JANWILLEM VAN DE WETERING
(Holland)
Outsider in Amsterdam
Tumbleweed
The Corpse on the Dike
Death of a Hawker
The Japanese Corpse
The Blond Baboon
The Maine Massacre
The Mind-Murders
The Streetbird
The Rattle-Rat
Hard Rain
Just a Corpse at Twilight
Hollow-Eyed Angel
The Perfidious Parrot
The Sergeant's Cat:
 Collected Stories

JACQUELINE WINSPEAR
(1920s England)
Maisie Dobbs
Birds of a Feather